A Christmas Wish on Arran

ALSO BY ELLIE HENDERSON

SCOTTISH ROMANCES
Book 1: A Summer Wedding On Arran
Book 2: A Christmas Escape To Arran
Book 3: A Summer House On Arran
Book 4: A Christmas Wish On Arran

A Christmas Wish on Arran

ELLIE HENDERSON

Scottish Romances Book 4

Choc Lit
A JOFFE BOOKS COMPANY

Choc Lit
A Joffe Books company
www.choc-lit.com

First published in Great Britain in 2024

Cover art by Jarmila Takač

ISBN: 978-1781898048

To my dear Dad, who taught me to have courage, determination, integrity and to always persevere. These values will always stay with me, and I will be eternally grateful to him for that.

PROLOGUE

Twenty-five years ago

It was early afternoon on a hazy September day as Elizabeth watched the steady stream of passengers hurrying across the concourse at Glasgow Central station. The constant mass of people were checking the noticeboard to find out which platform their train was departing from, clutching takeaway sandwiches, bags of crisps and glossy magazines. Elizabeth yawned, slightly bleary-eyed. This had to be the earliest she had been in this station for quite some time. Usually she would be out with the other weekend revellers, arriving several hours later and sprinting to catch the last train home after a night at the pub.

The train to London Euston was leaving from Platform One in just over twenty minutes. She really hoped he wouldn't be late. Elizabeth had arrived almost half an hour ago, positioning herself right under the clock in the middle of the station. When they had started making their plans, they had discussed meeting at the other popular spot, the Hielanman's Umbrella, where the trains came out of the station on Argyle Street between Hope Street and Union Street. But they settled on the clock. Elizabeth thought it would be more romantic, more like a scene from a movie, though she hadn't voiced that thought out loud to him of course. She didn't want him running for the hills.

As she continued to people-watch, she thought about the different characters who would come and go all day here; some being warmly welcomed off trains by loved ones, others slipping away quietly, unnoticed and unseen. *Everyone* had a story after all. Her eyes were drawn to a couple saying their farewells just a few metres away, and she felt herself well up as the sobbing girl clung to the boy. She was glad she would soon be throwing her arms around her boyfriend and saying hello and, at this rate, *hurry let's go catch the train*, rather than having to bid a sad goodbye. Looking at the couple, she wondered when they might next see each other. With a swirl of excited anticipation in her stomach, she realised she would be seeing her boyfriend again in just moments. Although it had only been a couple of weeks since she'd last seen him, it felt like months. This was a new adventure for them and she couldn't wait.

Tugging at her rucksack, she moved it closer to her feet, along with the large holdall that contained all she would need for this next chapter. A policeman sauntered past, clutching his walkie-talkie, his eyes darting around, as he half-listened to the drunk bloke who had befriended him talk intently about the weekend's football scores. Glancing at her watch she started to feel slightly anxious. *Where* was he? They had arranged to meet twenty minutes before the train departed. There were now fifteen minutes to go. Tapping her foot against her bag, she scanned the concourse, but there was no sign of him. A flash of worry rippled through her. Were they *definitely* meeting here at the clock? Maybe it *was* the Hielanman's Umbrella after all and she'd got her wires crossed. What if he was waiting round there for her and thinking the same thing? A few metres away stood an older lady, with soft white curls, who was dressed head to toe in purple tweed. Elizabeth caught her eye and smiled. Gesturing at her bags, she said, 'Do you mind watching these for a minute please? I'm worried that my boyfriend is waiting somewhere else. I just want to run and check. Our train is due to leave soon.'

'Of course dear,' said the woman, moving closer to take up guard. 'Off you go.'

Elizabeth ran as fast as she could, her eyes wildly scanning the crowds, looking for that familiar face she had fallen in love with. But when she reached the corner, hot and panting, he wasn't there. She spun on her heels just in case he was coming in the opposite direction. Looking at her watch she saw she had ten minutes to get to the platform and onto the train. She couldn't afford to miss it, and didn't have time to go to a payphone to call. And would he be home to answer, if he was here? *Think*, she urged herself, *think*.

When they'd spoken briefly on the phone a few days ago, he hadn't said anything that made her think he wasn't going to come with her. She quickly replayed the conversations they'd had about this move to London. When she was offered the job, she'd urged him to come with her. He had initially been reluctant but then seemed to warm up to the idea — and then he'd seemed excited. Or so she thought. Maybe he'd had a change of heart? Perhaps she had completely misread the signs. Maybe he *had* changed his mind, or actually didn't ever want to come and she hadn't listened to him. She knew she was headstrong and sometimes only heard what she wanted to hear. She thought back to their conversation several weeks ago when she had started making her plans. 'How about if you want to come . . . then I will wait at the clock for you,' she said.

He had smiled lazily at her and leaned over to kiss her on the lips. 'I will be there.'

'But if you decide not to come that's okay.' She gave him a lingering kiss back.

At the time he hadn't really responded to what she'd said, so she hadn't given it much thought. Now, as she jogged back inside the station and to her bags, she realised that she had obviously got it all completely wrong. She wondered, had he ever *wanted* to come with her? Her cheeks flushed with exertion

3

and utter mortification. How could she have been so stupid to think that he would give up everything for her? Thanking the woman in tweed profusely, she grabbed her bags.

'Was he not there, dear?' The woman's tone was sympathetic.

Elizabeth muttered something about a mix up and she hoisted her rucksack on her shoulders. 'Thanks anyway.'

The woman smiled kindly at Elizabeth.

The train for London Euston will depart from Platform One in five minutes. If you're not intending to travel on this train, please will you now leave the carriage before the doors close.'

'Bye,' Elizabeth mumbled to the woman, turning and walking briskly to the platform, where she hovered outside her carriage.

'Are you getting on, love?' asked the conductor. 'The doors are about to close any minute.'

Elizabeth desperately looked down the platform, willing him to appear and prove her wrong. But it was no use. There was no sign of him. She had to face facts. He wasn't coming.

'If you're intending on getting this train, I will have to ask you to board now please,' urged the conductor.

Elizabeth nodded. 'I was just waiting for my friend and . . .'

'Well if you don't get on the train in the next second, you might well find yourself waiting on an empty platform. Looks like your friend isn't coming.' The conductor raised his eyebrows and made a tutting noise.

She climbed on board, struggling to heave her bag on, trying her best to not consider what this meant. Storing her luggage in the rack, she took a breath — stifling back the tears, she made her way to her seat, urging herself to be strong. As the train blasted its horn and pulled out of the station, she dabbed her eyes with a tissue. She had to accept that he wasn't coming. They wanted different things and she had been too self-absorbed to realise. As she stared out the window, the train moved across the bridge, across the River Clyde and away from the sprawling city. Leaving Glasgow was what *she* wanted. She had always been determined to move to London, no matter what. This was her new start, and she now had to focus on making the absolute best of it — an exciting job in a city she'd always wanted to live. If he didn't want to come then she would just have to go it alone. She just wished he had been honest with her from the start.

CHAPTER ONE

Beth Ferguson trudged along the pavement, her nylon hood pulled up, her head tucked down and away from the autumnal rain as she made her way to work. It was a journey she made several times a week, normally always on autopilot, but lately things felt different. Normally on every walk she would make a point of looking up and appreciating the view of the River Thames as she walked across Deptford Creek, but today she couldn't be bothered to even lift her head. Maybe it was the change of season and the thought of a long autumn and winter looming ahead. With each step she took, she felt the sensation that something significant was about to happen. It was a feeling she had experienced several times over the past week, along with a dramatic decline in her mood.

Beth wasn't exactly sure of the moment she realised her life was starting to fall apart. Especially as she'd always tried to focus on the positives. She didn't exactly have a huge *aha* moment. More like a series of expletive-laden mutterings, usually under her breath, that she couldn't quite believe this was what her life now amounted to. The reality was that her day-to-day existence had continued to trundle on; she still got up every morning and showered, albeit in a cramped and mouldy old bathroom, where the shower curtain had a habit of clinging to her backside. She managed to make it out on time to get to work, which was a fifteen-minute walk from her poky room in a shared flat in Deptford, and she reminded herself how lucky she was that she didn't need to commute into the centre of London anymore like she'd done in her younger days. But working in a small café in Greenwich, even though it was a few moments from the River Thames, which she had always loved, wasn't entirely how she envisaged her career panning out. Not at her age and stage in life.

She kept telling herself that at least the job gave her a focus and paid regular money, which helped go towards the cost of her extortionate rent. If truth be told, her career in freelance journalism had dwindled — she was lucky to get the odd writing job, especially with the way the market had gone. All her regular sources of work had disappeared as budgets were repeatedly slashed, and so she had embraced her inner barista and listening skills at the café that welcomed regulars, locals and visitors every day of the week. Indeed *she* used to be one of the local regulars, when she would sit with a latte and type up her latest article. It was how she got to know the owner, Frankie, who then asked Beth if she would fancy doing some shifts, when Beth had confided that things were a bit bleak on the employment front.

'Come and work here then,' suggested Frankie. 'I was about to put an ad out saying we needed a server. It's yours if you want it, and hopefully you can still fit in some writing.'

Beth paused for a millisecond before answering. 'Done,' she replied. 'When can I start?' Fortunately she had inherited her father's Scottish Presbyterian work ethic, which meant she wasn't too proud to roll up her sleeves and get on with whatever needed to be done. Especially if it meant keeping a roof over her head. Mind you, she reminded herself with a sigh, it wasn't her own roof she was paying for. It was someone else's. She was just a tenant.

Was it really this time last year that she had her own flat and mortgage with a walk-in tiled shower that she could linger in as long as she wanted? The wistful moments of remembering those mornings, where she sang in the shower as she lathered up her expensive gels and shampoos, were becoming less frequent. There was no point in looking back. It was too painful. She had spent months going round in the same cycle of thoughts of *if only* and *maybe if*. Beth knew she had to focus on the here and now, and what she was going to do next to escape this trapped existence. She felt her phone buzz in her pocket and pulled it out. A message from her dad.

Hi dear, how are you? Haven't heard from you in a while. Hope all is okay. Love Dad x

Guilt washed over her and she held back the tears that these past few days seemed to be constantly on the verge of running down her cheeks. She'd intended to visit her dad over the summer but had put it off. *Again*. She knew she'd been evasive — not just with her dad but with her friends too. For as long as she could remember, Beth had always used her job as a high-flying journalist as an excuse for her missing out on family and social gatherings. She'd continued to do so even though things had changed quite radically over the past twelve months. That was putting it mildly. Her life had been completely upended, and she knew her dad would be horrified when he realised just how bad things had become. He would insist on helping her out in any way that he could, but she wanted to cling on to her last shreds of self-worth. She could hardly go scuttling back home at her age. She was forty-six, for goodness' sake. Anyway, her dad was now living in a retirement flat in a development just outside Glasgow. It wasn't exactly the type of place she could seek refuge in. She shuddered as she thought of the word "home" and what it actually meant. She was still having her mail redirected from her old flat — she couldn't quite bring herself to let go of it completely, even though she had sold it and it belonged to someone else. It was a home she had been so proud to call her own. The top-floor duplex conversion in Greenwich, an area she had always loved, was bright and welcoming and had two double bedrooms, with a beautiful large bathroom, a power shower and a roll-top bath. The open-plan kitchen and reception room had lovely views over the gardens, and she even had her own private patio area at the rear of the building, where she enjoyed pottering around and tending to her plants. Now, the closest she got to gardening was by walking through Greenwich Park, which she tried to do regularly to get her fix of nature.

For the past few months, Beth had been clinging to this existence by the tips of her chewed and chipped fingernails. Her younger self would be horrified by the state of them. But she'd given up her regular manicures quite some time ago, along with all the other luxuries she used to take for granted. She had tried to keep moving forward bit by bit with life, but this morning, as she walked into the café and hung up her coat in the small cloakroom through the back, she realised that she wasn't moving anywhere — certainly not in the direction she wanted to go.

'Morning love. You okay?' Frankie grinned at her.

She forced a smile. 'Yeah, fine.' At which point several customers arrived at once, so Beth had to focus on steaming milk, grinding coffee beans and telling people to "enjoy their day".

CHAPTER TWO

Later that night, as Beth plodded back to her rented room, having served what felt like at least one million customers and listened to people share their varied stories, she realised just how on edge she was. Her stomach churned with nerves, or perhaps anticipation, she thought wryly, that something would change for the better. As she slotted her keys in the front door and pushed it open, she was startled to find her flatmate Lara hovering around the hallway waiting for her.

'Hi there.' Beth wondered why the woman who did her best to avoid her at all times was now lingering by the door in a slightly weird manner. 'How's things?'

'All good thanks, all good.' She was dressed head to toe in cerise Lycra, and she put her hands on her hips and stared at Beth. 'I need to tell you something.'

'Sounds ominous.' Beth suspected she was going to tell her that she was heading to a Zumba class. But her comment landed like a lead balloon.

'I've got a new job in Dublin and I'll be moving out soon and you could take over the lease for the flat? What do you think? Will you let me know? Do you want to do that?'

Beth felt breathless on her behalf. She was worried that Lara had imparted all of that information in one go without pausing to inhale. As she processed the information dump — which totalled more than Lara had said to her in the last ten months since she had moved in to the flat — she started to feel the familiar ache of loss in her chest. Lara blinked back at her and clicked her tongue, tapping her foot noisily on the ground as she waited for a response. 'What do you want to do?'

'Oh, okay . . . erm, well, I wasn't expecting you to say that. But congratulations on your new job.'

Lara stared blankly at her. 'What do you think then? Shall I tell the landlord you'll take over the rent for the whole flat. Does that work, yeah?'

Beth's heart was now racing. *Stop talking*, she wanted to yell. 'No,' she shouted. 'Please don't do that.' *I can't afford a penny more*, she wanted to scream.

Lara took a step back, clearly startled by her tone.

Beth cleared her throat. 'Sorry, you've caught me a bit off guard with this news. What I mean is no thanks. It is very kind of you to think of me, but if you are moving out then I will too.'

'Righto,' said Lara. 'I will let them know. I *was* hoping that you would want to stay on and get someone in.' She paused in irritation. 'I start my new job at the beginning of October. I was hoping not to have to pay next month, but I guess we have to give a full calendar months' notice . . .'

Beth stared at a spot on the wall behind her, willing herself to say nothing.

'I'll tell him that we'll both be out the end of October. Which technically means you get the place to yourself for a few weeks as I'll be away at the end of this month. Is that okay?' Lara clearly didn't want to hear the answer, or whether it was okay or not, because she had already turned and disappeared into her room, closing the door firmly behind her.

That night, Beth sat on the narrow single bed in her cramped bedroom and let the tears fall. This was yet another

11

challenge to deal with. She really didn't think she had many tears left after this past shitshow of a year. In fact make it two years. But evidently, she did. All those boxes of guilt, embarrassment and shame she thought she'd managed to pack away started to spill open. As she stared at the mucky beige wall in front of her she thought about her dreams and hopes for her life. All those ambitions were now in huge dirty tatters.

Pulling out her phone, she knew she would have to look for somewhere else to stay in this city, which she had always loved but was now starting to feel like a lonely stranger in. Beth knew she was going to have to be brave and dig deep *again* if she was to get through this. She had spent so much time grieving that she knew she needed to move on and make a change. She didn't want her life to be defined by what had happened. Beth had lingered in the past too long. Yet she just didn't know if she had the energy to do this moving malarkey all again.

Scanning quickly through her emails, in case someone had miraculously decided they needed her journalistic skills and wanted to pay her loads and offer her free accommodation, she saw the latest message from a job site she was signed up to. Hesitating and almost deleting it, she shrugged. *Who knows, she thought, it might even cheer me up?* Last week's round up, with vacancies she was deemed to have suitable skills for, included being the night manager at a supermarket, retail assistant at a nationwide bakery, and chief electrician at the local university, as well as a lecturer in psychology. She had almost applied for that one for fun, citing her life experience, which had given her the perfect insight into the ways in which people behaved and misbehaved. As she quickly scanned the latest list of jobs, she did a double take when she saw an advert for the role of reporter on *The Arran News*.

That was a blast from the past. Wow, if only she could go back in time, maybe she should have taken that job when she was first offered it back in her younger days, she thought wryly. Instead, ambitious and eager to make a name for herself, she had left Scotland to come to London, where she thought the streets would be paved with gold. And look how that had turned out. How she wished she could go back to that time of her life when things were simpler, when she was full of optimism and the anticipation of new adventures. She kept reading down the list, which included openings as an art teacher, a property photographer and a marketing assistant. Her heart sank when she realised how little there was out there for her skillset, and how low the salaries were for one of the most expensive cities in the world. She found herself going back up the list, her finger hovering over the link for a few moments. Then she clicked on the reporter job, which took her to another page. She let out her breath as she started to read.

> *If you are looking for a job with a sea view then we need you. We are looking for an experienced and highly motivated reporter to join our team and serve the community on the Isle of Arran off the west coast of Scotland. This is a unique and brilliant opportunity for the right candidate to quickly obtain a working knowledge in a variety of areas important to the island community. The successful candidate must be capable of working on his or her own initiative to develop contacts, investigate stories and develop these through to publication. Experience in audio and video editing will also be an advantage.*

I could do all of that, thought Beth. *Couldn't I? Maybe seeing this advert is a sign?* Looking down at her coffee-stained T-shirt, and trousers that were smeared with food stains, she wrinkled her nose. She may have a stellar CV, and have worked all over the world, but it wasn't exactly opening up doors for her here anymore. Especially when a new, younger and eager generation of journalists were waiting and ready to do it all for so much less than they were worth. In fact, it was Beth who was now serving this new generation in the café, as they lined the tables clicking away on their laptops, swallowing espresso after espresso.

Could she really go back in time and revisit the place she had loved so much as a student, when she spent summers working there in a hotel, and go back to basics with her career? Would they even want her? Or was she being delusional and looking back at that time through rose-tinted glasses? Probably, she thought, as that was a safe place and it reminded her of a time when she had hope. These days, hope was something she needed more than ever. She'd become cynical and weary over the years and her hope had started to fade. Giving herself a shake, before she could talk herself out of it and change her mind, she quickly wrote a covering letter and attached her CV. Then she pressed send. *Nothing ventured, nothing gained*, she told herself. If she was meant to get the job she would. But something radical was going to have to change for her, or she would end up living with her dad in his retirement village, or have to go back to sleeping on a friend's sofa. She didn't want to do either.

CHAPTER THREE

Six weeks later and Beth had packed up her life in London, then celebrated Halloween with a crowd of rowdy pensioners in her dad's retirement complex. She didn't think she would ever forget the particularly gutsy version of Michael Jackson's *Thriller* that had been sung, and also *danced*, in the communal living area. The residents liked to gather there to celebrate everything and anything, play cards or drink tea, wine and brandy and debate the state of the world. Those robust discussions had given her *quite* the insight into the minds of some of the senior members of the population. She had learned *a lot*. It was fair to say that many of them were devoted *Daily Mail* readers, which made for interesting discussions with those who were on the opposite end of the political spectrum.

She quickly realised that her dad, Barry, and his friends all seemed to enjoy a celebration regardless of the date or time of year. They were always making excuses to bring out the whisky or pour a wee brandy and toast someone or something. Plans were already being made for the festive season, with a countdown of events that kicked off on the first of December. Beth had always loved the magic and sparkle of Christmas, but even she was exhausted when her dad ran through the schedule. It featured mulled wine tasting, festive wreath making, a reindeer rodeo — she had no idea what that was and wasn't sure she wanted to — and antler aerobics.

Beth had been staying with her dad for the past few days before she started her new job on Arran. She still had to keep pinching herself as she couldn't quite believe that she had *actually* landed the job at the newspaper. She didn't think it would sink in until she was there on the island and inside the office. It had been nice to have this time with her dad, who she quickly learned had a *very* specific routine he liked to stick to; chess on Wednesdays, line dancing on Thursday nights and pétanque on Friday mornings at the nearby park. There was also chat of a new book club starting up. When Barry, dressed as Elvis, invited her to join him and his friends for the Halloween party, she had politely declined and said she'd be happy to watch TV and leave them to it. But then Barry's neighbour, who had recently moved in — a twinkly-eyed woman called Margaret, or Granny Margaret as she was also known — insisted that she join them. She had come bustling through the front door wearing a blonde curly wig and a very tight dress singing, '*Working nine to five.*'

'No guesses for who you're going as,' said Barry, who was wearing a white jumpsuit and black wig.

'That's right, you guessed it. Maybe we could do a wee duet later. *Islands in the Stream?*'

'Aye, why not?'

Margaret chuckled.

Beth was momentarily horrified by their exchange. Was her dad, dressed as Elvis, actually trying to *flirt?* At *his* age? He was almost eighty for goodness' sake.

'I mean, I know he's a bit younger than me but I reckon I could just about get away with it.'

'What are you talking about Barry?' Margaret stood with her hands on her hips.

'David Beckham. Him and his missus did that duet. I saw it on Netflix.'

'Och away with you Barry. You couldn't even pass for Kenny Rogers. He had far more hair than you.'

Beth chuckled. Her dad's hair, or the wisps he still had, were also completely white.

'Aye, but I'm still handsome, aren't I? Especially with this wig on. It knocks the years off me. I'm always being told I look much younger than I am.' He grinned.

'Whoever says that is lying and they're after something.' Margaret smiled. 'Or else they need to go to Specsavers.'

Watching the banter between the two had been quite something to witness these past few days. She actually didn't mind their relationship as much as she thought she would. Beth's mum had died suddenly from a heart attack five years ago, just as she and Barry were about to move out of the family home and downsize to the retirement complex. Looking back to that dark time, she realised that perhaps it was then that her life started to disintegrate, as she tried her hardest to sweep her grief aside and focus on building her own family unit. She didn't even stop to think about her dad and how lonely he must have been. Especially as she was his only child, and she hadn't exactly been attentive these past few years.

'Right love, what can we dress you as?'

Beth felt herself backing into the corner of the room, hoping a hole would appear that she could disappear into.

Margaret wiggled her finger at her and put on her best southern drawl. 'Come on now. We need more powerful women in the room.' She winked at Beth. 'D'you get it? Powerful women? That song she did with that Pitbull chap.'

Dear God. Surely, Margaret wasn't expecting her to dress up as that American rapper.

'Is that not the name of a dog breed?' Barry scratched his wig, momentarily dislodging it from position.

Margaret shot him a look. '*Tsk*. Honestly you know *nothing*. Barry, you head downstairs. Me and Beth will see you down there. Beth, come with me. I'll get you sorted in a jiffy. You're going as Cher.'

Beth looked at her dad, her eyes pleading with him not to leave her. But he turned on his heels, whistling *A Little Less Conversation* as he disappeared out the front door.

Margaret shook her head. 'I know what you're thinking. You just want to stay in and watch *Bridgerton* or *Outlander* and eat a tub of ice cream. But you need some fun dear. Ice cream and the telly have their place, but it's not what you need tonight. Let's have a laugh, and I'm not taking no for an answer. Come on next door and I'll get you sorted.'

Five minutes later she was sat on a stool in Margaret's bedroom with a glass of wine in her hand, which she was quickly draining. Margaret had hauled a pile of clothes out of a bag. 'I knew these would come in handy. I found them in the loft when I was getting ready to move and wondered about chucking them. But then my Isobel borrowed them for a party and I thought they might be useful.'

Beth watched in fascination as Margaret held up a bright polka-dot polyester jumpsuit, then a pair of bell bottom jeans, a pair of gold hotpants and some corduroy flares. 'Right, I reckon all of these will suit you just fine. You're about the same size as Isobel.' Margaret chewed her lip thoughtfully, then disappeared back inside the walk-in wardrobe. 'Tada!' She held up a wig. 'I'm glad I kept hold of these wigs as well.'

Beth chuckled at her enthusiasm. She was a breath of fresh air, and seemed to know exactly what to say and do at the right time. When Beth thought back to last Halloween, she shuddered. She remembered the countless nights where she would wake gasping for breath as her splintered heart ached. 'Well,' she began tentatively, 'it has been a while since I got dressed up, and I suppose it could be fun.'

'Great.' Margaret clapped her hands in delight. 'That's my girl. Good on you. Do you trust me to do your make-up for you?'

'Oh . . . kay.' Beth swallowed the rest of her wine.

'I'll have you sorted out pronto and we'll go down and join the party.'

True to her word, Margaret busily applied make-up to Beth's face, then pulled the long dark wig over her scalp.

'Perfect.' She was clearly very pleased with her work.

Beth looked at herself in the mirror, bracing herself to be shocked. But she was pleasantly surprised at what she saw. Margaret had done an amazing job. 'Wow. How on earth did you do that?'

'Just one of my many hidden talents.' She cackled. 'Now you just need to go and choose something out of that lot to wear.' She pointed at the collection on the bed. 'I'll give you some space.' She shook her blonde curls and rearranged her amply padded bosom. 'Come out when you're ready.'

Beth grabbed the flares and a halter neck top, quickly pulling them on. When she saw her reflection in the mirror, she burst out laughing. This was all very surreal, but she had to admit it was also a lot of fun.

'Look at you,' exclaimed Margaret as Beth walked into her lounge. 'You're her absolute double. Come on then, let's get this party started.' She jumped up from her seat and linked her arm through Beth's. '*Babe . . . I got you babe*,' she sang loudly.

Beth felt her eyes tear up as she realised how much she appreciated the older woman's support tonight. She squeezed her arm and the two women, dressed as Dolly Parton and Cher, made their way into the corridor and down to the party.

CHAPTER FOUR

It was the day after the Halloween party and her final day with her dad. Her new beginning and her fresh start on Arran would officially begin tomorrow. Much as she appreciated the tiny spare bedroom at her dad's, she was looking forward to having some space of her own. She was reaching her limit of living from bags and trying to find things in the depths of her holdalls. Luckily, there was a flat above the office in Brodick available to rent. It was so much cheaper than the tiny room she'd been renting in London.

'Cup of tea, Dad?' she asked. Barry was flicking through the channels of the huge television that dominated the wall. Her mother never liked big TVs, and so Barry decided, if he could no longer have his wife, he would instead have a big screen. Beth didn't understand his reasoning but thought best to let him be in those early days of grieving.

'Please dear, that would be nice. I'll miss this when you go, you know,' he said vaguely. 'But at least you won't be so far away now. I can come over and visit when the weather gets a bit better. That's if you're not too busy.'

As she walked into the kitchen, she found herself wiping away a tear. It had been strangely cathartic to spend this time with him. Her dad wasn't a fan of cities, and had been so out of his comfort zone the one time he'd visited she hadn't extended the invitation again. There seemed little point.

Their time together here had been lovely. He had asked after Beth's former partner, Tim, a couple of times, and he must have noticed her flinch. Although she hadn't gone into the details of what had happened with him, she suspected he must have known it wasn't good, as he had patted her hand in sympathy on more than one occasion. Neither did he question the motivation behind her new job, which she had fully expected him to do. 'As long as you are happy dear, then that is all that matters,' he had said. She couldn't quite believe how much he had mellowed, and wondered if that had something to do with Margaret. Or perhaps she was finally just getting to know her dad.

The doorbell chimed and Beth jumped as she heard the door swing open.

'Coo-ee, it's just me.' Margaret let herself in.

'Cuppa?' called Beth. She was still trying to get her head around the fact they all just walked into each other's apartments whenever they felt like it. Sometimes it reminded her of being in the halls of residence at university. Especially when the visitors, more often than not, arrived holding a bottle or two of wine.

'Aw, go on then, twist my arm.' Margaret bustled into the kitchen, in which she was clearly *very* familiar. 'I've made some scones.' She reached into the cupboard for some plates, then got the butter from the fridge.

Beth dropped a tea bag in another mug and poured on the boiling water. After a wait, she squeezed the bag down with a teaspoon until it had turned a deep brown. Margaret had previously joked with her that she made weak-looking tea that was a bit "peely-wally". Beth had quickly learned to make it just the right strength for her.

'Look love, I was thinking . . . and I don't want you to take this the wrong way or anything. Or think I'm being presumptuous. But I know you're heading off tomorrow and, well, me and your dad have been talking . . .'

Beth watched Margaret slather the butter on the sliced scones with vigour. She had *no* idea what Margaret was about to say next.

'The thing is, the weather has been utterly Baltic, and it's not like it's going to get warm anytime soon. I mean I know Arran has palm trees and everything, but I don't think there will be much of a gulf stream at the moment. Spring is months away. Your dad mentioned that you're going to need a car for this new job and so . . . well, I would love it if you would take mine.'

Beth shook her head. 'I couldn't possibly do that Margaret. It's your car, and I will get one. Soon . . .'

Margaret gave her a knowing look, glancing over Beth's shoulder to check that her dad was still engrossed with the TV. 'You don't need to tell me anything lovey, but I have been around long enough to know that there's stuff you're not telling your dad. He's worried about you. And I know you're proud. I've got a daughter and a granddaughter who are exactly the same. If I was a betting woman, I'd put money on there being some muppet of a man being involved.' There was a question in her voice.

Beth felt her cheeks redden.

Margaret pursed her lips. 'I thought so. Honestly, I would take a swing for him if I could.'

When Beth didn't reply, Margaret turned back to the counter and started spreading the scones with jam.

Beth didn't have the heart to tell her that the *very* thick layer of butter was more than enough.

'Your dad has got one of those fancy cars with heated seats. I mean, when he first gave me a lift to Asda and he switched them on, I didn't know what was happening. I thought I'd wet myself. It's quite unnerving to feel your bum heat up when the rest of you is frozen. I wasn't sure I liked it at all.'

Beth couldn't help but laugh.

Margaret plonked the knife in the sink and, turning back to look at Beth, raised an eyebrow. 'I will tell you this though. It is a *very* handy feature to have when we go out to collect a takeaway. Keeps it warm on the way back, you know. Anyway, that's beside the point. My car is sitting there and you may as well use it. If I need to get anywhere, I can use my free bus pass. One of the advantages of being a pensioner. Besides, how else are you going to get about with this new job of yours?'

Beth hesitated, then clicked her tongue against the roof of her mouth. She knew Margaret was right. During the interview, which took place on Zoom, she had told a white lie when she said she had a car. She had hoped Jim, the editor, wouldn't notice her cheeks flush as she said it. She wasn't quite sure what she was going to do when she actually arrived on the island without wheels. Like everything else she did lately, she was planning just to wing it and make an excuse.

'But what about your family? They might want to use it?'

Margaret chuckled. 'Isobel has her own car, and Bella, my granddaughter, drives her mum's car. She's also previously told me that she wouldn't be seen dead in a red car.' She rolled her eyes. 'Apparently, it's not one of her colours and doesn't suit her complexion. Honestly, the youth of today. They don't know they're born.'

Beth chewed her bottom lip for a moment as she thought about Margaret's kind offer, which would help hugely. This past year she had been slowly getting used to accepting all the offers she could get. She took a deep breath. 'Okay . . . thank you Margaret. I appreciate it. Though it will be just a temporary thing until I get myself sorted out with my own car.'

'That's a deal,' said Margaret clapping her hands together. 'Now let's get this tea through to your dad before he expires on us. I don't fancy having to do CPR.'

CHAPTER FIVE

Callum Thompson wasn't having the greatest of mornings. He'd been up since the crack of dawn, having fed the chickens in the dark and then mended a leak in the bathroom ceiling. Ruby, his faithful Labrador, had been by his side throughout, and now she was curled up in her bed in the kitchen, eyeing him suspiciously as he paced the tiled floor and took yet another deep breath. She had become his shadow since his old Border Collie, Steve, had passed away a few years ago. Until then Steve hadn't let Ruby get too close to Callum — he viewed himself as top dog. Ruby must have watched and learned as a puppy. She now did a very good job of keeping the hens in check, rounding them up in the way that Steve used to.

Callum had planned to drop Daisy off early at her friend's house, then go and do the grocery shopping and some other errands in Brodick, the main village on the island. But Daisy, who was fourteen, had other ideas and insisted that, *yes*, she did need to straighten every single hair on her head, and that was his fault as he had bought a new shampoo that made her hair wavier than usual. He didn't understand how that worked. In his view shampoo was shampoo, and he tended to buy whatever was on offer in the supermarket. But in Daisy's opinion, this was a *catastrophic* problem, which he could never possibly understand, hence the meltdown. Suggesting that she put it in a ponytail, and telling her that it looked "fine", didn't land well with her either. She looked at him as though he'd told her to swim backwards to the mainland wearing a cowboy hat and nothing else. He really needed to remind himself that, when a thought floated through in his mind, he should say nothing at all. His attempts at trying to help usually made things worse.

'Daisy,' he called, in the most calming and soothing tone he could manage. 'I'm now thinking that you may as well just get the bus. It'll be here any minute.' He was kind of being sarcastic, but Daisy took his suggestion quite literally.

'Fine.' She appeared from her bedroom, quickly pulling on her shoes and jacket, then slamming the door on her way out. Their stone cottage, which had withstood all sorts of storms over the decades, practically shook. As she marched up the lane, he watched her pulling a beanie over her head and wondered, bemusedly, why she had bothered to straighten it if she was covering up with a hat.

Ruby whimpered — he crouched down and reached out a reassuring hand to pat her.

'Hey, it's okay,' he said gently. 'Teenage girls, eh? I'm not sure that I'll ever understand them. They are a mystery, Ruby. A complete and utter mystery.' He tickled her chin. 'I think I'll come back as a dog in my next life and be like you. Living the dream, eh girl.'

Ruby promptly licked his hand.

As he stood up, Callum was hugely relieved when he saw the bus rumble up to the end of their road, on time, and spotted Daisy climb onboard. He shook his head and sighed. 'I think I need another coffee before I do anything else.'

He flicked on the kettle. Ruby seemed to approve of his decision and soon she was lying on her back, legs in the air, snoring contently. He knew none of this was Daisy's fault, she was a teenager after all, and weren't these the toughest years? He let out a long breath. She didn't choose this life. Callum knew she would much rather have her mum here to love and guide her, but instead she had to make do with him. He was doing his best, he *really, really* tried. But what did he know about anything? Especially when it came to raising girls. He was just eternally grateful to his friends and neighbours who'd rallied around him to help in his time of need. In those early days his mum had been wonderful too, and stepped in to help everyone make the adjustment to this new and unexpected life they'd found themselves in. But she didn't live on the island and just came to visit, which, in Daisy's eyes, gave her super-star status, and he just became a bigger irritant. Callum was the person who reminded her to brush her teeth, who turned off the lights at night when she would rather have stayed up reading. Callum was also the person who said "no". He had always tried his hardest but he was beginning to wonder if that was enough.

Ruby sighed, deep in a doggy dream, and she gave a small bark. He shrugged. At least she was one female that he hadn't managed to upset. She had been a loyal friend to him these past seven years, always wagging her tail when she saw him. Ruby also didn't slam doors, stomp upstairs or scream at him. She certainly didn't care what her hair looked like either. Every greeting she gave him was heartfelt and enthusiastic — even if he had only been outside for a moment to fetch something from the car.

As he sipped his coffee, he looked out the large kitchen window overlooking the scraggly garden. It was yet another thing that needed his attention. He turned away and flicked his gaze across the calendar hanging next to the fridge. Daisy had designed it for him with some of the photos she'd taken over the past year. There were pictures of Ruby in various poses (who was an extremely patient dog), including a Santa hat for December and a pumpkin costume in October, as well as some of Daisy's arty beach shots, which included action shots of Ruby leaping around. Callum had always liked this time of year, and the lead up to Christmas, but he felt more tired than usual and not quite ready to embrace another cold winter on the island. He always seemed to be worrying about something — whether it was to do with securing more work for the joinery business he ran, balancing the books, making sure he was on top of the washing and remembering to make sure he had food in the fridge for Daisy. She had been off school the past few days with a heavy cold, and had gone a bit stir-crazy, hence her desperation to go and see her friend today. Perhaps that was all that was wrong and making them both feel out of sorts. Maybe they just needed to get back into some kind of routine. Surely things would soon settle down again. Dumping his mug in the sink, he felt marginally better and grabbed the shopping list from the kitchen table. He groaned when he scanned it and was reminded of Daisy's latest project.

'I'm going to become vegan,' she'd announced during the half-term break last month, just as he had pulled a large steak pie from the oven.

His mum had given him a wry smile and shook her head. He knew that was code for *don't say a word*.

'Okay . . .' He wondered what on earth he could rustle up that was entirely plant-based, or whatever the right language was these days. Everything in the world was so overly complicated and he usually got it wrong.

'That smells delicious,' said his mum. 'Is it the usual one from the butcher?'

He nodded. 'Yes, you always need to order them in the holidays, otherwise they sell out.'

'Well, Daisy dear,' his mum turned to Daisy, 'if you're not having yours then can I have it? I have been looking forward to that gravy and the buttery pastry all day. Would you just smell it? *Delicious*. You can have my potatoes though if you want Daisy? I'll enjoy the extra pastry.'

Callum had watched his mum in awe as Daisy looked at her hesitantly, then over to the pie that he'd placed on the table. 'Gran . . . I *am* going to go vegan but, maybe, not quite yet. I mean, Monday is a better day to start new things, don't you think?'

His mum chuckled. 'Yes, I agree. I think you should enjoy the steak pie while you can. Then you can embrace the vegan lifestyle as of next week.'

When his mum had left to return home to the mainland, Daisy had clearly decided that Plan Vegan was back on track. Her latest shopping list had left him in no doubt that she was keeping up with it. He shook his head again in despair, pulled on his thick coat and grabbed his car keys.

'Come on girl,' he said to Ruby and she dutifully followed him out to the car.

CHAPTER SIX

Beth woke early, having slept fitfully during the night. She was nervous, but also excited, about the day ahead as she swung her legs out of bed and pulled on her dressing gown. It was still dark and the flat was completely quiet, her dad still fast asleep. She shuffled into the kitchen to boil the kettle. Stifling a yawn, she stared out of the window, noticing the pool of moonlight in the residents' garden and the gentle mist of rain. It was quite a magical and calming sight, and she allowed her gaze to linger on it as she sipped her tea. She really hoped the mist wouldn't turn into a downpour as the weather was expected to change later. She could do with driving conditions being kind if she was to make the ferry. Indeed, she hoped the wind wouldn't pick up until she was safely on Arran. Her bags were packed, she had checked the boat actually was on time and now all she needed to do was quickly shower and dress.

It didn't take her long to get ready. When she came out of her room, her dad was waiting in the hallway in his striped pyjamas and the slippers she'd given him for his birthday.

'Good morning, dear. Are you all set?' His eyes were still bleary. 'Please do drive safely and let me know when you're there.'

She reached to him and pulled him into a tight hug. 'Thanks, Dad.' She felt a sob catch in the back of her throat.

'You do them proud, and remember I can come and visit anytime. Just get settled and then I will pop over. And you'll come back here for Christmas?'

'Of course I will, Dad. I wouldn't miss it for the world. We can make Christmas dinner together like we used to.' Beth felt a wave of guilt ripple through her. Last year she had made excuses not to come back to Scotland for Christmas. She couldn't face anyone or anything, and instead had spent it alone.

Her dad blinked back what looked like a tear and then reached across to the small hall table by the front door. 'This is for you.' He handed her an envelope. 'Please take it and use it. Please,' he pressed it to her palm as she started to refuse it, 'don't argue with me on this. I don't quite know what has happened, Beth. You can tell me when you're ready if you want, but equally you don't need to tell me anything. But just let me do this for you. It will make *me* feel better.'

Beth smiled gratefully. She didn't have the heart to disagree with him, so instead she took the envelope and tucked it safely into the bag slung across her body. 'Thank you. Thanks, Dad. I appreciate it, and all you've done for me. Margaret too.'

She had said her farewells to Margaret last night, and Margaret had promised to come and visit her soon with her dad.

'I was over there with the girls in the summer for the fête,' she'd said, referring to her daughter and granddaughter. 'It was quite the shindig.' Then she'd winked. 'But that's a story for another time. You'll not believe me when I tell you what happened . . . Anyway you'll have a ball. Mind you, it's going to be a big change from London isn't it. But the good thing is there are lots of nice-looking fellas there too . . .' She frowned as she thought about it. 'Though they all seemed to be taken when I was there. But anyway I'm sure you're bound to find yourself a new man. You're a great catch.'

Beth had winced and Margaret blushed, seemingly realising she had put her foot in it. She started to quickly backtrack.

'Sorry, ignore me. You don't need a man. They're useless. Nothing but trouble. You stay young, free and single. Ignore me and my big mouth. Sometimes I get a bit carried away and forget what I'm saying.'

Beth had grown increasingly fond of Margaret over the past week — especially after the Dolly-and-Cher bonding session — and now, as she stood there looking at her dad, who suddenly seemed older and smaller, she felt reassured that her dad had such a good neighbour, regardless of what their relationship was — and their questionable chat.

* * *

The weather forecast had been right, and by the time the ferry arrived at Brodick harbour, the wind had picked up and it was blowing a hooley. The grey water was furiously choppy. Beth had done all she could on the journey — focusing on the horizon — to avoid being sick. The dark, heavy skies looked as though a downpour of rain was imminent, and as she waited to get back down to the car deck, she heard people muttering about this being the last ferry of the day. As she turned to look at the rough seas behind her it was understandable that the ferry would dock in Brodick, not attempting the journey back to Ardrossan. Unfortunately, cancellations were par for the course if you lived on a Scottish island, even more so during the winter months. Even though it was just past noon, the fading daylight made it feel much later than it was. The shorter days were something she had managed to conveniently forget after living in the South of England for so long. As she looked out the smeared windows, she randomly thought about her old garden in Greenwich where she'd spent hot summer days enjoying glasses of ice-cold wine. She tried to push away the niggling voice of doubt that was starting to get louder in her head. *Is this really what you want? Have you made a mistake? Is it ever a good idea to revisit the past? What on earth are you doing? Surely the café would be better than this? There is no way you can do this.* But as she got into Margaret's car, silently thanking her again for that huge act of kindness, she reminded herself that she didn't have any other option. She no longer had a home *or* a job in London. This *had* to work. She had nothing to lose. Her inner cheerleader reminded her that, back in the day, she had flown all over the world in pursuit of stories. Interviewing Kofi Annan in New York when he was with the United Nations, actress Jennifer Anniston and all of One Direction were just a few highlights. Then the recession hit, and more and more jobs were axed and there were fewer prestigious jobs to cover. Beth had been a staff writer on a women's glossy magazine, which was forced to close when advertising revenue plummeted. Since then she had tried her best to make it as a freelancer, but the momentous effort it took to come up with new ideas and try and pitch them to no avail had left her exhausted. Sighing, she thought about why she became a journalist all those years ago. It wasn't about meeting celebrities. It was because she was young and naïve and thought that she could make a difference. Until she soon realised that sales were the bottom line.

Starting the ignition, she braced herself at the sound of the clunk as she followed the other vehicles driving over the ramp. The plan was to drive straight to *The Arran News* office where she would meet her colleague, Jim. He would in fact be her only workmate, so she really hoped they'd get along. Although they had only met on Zoom, he had been really enthusiastic about offering her the position, and delighted to hear about her connection of old with Arran. As she drove out of the ferry terminal, she looked at the foot passengers who were getting soaked in the rain that had turned torrential. The one person who had bothered to risk an umbrella was now fighting with it — the wind had blown it inside out. She was taken aback at the fancy terminal building, which was definitely new. It had been a much simpler harbour when she had last been there. The office was just a few minutes' drive away and she turned right and drove along the main road, briefly glancing at the cafés and shops that lined the left of the promenade. There had been lots of changes but, given that she hadn't been here for more than two decades, it all felt amazingly familiar. As she pulled up outside the front of the office, a shiver of nerves rippled through her. Being cocooned in the car made her feel safe and warm. Especially as the wind was now battering huge raindrops off the windscreen. As she approached the row where the office was, she could see Jim standing at the window waving.

Ordinarily Beth would have leaped out the car to say hello. But she was nervous and that jeering voice wasn't ready to quit. *What if he thinks I'm not up to the job? What if I get found out?* When she realised Jim was now waiting at the door and watching curiously, she summoned up the courage to get out of the car. *Come on,* she said to herself. *Local newspapers matter, and this is where I can try and make a difference.*

'Hi Jim. How are you?' She dashed towards the shelter of the doorway.

He ushered her in with a smile and gave her a warm handshake. 'What a lovely day, eh.' He laughed. 'Welcome Beth. It is great to see you . . . and I'm just glad you made it.' He gestured towards the bay. 'I believe the ferries are off now for the rest of the day.' He glanced at the sky. 'Though it looks like it could be a few days given the weather forecast.'

'I know. It was quite the bumpy ride. I just hoped I wouldn't vomit.' *Oh why did I say that?*

As if picking up on her anxious thoughts, he smiled reassuringly. 'Well you wouldn't be the first person to do that. I've never been great on boats, much to my wife's annoyance. She loves sailing.' He shrugged. 'Anyway, you're here now, Beth. There is no escape. Even if you wanted to leave you couldn't. I just hope you've brought your wellies.'

Beth wished she could come up with a witty response, but her mind went blank. 'Indeed.' She pictured the posh boots she'd bought to go away for a weekend in the country with Tim, which didn't happen. At least she could still get use of the boots.

'Now, come on, I can show you the office to begin with, which will take all of about ten seconds.' He pointed to the small open-plan office with a few desks. 'Welcome to our grand headquarters.' He chuckled. 'Let's just say you're not going to get lost.'

Beth looked around the room. 'It's absolutely fine,' she said brightly. A few wilting plants were dotted around the desks, looking as though they could do with a water.

'The kitchen is there and the toilets too.' Jim pointed through the back. 'And you'll appreciate, when the weather has improved a tad, we have that stunning sea view.' They both laughed as they looked at the dark churning waters in the distance. 'I'm fairly relaxed about where you want to work. You'll be out and about a fair bit, and we will always have a few meetings at certain times where we'll both be in the office. But if you want to write anything up from home that's okay. I tend to prefer coming in to be honest. I find I get a bit too distracted at home and end up in the kitchen or watching daytime telly.' He rolled his eyes and grinned.

'That all sounds good to me,' she said. 'And the flat? It's just upstairs?'

Jim hesitated and rubbed his hand over his chin. 'Ah, yes, it is.' He shifted his eyes from hers.

Beth felt a prickling sense of unease as she frowned.

'The only thing is, well, about the flat. I have to admit that we do have a *slight* problem.'

CHAPTER SEVEN

Beth watched as Jim jangled keys in his pocket. That in itself didn't bode well. In her experience, when people fidgeted it was a sign. They were usually trying to self-regulate because they were nervous about something.

'Ahem.' He coughed. 'The flat . . . and I am really sorry about this Beth, but the heating is knackered.' He pulled a face. 'I went in earlier to turn it on for you and make sure it was nice and cosy. Then I realised that the boiler had packed in.'

Beth shrugged, relieved that's all it was. 'Don't worry Jim, I'm sure I'll manage.' She was glad she'd packed her warmest layers. Margaret had also insisted she take a couple of extra blankets, "just in case", as it was always good to be prepared.

'Absolutely not.' Jim was firm. 'I've got a plumber coming out tomorrow, all being well, and so hopefully you should be in the flat soon. In the meantime I have taken the liberty of booking you into the Brodie Hotel for a few days. The last thing you need is being stuck in a freezing apartment when you've only just arrived. I don't want to put you off before you've even begun.'

Beth was completely touched but also taken aback. The Brodie was the hotel she used to work in all those summers ago, and had now been completely transformed. She'd looked at it recently online, out of curiosity, and had a nosy at the boutique bedrooms and annexe cabins. It was described as a cosy and secluded hotel, perfect for romantic escapes. She had also noticed the price tag and baulked slightly at the cost. She wasn't quite sure her credit card could take anything else right now and wondered how much this was going to cost her. Especially when she wasn't particularly in the market for a romantic or luxury break. The last thing she wanted to be was awkward, but she would have been happy to rent a caravan or stay in a hostel. That would have been better for her finances. Then she remembered the envelope of cash her dad had insisted on giving her earlier. That may well come in handy.

'The company will pick up the tab. This is for us to worry about, not you,' said Jim smoothly. 'I know the manager, we play golf together, and he has given us a deal for one of their cabins now that it's autumn and not quite so busy. It's lucky you came at the start of November and not December, when things ramp up for Christmas. Otherwise I'd be putting you in my spare bedroom.'

'Sounds good,' said a relieved Beth. 'And what a treat. Thank you so much. I have to admit it will be interesting to see it again after all these years.'

'Of course, I'm totally forgetting about your summer job there. That must feel like a lifetime ago now. Anyway, I think you'll notice a huge change since you last worked there. It was left empty for quite a few years, then bought over by the current owners around ten years ago. They have done a tremendous job with it.' He glanced at his watch and looked outside. 'Let's get you up there and settled and we can grab some lunch in the bar. I'll just jump in my car and you can follow me round. Let's make a dash for it as it looks like the rain has stopped. For now.'

Five minutes later, Beth pulled into the red gravel drive-way of the hotel and parked next to Jim. Before she got out the car, she quickly sent her dad a text to let him know she had arrived safely.

'It did *not* look like this when I worked here.' Beth looked up in wonder at the red sandstone building. During the two summers she spent working there she waitressed, covered the bar and also did a stint in housekeeping. They all mucked in and did what was needed and she realised that, actually, none of them had complained as it didn't actually feel like work. Now as she looked up at the hotel, she couldn't believe how much the building had completely transformed. She looked around in awe at the grounds, landscaped with beautiful shrubs and manicured lawns that, despite the weather, still looked immaculate — as though they had been combed — as well as neatly shaped hedges. The hotel was set in a peaceful location. The gardens had paved seating areas, possibly for al-fresco dining in the summer, with views across the sea. Beth recalled that the outdoor space was a real sun trap. Feelings of nostalgia came rushing back as she remembered how she and the other girls would soak up the sun whenever they had a break, making sure they got the best of summer tans. She shuddered to think of their lack of sunscreen protection back then and how they used a coconut-smelling cream, which maybe had factor one in it at the most. They must have fried their skin.

She was pulled from her sentimental thoughts when a tall and handsome man, with wavy black hair and a navy overcoat, came striding out the front door. He carried a huge golf umbrella shielding him from the rain that had started to fall again.

'Welcome.' He walked over to Jim and Beth and placed the huge umbrella over them. 'You must be Beth?'

She smiled and met his dark brown eyes as he reached to shake her hand. 'Hello.' He was very good-looking in a chiselled and groomed way.

'Beth. This is my friend Alessandro, who is also the hotel manager.'

'We are so pleased you're staying with us.' His smile was warm and engaging. 'Come on. Let me show you to your room and get you inside before the rain gets heavy again. Do you have bags?'

Beth quickly opened the boot, which was stuffed with all her possessions, and grabbed a holdall. 'This will do for now.'

'Jim, I will show Beth to her cabin. You wait in the bar and we'll be right back. That saves you getting wet and your hair being ruined.'

Jim, whose hair was very shortly cropped, let out a guffaw. 'Thanks for your consideration, mate. See you soon Beth.' He dashed towards the entrance.

CHAPTER EIGHT

Alessandro took Beth's bag from her. She followed as he led her down the path to the side of the building and the grounds at the back. It tapered off into a gravel walkway that was lined with shrubs and small lanterns, which were already glowing thanks to the lack of sunlight. As they followed the turn in the path through a small, wooded area, Beth gasped when it opened out to a grassy patch with three small log cabins. Each had a covered seating area at the front with a bench and small table.

'Wow,' she said. 'These are amazing.'

He nodded in approval. 'Yes, we have been very pleased with them. We had them built just before lockdown happened and they've been extremely popular with our guests. Especially when everyone was having a staycation these past few years.'

Beth gazed around and tried to recall what this part of the hotel used to be. She remembered that the hotel did have vast grounds, but she didn't appreciate just how much land it backed onto. When she worked here, this must have all been left to grow wild. Alessandro continued to the furthest cabin in the corner, which had a covered porch area, sheltering them from the rain. He gave the umbrella a shake and popped it down, placing it in the handy holder that sat right outside the door.

'You've really thought of everything,' said Beth admiringly.

'We like to make things as easy as possible for our guests. Nobody wants to take their wet umbrellas into the cabins and spoil the ambience with big wet puddles.' Alessandro slotted the keys in the lock and swung the door open. 'Here you are. Home for a few days. The larger cabins are booked out so I hope you don't mind this smaller one, which is more of a studio.' He placed her bag down by the door, pointing out where the heating switch was. He swivelled the dial round. 'I will increase the temperature now for you so it's toasty when you get back from lunch.'

It took a moment or two for Beth to absorb her surroundings — she didn't say anything. It was so far removed from what her life had become in London. For a moment she felt overcome with gratitude and joy. 'Crikey,' she said in awe. 'It is amazing.'

Alessandro looked at her curiously. 'Through here is the shower room.' He beckoned her through, pointing at the luxurious walk-in shower that had a huge round head. 'It should all just work with the flick of a switch, like so.'

Beth watched as he turned the water on and off. Then she caught sight of her reflection in the mirror. Her brown shoulder-length hair looked wild and unkempt. As her eyes connected with his as he looked at her, she felt her cheeks flush. It felt weirdly intimate to be in this tiny space with a man she had only just met. As she backed out into the main living area, she caught a whiff of his citrus aftershave, which smelt very familiar yet disconcertingly also filled her with dread. She tried to distract herself by quickly raking her fingers through her hair — hoping to tidy it up a bit — and looking around the studio. It was bright, spacious and open-plan, with a compact kitchen, a huge comfy sofa bed and a flat screen TV. It felt stylish yet homely, and she knew she would enjoy relaxing here the next few evenings, especially when it was so dark outside. Everything was decorated in a neutral colour, which helped to create a relaxing and tranquil feel.

'I do hope you will be very comfortable, Beth. I have taken the liberty of putting a few essentials in the fridge to keep you going as you won't want to be outside in this weather. But anything you need just let me know.' Alessandro smiled, showing his very white teeth. 'My number is here so do feel free to call me *anytime.*'

Beth wondered if he had overly lingered on the word "anytime" or whether she was just imagining it and she had to fight to suppress a sudden giggle. *What was wrong with her?*

He dropped his card on the coffee table and turned up the collar of his jacket. 'I will let you freshen up before you meet Jim in the bar.'

'Thank you,' she said gratefully, wondering what his story was and what had brought him to Arran. 'I really appreciate this. You are very kind.' Suddenly she wanted to know more. 'Have you worked here long?'

'A couple of years,' he said. 'Though on days like this it feels about a hundred years.' Alessandro laughed. 'I hope you've brought your boots and a big rain jacket.'

'I have come prepared,' she said. 'But I think I will just come across to the hotel with you now, so I can shelter under your brolly.'

'Of course. This will be a big change from London?' he asked curiously.

'Yes. But I was ready for something different . . .'

He raised an eyebrow at her but didn't ask any more questions. Beth assumed that he understood she wasn't ready to share any more information quite yet.

She pulled up her hood. 'Okay. Shall we? I am ready for an adventure.'

He laughed. 'That's what I like to hear.'

CHAPTER NINE

'I've made some porridge for you,' said Daisy as Callum came in the back door, rubbing his hands together.

'Oh brilliant. Thanks Daisy, you're a star. It's freezing out there and I am absolutely starving.'

It was still dark and Callum had just come in from walking Ruby and feeding the hens. He kicked off his boots, shrugged off his jacket and bent down to give Ruby another pat as she leaned into his legs.

'Come on, before it goes cold,' called Daisy.

Callum washed his hands at the sink, lathering them with soap and warm water. After drying them on a thick towel, he pulled out a seat at the table. He rubbed his hand over the reclaimed wood. It was the first piece of bespoke furniture he had made long before Daisy had come to live on the island. The table was a reminder of the kind of work he *wanted* to be doing rather than the functional joinery work that he had to do in order to pay the bills. Maybe one day he would when he had more time.

'You can add some seeds and raisins if you want,' suggested Daisy, passing him a packet of what looked suspiciously like bird seed. 'It's good for the gut,' she said knowingly.

'Though only have it if you want to. I don't want to tell you what to do,' she said in a sing-song voice. 'Or be bossy. Like you are with me.'

Callum grinned as he eyed the packet dubiously. 'I'll pass.' Picking up his spoon he took a mouthful of the porridge. It was surprisingly tasty. He could feel Daisy watching him and waiting for his response.

'You know, this is actually really nice. Especially after trudging about all morning in the cold and dark.' He took another spoonful and frowned. 'You have definitely made it differently though to how I would do it.'

'Urgh, of course I have,' she groaned. 'That's because you use water and salt which is absolutely disgusting. No wonder I never want to eat *your* porridge.' She didn't speak for a minute and then hesitantly spoke. 'Did my mum like porridge?'

'Sometimes,' he said gently. She'd caught him by surprise as she hadn't mentioned her for a while. 'And you did too when you were little. You loved it when she made you banana porridge.'

Daisy chewed her lip thoughtfully. 'It was really creamy I think. I do kind of remember that.'

'But when she was pregnant with you she preferred Coco Pops. She would eat boxes and boxes of them.'

Daisy pulled a face. 'Yuck. No wonder I don't like them. This is far nicer.'

'Right . . .' He didn't quite know whether to keep talking about Isla or change the subject. He paused, waiting to take her cue.

'Do you want to know how I made this?' she asked.

'Sure. Talk me through it then. What did you do? How did you make it?'

'Okay . . . well, I have been researching all the different ways that you can cook porridge. Did you know that you don't just have to use water?'

He nodded. The moment to talk about her mum had passed. 'I did know that. You can use milk or cream and sugar instead of salt . . . Gran said her parents used to make it with water and salt and then pour it into a drawer to set. Then they would slice it up into bars and eat it later.'

'That sounds horrid. A drawer? You mean like a drawer in the kitchen?'

'Yes, some of the old-fashioned kitchen tables had drawers in them, or some people would just use one of the bottom drawers in their dresser. If you Google it, you'll find pictures online.'

'But why on earth would they want to pour it into a random drawer? I mean there could be stuff in it.'

Callum smiled, knowing he could easily wind Daisy up with this, even though he shouldn't. 'Well I don't think health and safety was such a thing back then. But yes, sometimes they found old drawing pins and bits of fluff and stuff in the bars if they forgot to wipe the drawer our properly.'

Daisy's face was a picture of horror. 'That is totally gross. Yuck.'

'Actually I am kind of joking about that bit. But not about the drawer thing, although it does sound horrible doesn't it? What a mess it would make too.'

She sighed. 'You said your early New Year resolution was to stop making stuff up.'

He nodded. 'I know, you're right, but porridge drawers were actually very common in the olden days.' He grinned. 'Gran said they would be lined with a cloth before the porridge was poured in and left overnight to cool and set. And sometimes babies would be put in the drawer above to keep them warm.'

'Stop winding me up.'

He held up his hands. 'Honestly, I'm not. Ask Gran and she'll tell you. I promise you, I'm on my best behaviour and telling the truth.'

'I will ask her *and* I will tell her that you've already broken your New Year resolution about making fun of me.' She cleared her plate from the table and dumped it in the sink.

'Anyway, you said your early New Year resolution was to go vegan, and there is definitely milk or cream in here.'

The look of sheer triumph on her face told him he'd managed to assume wrong.

'You are *so* wrong. It has milk in it, but it's coconut milk, with a splash of maple syrup.'

'I was *not* expecting you to say that. Wow. Well done, Daisy. I really enjoyed it. I would definitely eat that again if you made it for me.'

Daisy rolled her eyes and tutted. 'What's the magic word?'

'Soon . . . sorry, I meant, please.' Crikey, she was a hard taskmaster.

'Maybe you could go vegan as well?' She grinned.

'I love you very much, Daisy Thompson, but that is a step *too* far.' Based on what he had picked up for her at the supermarket there was no way he was going to be eating any of the vegan stuff. Callum was a meat and two veg kind of guy and nothing was going to change that. Not even Daisy. Glancing at the clock he realised the school bus would soon be there.

'Sorry, I don't think I've time to clear up,' she said sheepishly.

'It's okay,' he said. 'Get your stuff and I'll do it.'

'Thank you,' she sang, looking very relieved. 'You're the best. Oh, and remember I won't be home at the usual time. Murray and I are going to start working on the school newspaper this afternoon.'

He nodded thoughtfully. 'It's marked on the calendar. Shall I pick you up from school later?'

'I'll message you and let you know where we are. We may go back to his house and work from there.'

'Okay, just keep in touch.'

Murray was one of Daisy's best friends so Callum didn't question it. If it had been any other boy he might not have been quite so relaxed. He knew that she was going to soon be attracting a lot of attention from the opposite sex, and he hadn't prepared himself for just how protective he would feel over her. She was growing up to be such a beautiful girl — and she was *so* like her mother. Sometimes the likeness caught Callum by surprise and he felt as though Isla was actually in the room. He caught his mum watching her over the holidays, wiping away a few tears when she thought he wasn't looking. Both Daisy and her mother had long and wavy blonde hair, with a dusting of freckles across their noses, and rosebud lips. Daisy was also very headstrong in the same way that Isla had been and had the same mannerisms. She'd started putting her hands on her hips when she was arguing, which was becoming more common, especially as she loved modern studies at school. He was glad it was a subject she enjoyed, as there was a lot about school that she didn't seem to like at the moment.

'See you later,' called Daisy as she ran to the front door, pulling on her coat.

'Bye D,' he said, feeling an unexpected sob catch at the back of his throat.

Smiling, oblivious to the fact he was trying to choke back tears, she left him with a wave and ran out the door. He stood up and walked to the window, watching as she ran up the lane. His every instinct was to protect Daisy and keep her wrapped in cotton wool, away from the world in a way that he hadn't been able to do with Isla. That was something he would always regret until the day he died.

CHAPTER TEN

Over the next couple of days, memories of Beth's time on Arran came flooding back as she explored and refamiliarized herself with her new surroundings, as well as the places she had such fond memories of. Fortunately the rain had let up and the winds had died down, which made life a bit easier. She was so grateful that Margaret had suggested she borrow her car. It meant she could drive the whole way around the island from Brodick through the villages of Lamlash and then round to Whiting Bay down to Kildonan — an area she had always loved swimming at when she was younger — then to Blackwaterfoot and all the way up to Lochranza, where you could catch the ferry to Claonaig on the mainland, and then round to Corrie. It was exactly as she had remembered, which was such a relief. She would have been so disappointed if the island had lost its charm and appeal. Plenty of years had passed but, if anything, it felt as though things had mainly stayed the same. Yes, there were new places, but nothing significant or transformative that had changed its essence. It all felt reassuringly familiar. She felt a sense of belonging, which was an unusual feeling, and so far removed from what her life had been like last year. It felt like *home*.

A plumber had been called out to fix the heating in the flat, however, it looked as though a new boiler was needed, so the problem was going to take a bit longer than a few days to fix. In the meantime Beth had unpacked a few more of her clothes and made herself at home in the cabin, despite her attempts not to get too comfortable. The flat that she was going to was fine, but not a patch on the stylish hotel accommodation.

Today Jim had kindly invited her to have Sunday lunch with his family. He lived just outside the village of Lamlash with his wife, Freya, and their sons, who were twelve and fourteen. Beth stopped at the local shop in the village to pick up some flowers and chocolates for them. As she walked back towards the car she glanced up and noticed a café with floor-to-ceiling windows. The sign said *Cèic* and the windows were strung with twinkling fairy lights that made it look very cosy and welcoming. She was tempted to go in but was short of time. Instead, she made a promise to herself that she would definitely return to check it out. As she opened the car door, she glanced over at the verge by the beach and saw a man walking his dog. Her stomach started to flutter. There was something familiar about his gait and the casual but confident way he strolled across the grass. He turned to call the dog and, when she saw his face, her head started to spin. Beth quickly got into the car and sat in the driver's seat for a moment to gather her thoughts. *It was just a coincidence*, she told herself. It wasn't him. Not after all this time. It was just someone who looked like him, and she felt a pang of wistfulness as she thought back to those intense and heady days when life seemed far much simpler. She allowed her mind to drift for a moment, thinking back to how different her life might have been if he had arrived at the train station that day. Then she gave herself a shake and remembered that she had somewhere to be. There was no point in dwelling in the past. There was no way he was still here after all this time.

A few minutes later she pulled into the driveway of Jim's split-level bungalow, which had wonderful views towards the

Holy Isle. She paused for a moment as she looked at the small island in the bay. It was a place dedicated to peace and well-being and it was only now, when she had the perspective of a weary adult, that she understood why people would go there on retreats, to take a break from life and get back in touch with themselves. It did sound very appealing. As she turned and walked towards the front door of the house it swung open just as she reached it.

'Well hello there,' said Freya, a petite woman with curly red hair and a broad smile. 'You must be Beth. I've heard so much about you. Welcome. Come on in.'

Beth warmed to her immediately as she followed her into a bright hallway where she kicked off her boots.

'Och, you don't have to do that Beth,' said Freya, who was wearing just warm socks on her feet. 'But I appreciate it. I feel as though I spend all my time mopping the floors at the moment, especially with all this rain. As you can imagine the boys tramp in and out with muddy boots and don't give it a second thought. Come on through here.' She walked into a huge open-plan kitchen with a large island and barstools.

'This is Rory, our younger son.' She pointed to a shy-looking boy who was sitting on a stool swinging his legs.

'Hi Rory, nice to meet you,' said Beth.

'Hello.' His cheeks flushed.

'Where's your brother?' asked Freya.

Rory shrugged. 'I'll go find him.' He slipped off the stool and went to look for him.

Beth handed the flowers and chocolates to Freya. 'These are for you.'

'They're gorgeous,' said Freya. 'Though there was no need.'

'I wanted you to know I appreciate you having me.'

Freya gave her a reassuring smile. 'Thank you.' She took the flowers to the sink and reached for a vase from a cupboard. 'It's great to have you here, and I know Jim is just relieved that it's no longer just down to him.'

'I'm excited about it.' Beth watched as Freya snipped the end of the flowers, then poured boiling water over the ends.

'Just a wee tip I picked up along the way. It makes them last longer.' Freya had seen Beth watching.

Beth smiled. 'Thanks for that. I will try and remember the next time I have flowers.' She gestured around the room and towards the window that framed the bay. 'You have a beautiful home. And what an amazing view.'

'Thank you.' Freya smiled and put the vase of flowers on the window ledge. 'I do love sitting there and just looking out when I'm in the house on my own and all is quiet. It changes every day. I often think of it as being like a live picture frame.'

Beth nodded in agreement. 'I can see how that would appeal.'

Freya pointed to one of the stools at the breakfast bar. 'Take a seat while we wait for the boys to come down. I have to say, I do think you're very brave to come here.'

Beth shrugged as she perched on the barstool. 'At least it's not completely new to me. I think that would be much scarier. I'm not quite sure I could go somewhere I don't know at all. And it's actually really nice to be back.'

'Of course, that's right. Jim said that you worked here when you were a student?'

'Yes, that was a very long time ago. But it was a really happy time. I've got some great memories.'

'I'm not surprised. That time in your life when you have no worries and everything is carefree. Then it all goes downhill.' Her tone was knowing, but she smiled. 'It has been a great place to raise the boys, and they love the summers here. But I have a feeling they'll be off to the mainland as soon as they can.' Freya took a seat opposite her. 'Did you keep in touch with anyone from your time here?'

'Not really. We all had good intentions to begin with, and then things kind of fizzled out. Life happened, I guess. I don't know anyone here anymore. I suspect most people will have left and gone on to other things.'

'Yes, I know what you mean. We didn't have Facebook back in the day did we. It was harder to stay in touch, as I keep telling the boys. Mind you, it was also easier to be a bit more elusive, which I have to say I prefer. I will never get used to everyone feeling the need to share every minute detail of their lives.'

Beth nodded thoughtfully. Even now some people avoided social media like the plague. They clearly just didn't want to be found.

CHAPTER ELEVEN

After Freya and Beth chatted for a while, Jim appeared with who Beth assumed was their older son.

'Hi there,' she said brightly.

'Good to see you Beth,' said Jim. 'This is Murray. We were just trying to get some maths homework done.'

Murray was less shy than his brother — he stepped forward and held out his hand. 'Nice to meet you, Beth.'

'Oh, I don't envy you. Maths was never my strong point,' admitted Beth.

'Aye and I don't think it's my dad's either.'

Beth chuckled.

'Oi,' said Jim, 'do you mind? Did I or did I not help you with the problem?' He rolled his eyes. 'Honestly! Grab a seat at the table and I'll get lunch sorted. It won't be long.'

'Jim has been cooking so we are in for a treat.' Freya chuckled. 'Beth, if you and the boys grab a seat at the table and I'll just bring over some water.'

The large table in the dining area of the kitchen was covered in a pale blue oilskin cover, was flanked on either side by pine benches.

'Beth, I've done a roast chicken. I hope that's okay. And I believe Rory has been busy making an apple crumble.' Jim had a tea towel sling over his shoulder and looked very much at home in the kitchen.

'That sounds perfect. Thank you. And Rory, how did you know that crumble is my favourite?'

Rory blushed but smiled as he followed Beth to the table, taking a seat next to her. 'We did it in food tech.'

'Food tech, is that like home economics?'

Freya nodded as she sat opposite Beth. 'Yes, it was home ec back in our day, wasn't it? But it's pretty much the same thing.'

'And do you like cooking, Rory?' asked Beth.

'Yes.' He nodded enthusiastically.

'What sort of things do you like making?'

'Pastas, cakes, curries, omelettes.' His voice bubbled with excitement. 'And we're going to start doing Christmas baking soon. Shortbread and a Yuletide log.'

'Wow. I wish I could do all of that.'

Rory flushed with embarrassment but smiled, clearly delighted by her praise.

'The school has a winter market later this month,' said Freya. 'You'll need to come to that Beth. Rory has volunteered to help with the cake stall.'

'I will be there.' Beth smiled at Rory. 'I love cake, and it's been ages since I've gone to anything like that. Count me in.'

'And there's the Christmas fair too. That's at the start of December, when the lights are switched on.' Rory's eyes sparkled with excitement.

Jim chuckled. 'And that's just in Lamlash. You've joined us at the right time, Beth. It's going to be a busy few weeks for you.'

'It sounds perfect. I can't wait.' And Beth meant it.

Perhaps it was Rory's youthful enthusiasm, or the cosy ambience that Jim and his wife had created in their home, but Beth realised she felt a sense of happy anticipation at the thought of Christmas. She was looking forward to being part of this community as all the festivities began. It was a sign of how far she'd come since this time last year.

The conversation flowed over lunch as they talked about the boys' school and their other subjects. Some favourite and others not so much. Freya spoke of her reluctance to move to the island when Jim was offered the job. 'We were living in Aberdeen, close to my parents, and Murray was about to start school and Rory was a toddler,' she explained. 'I thought it was one of the worst ideas Jim had ever had.'

Jim smiled at her affectionately. 'But it turns out I was right though, wasn't I?'

She grinned at him. 'Yes, you were. And it was the best decision we made. We moved into this amazing house, the boys settled into school and I even managed to get a teaching job in the primary school. It all seemed to fall into place.'

'Then the in-laws moved over too,' said Jim wryly.

Freya took a sip of her water. 'It has worked out well for babysitting though. We've been really lucky to have them here. But enough about us.' Freya set her glass back down. 'Tell us about London. How did you like working there?'

'It was a great place to be as a young journalist, when papers and magazines had budgets.'

'You must have seen some sights? Jim said your CV is incredible.'

'I was very lucky.' She felt her cheeks flush. 'I did get to travel quite a bit.'

'I can't believe you wanted to come *here*, after doing all of that exciting stuff,' said Murray. 'Won't you be bored?'

'Ah, well, things tend to change as you get older.' She shrugged. 'I was ready for a quieter pace of life.' Beth wasn't quite ready to talk about or dwell on her past. She rested her fork on her plate and looked at Murray and Rory appraisingly. 'Now, tell me what you like to do when you're not at school.'

Jim cleared away the main course and brought the crumble dish to the table, scooping large helpings into bowls.

Beth listened intently to both boys as they talked about their hopes for the future and things they did at the weekend, including football and rugby and kayaking when the weather got a bit warmer. They also said they were hopeful that the year ahead might involve a trip to see Scotland win a rugby game at Murrayfield Stadium in Edinburgh.

'You may have a long wait,' said Jim drily. 'They're not doing so well right now. I think just be content with watching them play a game at Murrayfield rather than them necessarily winning.'

Beth raised her eyebrows, smiling as Jim and the boys started to debate, in impressive detail, the strengths and weaknesses of the national squad.

Freya shook her head. 'You see what I have to put up with? If it's not rugby, it's football, and I know it's clichéd but I don't like either.'

Beth chuckled and realised how much she was enjoying being part of this household that was full of love and chatter and stories. She took a final mouthful of crumble and put her spoon back in her bowl. 'I'm absolutely stuffed. That was delicious. Thank you so much. I insist that you let me help with the washing up.'

'Not at all. That's for Murray and Freya to sort. We have a rule in the family that whoever cooks doesn't do the tidying,' said Jim.

Freya grinned. 'Yep, and when Murray and I cook we also, very thoughtfully, don't use absolutely *every* single dish in the kitchen.'

Murray nodded in agreement, then turned to look at Beth, focusing his dark brown eyes on her. 'I wondered Beth . . . would you be able to help me with a school project please?'

'Of course — well, as long as it's not maths.' Beth couldn't help smiling. 'I'm afraid it was never my strength.'

He shook his head. 'No, it's not maths, don't worry. A few of us are keen to start a school newspaper and I wondered if you might come in and speak to the group and give us some advice, please. We have started trying to make a plan but we're a bit stuck.'

'Of course I will,' said Beth carefully. 'Though you do have a bit of an expert here in your dad. Don't you want to ask him? I don't want to step on his toes.'

Jim had a huge grin on his face. 'It's not quite the same when it's your old man though, is it? You can imagine how embarrassing it would be for him to have me traipse into school and lecture them. I mean, what do I know about anything?'

Beth gave Murray a conspiratorial wink. 'That is very true. I can totally see what you mean. Look, don't worry, we can't possibly have your dad embarrassing you. I would be delighted to help. Just let me know when and where and I'll be there.'

Murray jumped up from the table with a huge smile on his face. 'Brilliant. Thanks so much Beth. When can you come in?'

'As soon as you would like. Next week if that helps? You have a chat with the group and the teachers and work out when would suit. I am assuming that I would need the head-teacher's permission to work with you? I actually have my DBS, the English criminal record check, if they'll accept that?'

Jim nodded. 'Don't worry, it's all fine as I forgot to tell you that I did the Disclosure Scotland check for you when you accepted the job. Your certificate should be in your desk drawer in the office.'

Beth raised her glass. 'Thank you. Thanks for making me feel so welcome. It's been such a lovely afternoon and I am happy to help with anything that I can. Same goes for you too, Rory.'

Freya, Jim, Murray and Rory clinked their glasses against Beth's.

'To a new beginning and a brilliant New Year on Arran. Cheers everyone,' said Freya.

'Cheers,' said the rest of them unanimously.

CHAPTER TWELVE

Beth walked into the small kitchen in the corner of the office and filled the kettle, feeling a mixture of positive emotions. Her happiness felt heightened, as though the screen had been pulled back on her grey world and she was rediscovering colour for the first time. It was like being in the opening scenes of *The Wizard of Oz* when everything began in black and white and then became vibrant. As she waited for the water to boil, she thought back to the day she spotted the advert for the new job. Since then it seemed as though things were now slotting in to place, bit by bit, and the overriding feeling she had was one of joy. She was truly grateful that she was here doing a job she loved.

The plumber had deemed the flat almost fit for purpose, and tomorrow it would be ready to move into. She had been scouring previous editions of the paper to get a feel of what mattered most to locals, and Jim had introduced her to some of his key contacts on the island.

This morning she had noted possible ideas for future editions, jotted down some thoughts around audio and video content to contribute to the online edition, as well as checked the diary for significant dates and events — it was due to be really busy thanks to the time of year — while Jim chatted to her in between calls and queries.

Jim was very much the hands-on type, which Beth respected. Even though he had a senior position he wasn't afraid to roll up his sleeves and just get on with what needed to be done, whether that was writing up stories, interviewing locals, taking photos or making the coffee and running out to get milk when they ran out. He was a breath of fresh air compared to the many bullying editors she'd worked with who had monstrous egos. All the design and advertising for the paper was handled at the company's Glasgow headquarters, which also oversaw the running and production of six other local newspapers across Scotland. That meant she and Jim could focus on the content.

'There you go.' She placed a mug of coffee on Jim's desk.

'Thank you.' He lifted it up and curled his hands around the warm cup. 'Just what I needed.'

She sat back down at her own desk and looked at him curiously. 'This must have been an awful lot of work for you when you were here on your own.' The previous reporter had left more than six months ago to work abroad, and Jim had since told her they'd struggled to fill the post.

Jim shrugged. 'Yes and no. I'm quite used to multitasking so just got on with it. That said, I am glad that you're here now. As is Freya. I think she was getting quite cheesed off with all the late nights, of me calling home to say I was "just doing one more thing" and then would get back hours later.'

'I'm sure.' Beth gave a wry smile. 'It can be hard being partnered with a journalist. I know how work can become a consuming passion.'

Jim chuckled. 'Aye, I think Freya would agree with you. She's been very patient over the years. But there have been a lot of comments about the paper being my other woman.'

'Did you ever want to go and work for one of the big papers?'

'Not at all. The biggest paper I worked for, before coming here, was the *Press and Journal* in Aberdeen, and that was full on, especially with the kids being little. I lost count of how many times I missed their bedtimes because I was working late or got called in at the weekends when a big story broke. That's why I jumped at the chance for this job when I was offered it. I wanted something more settled, and I didn't want my marriage to fall apart.' He grimaced. 'I'd seen it happen too many times to colleagues who had no boundaries between their lives and work.' He looked around the office and shrugged. 'I know this is a small operation, but to be honest my heart was always in local news, and I think regional newspapers are more important than ever. Especially nowadays. They can help to strengthen connections in communities. Local news really does matter.'

Beth thought about how driven and ambitious she had been as a young journalist. Her focus had been all about getting to London as soon as possible. She knew that staying in Scotland wasn't enough for her back then, and that was why she was so quick to turn down the job of trainee reporter here and head south to a junior position with a news agency.

'What about you? What have you enjoyed most about your career?' Jim leaned back on his chair.

Beth tucked a leg underneath her on the seat and frowned as she thought about it. 'Meeting lots of incredible people and helping them tell their stories . . . Travelling to places I might otherwise never have been . . . that has been amazing . . .'

'Where was the best place you went to?'

'I loved New York for obvious reasons. But I think the most memorable place I went to was Bosnia. To interview people impacted by the war. It's always good to try and shine a light on places and people who are left affected by a war, yet the rest of the world seems to have moved on and forgotten them.'

They were both quiet for a moment, lost in thought.

Jim broke the silence. 'What else?'

'The parties and the social life . . . though saying that out loud all sounds quite trite, doesn't it?' For a while Beth had lived the high life and mixed with people as ambitious as her, until she realised something was missing, in more ways than one. Then, when her carefully constructed life started to crumble, she found herself unconsciously avoiding the people she had once called friends until she slipped off their radar. There had been no contact from them, when she could *really* have done with friends, when she'd been at rock bottom. It had been a harsh life lesson, making her think about the impermanence of life and of people, and how colleagues, contacts, friends came into your life and then just as easily drifted out of it. She often wondered whether the sacrifices she had made over the years had been worth it.

'Anyway,' she forced a smile, 'that all seems like a million years ago now.'

Jim glanced out the window and waved at Laura, the post-woman, who had just walked past. 'Remind me to introduce you to Laura. She knows everyone and quite often everything . . . I often think she's an honorary team member. If I have a question she generally will have an answer.' He finished his coffee and placed the mug on his desk. 'Well I for one am glad to have you here with all your experience and enthusiasm. We maybe don't offer the glamourous life of London, but what we lack in fancy nights out and travel we make up for in friendliness.'

Beth shuddered at the thought of returning to her old life — she realised what she'd been missing in London. She missed having friends who were authentic and there for her. She had so much to be grateful for right now, and she wanted to make sure she focused on that rather than looking back. She had tried so hard to make things work in London, and then tried again, always trying to focus on being as positive as she could, until those last few months in particular. But it clearly wasn't meant to be.

She was grateful that things hadn't worked out because then she would never have come back to Arran. Her excitement at being here was also mixed with nerves — she wanted to make sure she lived up to Jim's expectations. Apart from anything else, *The Arran News* was one of the best-performing weekly newspapers in the country and had a really loyal readership. She felt privileged to be part of it, as though she was now able to do something positive for the place she once loved.

'Not at all. It feels good to be doing something different and worthwhile, Jim, and I'm grateful you've given me this chance.'

CHAPTER THIRTEEN

Later that night, Beth walked along the promenade and followed the road that swept round to the hotel. The weather was settled and still. The sea was calm. She crossed the road to look out over the water towards the twinkling lights of the mainland. There was something quite reassuring about the stretch of dark water that separated her in this new life from the rest of the world. Although she wasn't quite sure she would ever get used to the cooler temperatures in Scotland. Shivering, she pulled her hat down over her ears and turned to make her way back to the cabin. As she reached the driveway, she looked at the welcoming fairy lights in the window of the restaurant, the guests cosy inside and enjoying dinner. For a moment she stood watching and breathing in the cool, night air. Going to fancy restaurants for dinner, or meeting friends in bars for drinks, was such a big part of her life for so long that she took it for granted. She'd been completely unaware of the people on the other side of the window — those outside and looking in, like she was now. Eventually she turned her attention to the lit pathway that took her to the cabin. As she walked, she looked up at the stars in the dark sky. It was so peaceful tonight without the wind howling and no revving engines or blaring sirens like there would have been in Deptford.

Two years ago she and Tim had spent a couple of nights on a stargazing break in Northumberland. During the day they had visited the remnants of Hadrian's Wall and the tree at the Sycamore Gap. She still couldn't believe that someone had hacked it down. At night an astronomer gave them a laser-guided tour of the constellations, and she remembered her excitement when she realised she could see the Milky Way arching its way across the sky. Beth wasn't quite sure that she could remember all of the planets and galaxies, but as she stood now peering up at the dark sky, she could see clusters of stars. It was another romantic spot just like Northumberland had been, which wasn't lost on her, but she felt quite empowered to be standing here at this moment *and* even more so that she was alone. Beth realised she had almost forgotten what that kind of confidence felt like. She couldn't remember the last time she felt content and comfortable enough to just be like this. For a few moments she stood enjoying the glittering vast sky and felt very at peace. Until she heard the sound of footsteps crunching on the path behind her. She turned to see who was coming.

'I see you are enjoying the lovely evening and beautiful sky.' Alessandro walked confidently towards her with a huge silver platter. His smile lit up his face and his gaze lingered on her.

'I can't believe how clear it is. Isn't it amazing? Though it's starting to feel quite raw.' She shivered. 'I'd better get inside and warm up.'

She began walking, and he accompanied her in a comfortable silence. 'I'm not sure if Jim mentioned,' she said, 'the flat will be ready for me tomorrow so I'll move my stuff out then.'

His face fell. 'Yes, we will be sorry to lose you.'

Beth wasn't quite sure how to respond to that. 'Uh, well, it has been lovely staying here. Thank you for making the space and for looking after me so well.'

'It has been my pleasure. Don't be a stranger.'

She gestured at the platter. 'I'd better let you deliver that, otherwise it will get cold.'

He laughed. 'Ciao for now.'

'Bye Alessandro.'

'Maybe we could get a drink sometime?' he asked over his shoulder as he walked away.

She froze for a moment, telling herself not to jump to conclusions as he was just being friendly. 'Erm, maybe. Goodnight.'

She let herself into the cabin and closed the door firmly behind her. Her cheeks were flushed and she couldn't work out why she was so flustered. Then she realised that, for the first time in a long time, she'd actually felt seen. So much for feeling empowered. He was the first man who had paid her any attention for a long time and she'd turned into a bag of nerves. She gave herself a shake and reminded herself she didn't need anyone else's approval or attention. She was managing fine as she was.

CHAPTER FOURTEEN

Callum had driven to Lamlash this morning especially to pick up an almond croissant for his elderly neighbour, Maisie, who lived in the small stone cottage just along from Callum's house. It was her birthday today and, at ninety-two, she showed no signs of slowing down. Even as he'd driven past her house earlier, she'd given him a wee wave and a wide smile as she'd pegged her sheets outside on the washing line. Despite the cold temperature, the sky was blue, the sun shone and there was enough of a breeze to ensure her sheets got a good airing. Callum often envied her boundless energy and razor-sharp wit.

He got out the truck, followed by Ruby, and smiled at the lollipop man, who was just packing his things away now the kids were safely in school. 'Morning,' he said as he passed and made his way towards Cèic, the bakery and café that produced the famous croissants that Maisie was so fond of. The slate chalkboard sign outside said, "*Come in and start your day the Cèic way. Furry friends are welcome.*"

Callum wasn't a regular visitor to the café, mainly as he was usually busy working or doing errands and didn't have time to sit around sipping fancy coffee. He just made do with the instant stuff at home, which he would quickly swig as he went about his task list. But this morning, as he admired the view and saw the basket of freshly baked scones that the owner, Cano, had just put on the counter, he decided to live a little and ordered himself a latte and a blueberry scone. 'Oh, and I'd better not forget, an almond croissant too please. To take away.' He watched as Cano reached for his tongs and put the pastry carefully into a paper bag.

'No problem, take a seat and I'll bring your scone and coffee over,' he said cheerfully.

Callum walked over to a seat at the window. Ruby curled up and lay at his feet. He always felt uncomfortable in some of the super trendy coffee shops he'd been to in Glasgow, with their hard-edged chairs and fancy interiors. But this morning, as he sat there and people watched — something he *never* usually did — he realised it was like the hub of the community as people passed in and out to collect their coffee and morning pastries. A long wooden table ran along the front of the huge floor-to-ceiling windows that overlooked the bay. The oak floors were lightly scuffed. Plants were dotted around, offering bursts of vivid green. There was a constant sound of chatter and laughter above the noise of the coffee machine whirring in the background. Wonderful smells of nutmeg and cinnamon wafted from the kitchen, which he inhaled.

'Hey Callum.' Fergus, who worked at the outdoor centre in the village, was clutching two takeaway cups. 'I wondered if it was you. Long time no see. How's tricks?'

'Alright.' Callum felt slightly mortified that he had been caught sitting in a café. Especially when he had been keeping a very low profile lately.

'There you go.' Cano arrived with his coffee and scone, setting them on the table before returning to his post.

'Treating yourself?' asked Fergus light-heartedly.

'Aye something like that.' Callum felt his cheeks colour.

'Quite right. You deserve a break. You work too hard man, been ages since we've seen you. When was the last time you got out on a kayak?'

Callum shrugged. Fergus was right. It had been months, possibly more than a year since he had been out on his kayak. 'Aye, it's been a while. There never seems to be a minute with everything that's going on. And the weather hasn't exactly been encouraging.'

'I know.' Fergus nodded. 'It's been rubbish. How's things?'

'Aye good.' Callum took a sip from his cup, realising how much he enjoyed a coffee that someone else had made for him. 'Mum came over a couple of weeks ago and that was great. Daisy loved seeing her. How about you? Things still going well with Amelia?'

Fergus grinned in response. 'All good thanks. Work is fine and Amelia is great.' He rubbed his hands together. 'Getting a bit chilly now, isn't it?'

Callum nodded and gestured at the scone in front of him. 'This is not my normal routine, honest. It is very out of character for me. Just thought, well, why not?'

'Quite right,' said Fergus. 'Mind you, if I start seeing you here every morning, I would think that was strange, but you are allowed a break Callum. Listen, how about you come out with me and Grant for a beer one night? Do you fancy it?' Fergus put his cups down on the table and bent down to scratch Ruby's ears.

'Sounds good.' Callum had got used to uttering these words over the years to people's invitations when he rarely followed up on it. But this time he genuinely meant it. He knew he had neglected his friends these past few years. They'd been great about stepping in to support and help with Daisy when she was younger. But he'd been so overwhelmed with everything that sometimes it felt easier just to withdraw. He couldn't blame his friends for getting fed up with him when he never replied to their texts or cancelled plans at the last minute. But now Daisy was older and more independent, he knew he really needed to make more of an effort. Otherwise he was going to end up friendless. Fergus had moved back to the island a couple of years ago, and Callum had met him through his old friend Grant who worked at the outdoor centre. Fortunately they were both very laidback and didn't seem to mind their erratic friendship, or that Callum would drift in and out of their lives depending on what was happening with his.

'Right, I'll give you a shout and we'll plan to do something soon? I'd better get back to the centre. Grant will be raging if I don't get his coffee to him. He likes it piping hot.'

Callum laughed at his sarcasm. Grant and rage were two words that couldn't have been more mismatched. He watched as an older woman, who looked like Edie, approached Fergus from behind and placed a hand on his shoulder.

'Good morning, Fergus.' Her dog, a spaniel, wagged its tail so furiously at Fergus that her whole bottom moved back and forth.

'Edie.' He turned and beamed at her in delight. 'Nice to see you. Oh, and you too Molly.' He laughed as she settled herself at his feet and stared up in adoration.

'Oh Molly,' said Edie. 'You are a shameless flirt.'

The dog wandered over to sniff Ruby's head — she raised it briefly before sinking it back down between her paws.

'Molly come here and stop bothering the poor dog. She looks like she's quite happy as she is.' Edie smiled warmly at Callum.

'Edie, you know my mate Callum who lives up near Maisie in the old cottage. And Ruby his dog,' said Fergus.

'Ah, yes, of course,' she said. 'Hi Callum.' She looked at Callum and chuckled. 'Maisie always speaks very highly of you.'

Callum had always had a soft spot for Edie, and he immediately warmed to her again this morning. She had twinkling eyes and a bright orange coat. A yellow scarf was draped round her neck and she looked like a burst of sunshine, with her vibrant energy and kind smile. 'Nice to see you Edie.'

'Right I'd better be off,' said Fergus. 'Or Grant really will be raging. Callum, you enjoy your five minutes' peace and let's arrange to catch up soon. See you.'

Callum gave his friend a wave. 'Nice to see you too Edie.'

She paused and Callum waited, fully expecting her to say goodbye. But she suddenly sat down. 'I know this is a bit forward of me dear, and I hope you don't mind, but I need you to be my decoy. I'm trying to avoid Doris over there.'

Callum glanced over at the door and raised his eyebrows questioningly.

'She's in charge of the Christmas fair and she's driving me mad. I can't bear to listen to her rant on about Santa's grotto yet again. Or debate how many mini-marshmallows should be sprinkled on the cups of hot chocolate. Once she gets going there's no stopping her. And if you're not careful she'll have you signed up as Santa. She managed to rope Fergus into it last year.'

Callum chuckled. 'Yes, I remember that. Looks like the coast is clear. She's away.'

'Oh thank goodness for that. Actually, while I am sitting here, and I know this is a bit cheeky of me. But, well, I'll strike while the iron's hot and all of that . . . It's just that I'm looking for someone to do some nice shelves for my study. I've books all over the place and I keep tripping over them. Well, I know you're a bit of an expert with joinery and woodwork . . .'

Callum smiled at her. 'I'd love to help. Just give me a call and I can come and have a look.' He passed her a business card.

'Oh thank you dear, I'm so glad I was bold enough to ask. It's been on my to-do list for yonks! Anyway, I'd say it's time for me to get my coffee. Otherwise I'm going to expire. Toodle-oo. I'll be in touch.' She grinned. 'And thanks for being my decoy.' With that, she gave Molly's lead a gentle tug and turned to make her way to the counter.

Callum took a bite of his scone and chewed. The thought of making some bespoke shelves for Edie had left him feeling excited. It had been a while since he'd done anything other than the usual joinery jobs, which had involved a lot of window frames lately. This would make a nice change — he could be more creative. Feeling buoyed, he realised he really needed to make more of an effort to get out and connect with people. It felt good just to chat. He should make more effort to come here and socialise. There was kindness and authenticity to Edie's smile, and her request for help and the interaction with both her and Fergus this morning was a reminder that there were genuine people out there who cared for him.

He glanced at the door and did a double take when he saw an attractive woman exiting with her takeaway coffee. There was something familiar about her and he watched her through the window, frowning as he tried to place her. Then his heart skipped a beat as he realised who she reminded him of. It had been years since he'd thought about Elizabeth. He couldn't. She was from a different lifetime — a lifetime that was very different to where he had ended up. Realising he was getting wistful, he gave himself a shake. She was long gone and firmly in the past. He picked up the paper bag with Maisie's croissant. 'We better get this to the birthday girl.' He stood up and Ruby jumped to her feet.

Stopping at the café that morning had been a nice reminder that, even though life could be tough, he did have friends and he wasn't alone.

CHAPTER FIFTEEN

Later that night Beth pulled on her pyjamas and warm socks, curled up on the sofa and called her dad, letting him know she had now moved all her things into the flat. She had barely spoken to him since her arrival on Arran as she had been so busy settling into the new job. But she really did want to let him know everything was okay.

He picked up in two rings.

'Hey Dad. How are you?'

'Better for hearing you dear. Tell me how are you? Are you all settled and enjoying island life?'

She smiled at the sound of his reassuring voice. 'Yes, I am, and sorry I haven't been in touch. It's been hectic trying to get settled and learn the ropes. But you'll be glad to know that I am now in the flat above the office. I moved in this afternoon.'

'That's good news. You said in your message that the boiler was broken. I hope it's been fixed now. Is it nice and warm?'

She looked around at the sparsely decorated room and chewed her bottom lip. It was definitely a contrast to her surroundings in the lodge at the Brodie Hotel. The flat was charming. It had a bright and airy sitting room, neutrally decorated. The bedrooms were off the living room, and there was a small galley kitchen.

'Yes, it is nice and cosy, and once I've added a few bits and pieces it will definitely feel a bit more homely. And guess what? There is even a spare room for when you come and visit. Mind you it is quite small.' She wasn't quite sure what the deal was with Margaret, and whether she would also want to come along.

'Oh that's good. Though I don't want to put you out Beth. You just get yourself all settled and I will come over when it suits you. That's if it's okay with you of course.' His voice was full of uncharacteristic enthusiasm.

Beth nodded, as her eyes filled with tears. 'Of course you can come over, Dad. In fact, what about if you come over for the last weekend of the month when the Christmas lights are switched on?'

'Sounds good, let me just check those dates.'

She listened as he flicked through the large desk diary that he kept by the phone. 'You're in luck. That weekend is free, dear. The Christmas events kick off on the first of December. But it's a Christmas charades night and I could definitely do with avoiding that.' He chuckled.

'That's great, Dad. You could come over on the Friday and stay until the Monday? There's a Christmas fair on in Lamlash that weekend as well as the light switch-on in Brodick.'

'Wonderful. I can't wait to see where you are and what it all looks like. It's been years since I was in Arran.'

'Tell me how you are and what you've been up to?' Beth listened as he told her about the latest news from the retirement flats, which included an in-depth description of the latest Bridge tournament, plans for several Christmas lunches and a golf game he had planned for later in the week — all dependent on the weather.

'What about you?'

'What do you mean?' She reached to the floor for her glass of water and took a sip.

'I just hope that it's not all work. You deserve to have some fun too Beth. Have you met any nice people yet?'

Beth knew he was right. Pausing before she answered, she put her glass back down on the floor. But her dad continued before she could speak. 'I know I may be speaking out of turn, but you have always worked so hard. Just please look after yourself Beth. You only get one life you know.'

Beth wasn't quite sure what to say. Everything he said was correct, and yet she felt annoyed. She couldn't help but take his words as criticism. 'Okay, you don't need to lecture me,' she snapped.

Then she immediately felt remorse for being so insensitive, especially when she knew that her dad was only trying to help. And had been such a *huge* support these past few weeks, even when she had been such a crap daughter for years.

'Sorry Beth. I'm just trying to help. I worry about you.'

Beth took a long breath and silently reprimanded herself again. 'No need to apologise. I am the one who is sorry, Dad. I didn't mean to snap at you. Everything you said is true and I know you're trying to help . . . I'm just not very good at taking advice.' Her face softened a little as she thought about her dad, who was probably standing scratching his head as he paced around his flat, wondering what he should be saying to her. Her mum had always been the one to dispense the parental words of wisdom. 'I really appreciate all you've done to help me, and I know I owe you an explanation. I've not been a very good daughter for a long time now. But I promise I will make that up to you. I will tell you what happened one day. When I'm ready.' Though at this moment in time she didn't know if she would ever again want to rake up the details of what happened with Tim. Aside from anything else, she knew her dad would be livid and want to hunt him down and throttle him.

'Beth.' His voice was calm. 'If I was there beside you, I would give you a hug and remind you that I am always here for you and I love you. Please never forget that.'

She wiped away a tear that had rolled down her cheek. 'I know. Thanks, Dad.' She forced back the choking sob rising up the back of her throat. 'I promise I will make sure it's not all work and no play.'

'Good,' he said. 'I'm glad to hear it. Oh, and before I forget, Margaret sends her love and hopes the car is behaving.'

Beth smiled fondly. 'Tell her it has been a lifesaver. I'm not quite sure what I would have done without it.'

'I will tell her. She will be delighted to hear that.'

'How is she doing?'

He chuckled. 'She is just fine and keeping me on my toes. And tell me, what's on the rest of the week for you?'

Beth gave her dad a vague rundown of some of the meetings she had lined up for work. 'I've also been familiarising myself with all the local coffee shops. I might even make the effort to go to an exercise class in the community centre.' She had no intention of doing this, but wanted to make sure that her dad wouldn't be worrying about her sitting alone in the flat night after night.

'That sounds nice. And outside work is there anyone to socialise with?'

Thoughts of Alessandro floated through her head. He had popped into the office that morning, although she had been out on an errand, and left a message with Jim asking her to call him sometime. Jim had merely raised an eyebrow as he relayed what Alessandro had said. She still wasn't quite sure that getting involved with him, even as friends, was a good idea at this stage. He was the type of guy who thought he had the gift of the gab. Beth wasn't convinced that his charm was genuine.

'It's still early days for that.' She tried to reassure herself as much as her dad. 'But don't worry, I will keep you posted.'

They chatted for a few more minutes and then she ended the call, promising to be in touch again soon. For a moment she wondered if she should drop Alessandro a text, but then decided there was no rush. In spite of her initial misgivings, Alessandro had been really welcoming and friendly to her and she didn't want to let things that had happened with Tim cloud her view on men for the rest of her life. But she needed to give herself some time and space before she reached out to anyone.

CHAPTER SIXTEEN

When Beth woke up the next morning it took her a few
moments to work out where she was. It was quiet and dark —
she felt as though she could be absolutely anywhere. Reaching
to switch on the bedside light, her eyes adjusted and the bland
décor reminded her that she was in the flat in Arran. Her mind
raced through the numerous beds she had stayed in this past
year, including the hotel she had just left, her dad's flat and the
flat share in Deptford with Lara. Was it really only a couple of
months ago that she lived there? As she lay on her back, cosy
and propped up by pillows, she stared at the ceiling, wondering if it would take her long to get used to living alone. She
couldn't quite believe that she now had a place to call her very
own. She could take as long in the shower as she wanted, leave
her dishes in the sink and do them when it suited her. The
freedom of having a place to call home again made her feel as
though she was in her twenties again. Though her reflection
in the mirror of course told a different story, with her lined
forehead and long brown hair that was starting to show streaks
of silver. As she stretched her toes and pointed them towards
the end of the bed, she realised she *hadn't* woken with the
familiar feel of dread that she'd carried like a cumbersome

weight for months. She felt a shiver go down her spine, then a sense of anticipation in her stomach. It felt liberating and she grinned. Looking at her watch, and realising it was only just past seven, she was now wide awake and ready to embrace the day. She sat up, swung her feet round onto the floor and slid them into the slippers that Margaret had kindly given to her. They were huge furry reindeers, complete with antlers, which looked utterly ridiculous on her small feet.

'They'll keep you all toasty through the winter,' Margaret had said knowingly when Beth had unwrapped them. 'And get you in the festive spirit.'

Beth smiled as she now looked down at her feet. She'd been slightly resistant to wearing them when she first opened up the parcel. Reindeer slippers were so *not* her thing. But Margaret had been right. They *were* lovely and warm. Beth stretched her arms above her head, then padded through to the kitchen and filled the kettle to make a cup of tea. As she squeezed the teabag against the side of the cup, she managed to spill some water on the worktop. Automatically reaching for a cloth, she realised there were lots of things in the flat that she needed to get. Grabbing a piece of paper she started to make a list. She would try and go to the shops if she had time at lunch.

* * *

She was in the office alone today as Jim had a meeting in Glasgow, catching the early ferry over to Ardrossan. Things had been busy that morning as she tried to work through her task list and, by lunchtime, Beth's stomach was rumbling. She decided to go to the large Co-op to get a sandwich and the other things on her list. As she pushed the trolley up and down the aisles, she scanned the bit of paper that she had scribbled quickly on earlier, trying to remember what else she might need. There were the practical things, like kitchen roll and toilet paper, washing-up liquid and laundry detergent, bread, teabags, pasta, sauce, tinned tomatoes, sardines and eggs. She reminded herself to buy some fruit and salad. It was a random assortment but, as she looked into the trolley, she knew there was enough in there to keep her going until she got a bit more organised. Beth had never been a keen cook, despite her attempts to embrace it over the years. But she could manage to make herself basic meals like sardines on toast, omelettes, stir-fries and pasta dishes. When she thought back to Jim's son Rory the other day, how excited he was to be around food, she smiled. As she steered the trolley round the corner and into the cleaning products aisle, she glanced up at the customer coming towards her. It was a woman who was about the same age as Beth — as she got closer, Beth tried to steal a few more furtive glances without worrying the woman that she was some kind of stalker. There was something very familiar about her gait, and Beth paused as she desperately tried to put a name to her face. This had happened frequently in London and could be *very* embarrassing. She would pass people in the street, recognise them and quickly try and rack her brains as to how she knew them. Was it from college or work or school? Was it someone she had interviewed? She had a terrible tendency to mix up names and faces and places and wrongly associate them. She still cringed when she remembered the time she had been in Covent Garden and walked past a guy who was the features editor on a newspaper she had once worked on. Except she couldn't remember his name. He had a beanie pulled down over his head and was minding his own business as he sauntered along the street. He happened to make eye contact for a second and she waved at him. 'Hey, how are you?' she'd said. 'Long time no see.'

He paused and looked at her with bemusement. 'Hello.' He'd sounded a bit nervous.

'How are you?' She'd tried desperately to recall his name, wondering why the hell she hadn't noticed how spectacularly good-looking he was when she worked with him. She didn't remember his eyes being so stunningly blue. Or those dimples either.

'Um, okay, thanks.' He looked like he was trying to edge away.

She couldn't understand why he didn't want to engage. 'We worked together. At *The Review*?'

He shook his head. 'I think you're maybe mixing me up with someone else.'

It was only then, as she heard his Northern Irish lilt, that she remembered Nathan (that was his name!) having a different kind of accent. In fact she was sure that he was from Manchester.

'Oh God, I am so sorry.' She felt her cheeks flush.

He shrugged and flashed a smile, which turned her insides into mush. He really was extremely good-looking. 'No worries.' He turned and walked briskly away.

Moments later, the penny dropped and she realised just who it was. The actor Jamie Dornan. She was absolutely mortified.

Now, as she stood in the supermarket on this Scottish island, she knew that the woman coming towards her definitely wasn't a celebrity. For a moment she turned away to examine the laundry detergent in great detail, desperately trying to work it out. Then the penny dropped. Behind her was a blast from her long-ago and forgotten past, and she didn't quite know what to do or say.

'Excuse me please,' said the woman behind her. 'Can I just get in there for a moment?'

Beth had no choice but to turn round and step aside. 'Of course.' She tried to make soft eye contact with her.

The woman looked at her curiously and then also did a double take. 'Thank you.' A little frown played on her lips as she evidently also tried to place who Beth was. She reached for a huge box of laundry tablets. 'Living the dream, eh?'

After putting them in her trolley, she started to manoeuvre it down the aisle but then stopped to glance over her shoulder again. Then she wheeled it back and pushed it back towards Beth. 'I know this is going to sound really weird . . .

but do I know you from somewhere? You look really familiar. And I just can't place you.'

Beth nodded. 'I was thinking the exact same thing. Except I usually mistake celebrities for people I know.'

The woman's eyes were bright as she laughed. 'I'm definitely not famous. I'm awful with names, so you may need to help me. I've got a brain like a sieve.'

'I've just moved here.' Her voice was artificially cheerful. She had been so naïve to think that, after twenty-five years, she wouldn't know anyone here. Or that they wouldn't know her.

'Ah, I see. Well maybe you've just got one of those familiar faces,' she said. 'Maybe I've just seen you around.'

Beth was aware of other shoppers passing them who probably thought they were having an in-depth chat about the weather. She was glad they had met here, which was quieter compared to say the fresh produce aisle.

'No, you're right.' Beth nodded. 'I've just worked it out. We do know each other. Though it was from a very long time ago. In fact it was a lifetime ago. You're Kirsty?'

There was a moment of stunned silence as Kirsty looked back at her in surprise. 'Yes and . . .' Her voice trailed away as the penny started to drop. 'Elizabeth?' She reached out to touch Beth's arm. 'From the summers at the hotel. The Brodie? Way back when we were just kids?'

To Beth's surprise, Kirsty's face lit up in a warm smile. 'Yes. A blast from the past, eh?'

'Oh wow. It is so strange but so nice to see you. After all this time. As you say, that was a lifetime ago.'

For a moment, Beth allowed her mind to go back to the last summer they worked together. It was 1999 and the soundtrack for that happy time had been *Bring It All Back* by S Club 7. The group she'd made friends with were all young and full of excitement and heady enthusiasm for the next chapter of their lives. All they cared about was being in the moment and enjoying themselves. "*Let the world see what you have got, bring it all back to you,*" was a line she and Kirsty frequently

79

chanted as they cleaned the rooms of the hotel, knowing they wouldn't be there forever. It was funny how many of the lines of the song had resonated with her in the coming weeks after she had left Arran. "*Hold your head high and reach the top,*" had become her mantra.

'I can't believe you're here.' Kirsty drew her back to the present moment. 'Gosh, I always wondered what had happened and where you'd gone. I know you went to London, and I moved down not long after but I had no way of getting in touch . . . you just seemed to vanish.'

'I know. I'm sorry we lost touch.' Beth felt her cheeks flush.

'And what are you doing here *now?* You said you'd just moved here?' Kirsty looked completely puzzled.

'That's right. I arrived just last week. I've come to work on the newspaper.'

Kirsty looked baffled as she processed what Beth had just said. 'So you're the new reporter? Well, what a surprise. I had no idea.'

Beth felt slightly sick and overwhelmed with regret. She and Kirsty had always promised they would keep in touch. But then Beth had gone to London to start her career and things had just drifted. The longer they weren't in touch, the harder it was to make the effort. It all felt very surreal — standing there with their trollies with no idea about what had happened to each of them in the past couple of decades. Beth was grateful that Kirsty did look genuinely pleased to see her and wasn't nervously backing away or abandoning her trolley and hotfooting it out the shop.

'It was a bit of an unexpected move.' Beth smiled uncertainly.

'Look,' Kirsty glanced at her watch, 'I need to get back home, but I would *love* to see you and catch up properly.' She reached into her handbag and found a pen. Scribbling her number on the back of an old receipt, she then ripped it off and handed it to Beth. 'Please do drop me a message and we can catch up and share what we've been doing with our lives.'

'Where do you live now?'

Kirsty rolled her eyes. 'It's a long story, which I will fill you in on properly when we meet, but I live back at the house I was brought up in. Although it's now a guesthouse as well as being my home. But do let's get together and chat. In fact, why don't you come round for a coffee sometime? Do you remember where it is?'

'Oh Kirsty, I would really like that. It would be wonderful to catch up properly and hear about what you've been doing.' Although was feeling a bit flummoxed as to where she would even start. She had spent so long avoiding getting close to people so that she didn't need to tell them the details of where life had all gone wrong.

Kirsty laughed. 'And remember I know where you work now, so there will be no avoiding me.'

Beth nodded. Kirsty had always been kind and genuine. It would have surely taken a lot for that to change. And Kirsty still radiated an authentic warmth. She knew she could do with some friends in her life. Maybe it was time to take a bit of a leap of faith. After all, what did she have to lose?

CHAPTER SEVENTEEN

'It's about finding pockets of time where you can do this. We can all find time in our day to do make changes if we want to,' said the assertive voice speaking in Callum's ear. 'If you want to transform your life then you have to do it yourself. Step into your own power. Prioritise yourself and your connections.'

He was leaning on the kitchen counter, staring out the window and admiring the patchwork of fields in the distance. He didn't think he would ever tire of the view — all that space and the vastness of the sky. The thought of being in a city had never appealed, yet he had tried it for a few years in his twenties, as he felt he had to. But it didn't end well. City life wasn't for him. In fact, he wanted to protect Daisy from busy, dangerous cities as long as he could. Although he knew, at some point, he would have to let her go. She would have her own life to lead. But the thought of not being able to keep watch over her completely petrified him. As he stood there, lost in his thoughts, he jumped when he felt a hand on his shoulder.

He turned to see Daisy glaring at him and, embarrassed that she'd caught him indulging in his guilty podcast pleasure, he pulled the pods from his ears and pressed pause.

'Honestly, you tell *me* off for not replying when you call for me.' Daisy flicked her hair over her shoulders.

'You're absolutely right. I should be available at all times at your beck and call, just in case you decide to holler.' Stretching his arms up, he then placed his phone on the worktop.

'Urgh.' Daisy had looked at his phone and seen that it wasn't a music playlist he'd had on. 'Not another coaching session from one of those gurus again. Honestly, it's like you're permanently listening to them. Why don't you let me make you up a playlist, then you can dance and connect with your inner creative. You need to have more fun. Like get out and meet a proper woman, rather than listening to all these voices in your head.' She gestured at the ear pods. 'Literally.'

Callum laughed. 'Thanks for that, Daisy.' He was always amazed at how much wisdom she possessed for someone who was so young. Yet it shouldn't surprise him — her mother had been exactly the same. Isla had always been a free spirit, a woman who was wiser than her years. Part of the reason he listened to so many podcasts — apart from the fact he found them fascinating, particularly the self-help ones — was so he could get the female perspective on things now he no longer had Isla to talk to. Maisie was helpful with some stuff, and had been a good friend to him and like a surrogate grandma to Daisy, which they'd appreciated. Especially as his own mum didn't live close by, although she was great at Facetiming and keeping in touch with Daisy. Having Maisie so close was an added bonus. She was a great storyteller, and so unassuming about how much she'd achieved in her ninety plus years. She always insisted that her good health was down to her daily dose of red wine.

'Right,' said Daisy, 'just to let you know that I need to stay at school later today for the newspaper. One of the journalists from the paper is coming in to talk to us and give us some advice. Hopefully she'll help us with the school newspaper.'

'I'm sure you'll probably be the one giving the advice.'

Daisy shrugged and gave a coy smile. 'I will be on my best behaviour and just ask lots of questions.' Then her expression changed, becoming a bit huffy. 'That reminds me, parents' night is fairly soon. It's the week after the winter market. That's going to be a treat.'

Callum nodded. 'Yes, they're both on the calendar. Which reminds me, do you need me to do anything for the market?'

Daisy shook her head. 'I don't think so. I will do some baking. All you need to do is just come and splash some cash.'

Callum nodded. 'I can do that.' He frowned when he realised Daisy's brows were furrowed. 'Is there something you're worried about, or need to tell me about school and parents' night?'

Daisy smiled weakly. 'No, not really . . .'

'*Daisy*?'

'Everything's fine. I'd better go or I'll miss the bus.'

Over the years Callum had learned to pick his battles with Daisy, and he realised this was not the time or place to get into what was going on at school. He shrugged. 'Okay. Do you want to text and let me know when I've to pick you up?'

'Thank you.' She gave him a hug. 'See you later. By the way, I put the latest cake in the tin for you. Let me know what you think?'

Callum smiled weakly. He had been the guinea pig for Daisy's vegan experiments since she announced her change of diet. It was fair to say that some were better than others. She kept telling him she was refining the art of how to make the perfect cake. He didn't have the heart to tell her that he didn't think that baking was her forte.

Just then his phone started to buzz. 'Hello?'

'Hi Callum. It's just me, Maisie. Do you mind popping by when you have a minute, please? I need help with the logs.'

'Of course. I'll pop up over in ten minutes if that suits?'

'Oh thank you Callum. Where would I be without you?'

'What are you doing today?' Daisy pulled on her jacket.

'That was Maisie. I'll go and help her with the logs and then I've a few work calls to make.' Callum hadn't yet told Daisy about the job Edie had asked him to do. He planned to make a start on drawing up a few ideas for that today and was really looking forward to it.

Daisy leaned down to kiss Ruby on the head. 'Bye Rubes.'

Callum sighed as she slammed the door and flew up the lane. Inwardly he was glad she was growing up and becoming more independent, but he was starting to realise that he felt a bit discombobulated. For as long as he could remember, Daisy had been his sole focus in life — he'd put his life on hold. Maybe he needed to make an effort to get out more. That podcaster was right. He needed to prioritise himself and make some connections. Looking down at Ruby, who was gazing up at him in adoration, he tried to reason with himself that she was the only female companion he needed. But then the voice in his head reminded him that he'd been hiding himself away for far too long now. It was in Daisy's interests for him to become less introverted. He didn't want people to think she was the poor girl who lived with the weird farm man. Before he could change his mind, he picked up his phone and sent Fergus a text.

Fancy a beer sometime soon? Callum.

He didn't have to wait long for a reply.

How about tonight? 6 pm at the Inn?

Callum did a quick calculation in his head. That should give him enough time to collect Daisy from school and drop her off home. He was sure she'd be delighted at the thought of having the house to herself for a couple of hours. He smiled as he typed his reply.

See you there. Looking forward to it.

He pulled on his jacket and walked briskly towards Maisie's cottage. She was already outside in the back garden having stacked up her basket with logs.

'Dearie me.' She huffed and puffed. 'It's harder work than you think.'

'I know, and I'm glad you phoned me Maisie. Though you should have called me before you gathered them all up. I could have done that for you and brought them in, save you getting cold.'

'Oh don't worry about that. I'm not an invalid. It's good to keep busy.'

Callum shook his head fondly at her. She was fitter and more agile than lots of folk he knew in their fifties.

'Thanks for that croissant the other day. It was delicious. And the flowers you and Daisy gave me are beautiful. Look,' she pointed at the kitchen window, 'aren't they lovely?'

Callum nodded as he looked at the jug of multi-coloured flowers that brightened up the space. 'Did you have a good day?'

'Yes. Met the girls down at the hotel and we had a nice lunch. Along with a gin or two.' She grinned wickedly. 'There's still life in me yet.'

Callum didn't doubt it. She was a force of nature, and he hoped that he would grow old as gracefully as she had.

'Which reminds me, are there any nice ladies on the scene that you want to tell me about?'

He shook his head and grunted.

'You know that it's okay to move on with your life son. Life has to go on.'

He looked at her — she stared back at him earnestly. 'I know Maisie. I guess it's just all about the timing. But I am going to meet some friends for a beer tonight. I was going to ask if it was okay if Daisy pops in to see you for a while.'

'Of course,' she chuckled, 'I'm sure she'll be quite happy having an empty house.'

'Yes, maybe for a while, until her stomach starts to rumble.'

'Just tell her to come to me if she's hungry. I'll be making a pot of stovies later.'

'That's almost worth me cancelling *my* plans for.' Callum's mouth watered at the thought of her comforting dish made from potatoes, meat and onions. 'Mind you, has she told you that she's gone vegan?' Callum remembered that she wouldn't be able to eat the stovies.

'Aye, well, she didn't turn down one of my sausage rolls when she was in the other day.' Maisie chuckled. 'Don't worry,

I will see what she says, and if she decides against it, I'll make her some toast and cheese. Though I guess she can't have that either can she?' She frowned. 'I guess I could do beans on toast. Anyway don't worry, she'll be fine. As long as she doesn't start trying to convert me. She will have no chance! Either way, I will send some stovies back with her so you can have them when you get back from the pub.'

'Maisie, you are an angel. Thank you.'

She blushed and clapped her hands. 'Och, away with you. Now, if you don't mind lifting the basket of logs in, I will let you get on with your day.' She glanced at her watch. '*A Place in the Sun* is on soon.'

Callum knew that was his cue to get the job done and exit. He loved that she didn't mince her words and wanted to get on with watching her favourite television programme. He did as she asked, then left her in peace and walked back towards the farmhouse, whistling as he walked. He genuinely was looking forward to going out later. Maisie was right. He needed to make the effort and make a change. Otherwise he would be alone and potentially miserable forever. Life did have to move on.

CHAPTER EIGHTEEN

Through the office window, Beth could just about see the waves, grey and frothy, against the heavy, dark November sky. Jim had just left to head home. He and Freya and the boys had a pizza and movie night planned.

'See you Monday,' he'd called, after enquiring if she had any plans for the weekend.

She didn't, but was quite happy about not having to be anywhere or answer to anyone except herself. Working full-time at the paper was an adjustment, and when she made it upstairs each night, she found she was ready for a nap before cooking dinner. That would have to change, she'd told herself, on more than once occasion. Perhaps she should join the gym or at least go swimming at the local pool. Otherwise it would be a very long and lethargic winter.

She smiled as she thought about her afternoon spent with the kids at the high school. Jim's son, Murray, had introduced her to the newspaper team, who were all much more intelligent and confident than she ever remembered being when she was fourteen. At times she wondered if she could actually be of any help to them — they all seemed to be so efficient and in the know, exchanging views on politics and celebrities.

However, once she started chatting to them and they started to ask her questions, she found that they were curious and keen to learn how to plan their content, and what sort of things they should be asking when interviewing people.

'Remember the basic questions to ask when you're writing a story,' Beth had explained. 'What, where, when, how and why? Those are the main questions to remember, and will give you a good structure to work from. And if you're interviewing, then it is vital to allow a silence. Give people a chance to answer your questions.'

All in all it had been a good week, and she still couldn't quite believe this was now her life. Which reminded her, she still hadn't gotten in touch with Kirsty, and had been meaning to text her since seeing her earlier in the week. Pulling out her phone she sent her a quick message, saying it was a lovely surprise seeing her in the supermarket and it would be nice to catch up. Then she turned back to her computer to finish her final emails for the week. Her phone started to buzz and move across the desk. It was a message from Kirsty.

Fancy a coffee here tomorrow morning?

Beth felt a flutter of nerves in her stomach. She hadn't expected Kirsty to respond so quickly.

Sounds great. Just let me know best time.

Her phone buzzed again.

How about 1030?

She replied immediately again.

That is perfect. See you then!

She logged out of the system, switched off the computer and was pulling on her coat, wondering what to make for dinner that night, when the door swung open. She groaned inwardly, especially as she had mentally logged off from work as well as physically. Then she realised it was Alessandro. But her stomach still continued to sink.

'Hello there.' He smiled brightly.

'Oh, hi Alessandro. I was just about to lock up. I'm afraid Jim has already left for the night.'

He shook his head and grinned, his white teeth practically lighting up the dark office. 'I've come to see *you*. I was just passing and thought I would check, on the off chance you were still here. Did you get my message?'

Shit. She was momentarily lost for words. 'Sorry, I just haven't had a chance to reply. It's all been a bit hectic this week. Jim did let me know you had popped by. Thanks, that was kind of you.' She knew she was babbling — she willed herself to pause.

'I wondered if you fancied a quick drink? It's just that I've got a quick errand to run in Lamlash and wondered if you wanted to come along for the ride?'

She hesitated before answering, unnerved slightly by the knot of tension forming in her stomach. But she couldn't work out whether that was because she'd gotten so used to doing her own thing and *not* meeting any blokes for drinks. Or it was because she did genuinely just want to go upstairs to the flat and chill out. Alone. Then the voice in her head reminded her that was the easy option. *Maybe you should push yourself out of your comfort zone and just go for a drink with the man? What harm could it do?*

She nodded, though felt slightly wary and weary. *You need to try and fit in.*

'Sure. Why not,' she said. 'Though just a quick one if that's okay. I've got a few things I need to do tonight.'

He grinned back at her playfully. 'Wonderful.'

Beth pushed her hands through her hair, hoping she looked presentable. Pyjamas and Netflix would have to wait.

CHAPTER NINETEEN

'How are you settling into the flat?' asked Alessandro as they walked towards his car, which was parked across from the office. He clicked it open with his key and gestured towards the passenger seat, opening the door for her.

'Fine thanks. Not quite the same standard as your hotel, but it is very comfortable.' She got into the car and he closed the door. There was no doubt he was extremely charming, but Beth realised that it was no longer an attribute that she found appealing.

As he started the ignition, she felt herself babbling again. 'How come you're off on a Friday night? I thought it would be busy at the hotel. What do you normally do at the weekends? Or are you usually working?' She paused for breath before continuing. 'It's been ages since I've been to Lamlash. You must like going there to get a change of scene?'

He glanced over at her, a small smile playing on his lips. 'That's a lot of questions. I can see why you're a journalist.'

She felt her cheeks flushing and was grateful to be shrouded in darkness. 'Just taking an interest.' She hoped he wouldn't realise how nervous she was. To think she had been lecturing the kids earlier about the importance of allowing people the chance to answer questions.

'It's okay. I don't mind. It's actually quite nice to be asked. Now, let me try and remember your questions. Yes, you're right, I do normally work at the weekend, but because things are a bit quieter I took the night off.' He sighed. 'Sometimes it feels like all I do is work. What else did you ask?'

'Erm, I asked if you'd like to go to Lamlash for a change. Rather than bars in Brodick?'

'Yes.' His eyes twinkled. 'If I go out in Brodick then there can be guests there and it can feel as though I'm at work. It is nice to go somewhere else where I can switch off a bit. Less chance of an amorous customer taking advantage.' He chuckled, lightening the mood.

'No, surely that doesn't really happen?' Beth couldn't imagine the guests she'd seen at the hotel making advances on the manager, however handsome he might be. They were all ladies of a certain age.

'You would be surprised,' said Alessandro spiritedly.

The road was dark between villages. As they drove down the hill into Lamlash, Beth could just about make out the dark shape of the Holy Isle in the distance. Then a few moments later he pulled over and parked outside the pub. 'Here we are.'

'Didn't you say you had to drop something off somewhere?' Beth shivered as she got out the car and looked over at the dark water of the bay. She reached into her bag for her scarf and wound it around her neck. 'It's so cold.'

'I know. Come on, let's go in. I just need to drop a package off for my friend who works in the pub.' He opened the boot and pulled out a jiffy bag.

Beth looked at it speculatively, immediately wondering what it was, and Alessandro must have read her mind. 'It's nothing dodgy, if that's what you're thinking.'

Beth groaned. 'Am I that obvious?'

Alessandro nodded. 'You're so like Jim. Always *so* suspicious. A journalist through and through. It's just some keys I need to drop off.'

Beth had to smile. He was absolutely right. She did tend to question things, though she reminded herself that she should have listened to her instinct and interrogated Tim from the outset. But, somehow, she'd had a rush of blood to the head, which had left her broken in more ways than one. She followed as he led the way and held the door open for her. As they entered the pub she was immediately hit by the welcoming warmth of the log fire and the background noise of chatter and laughter. Following Alessandro to the bar, he turned and looked at her.

'What would you like to drink?'

'A glass of red wine would be great thanks.' She watched as he warmly clasped the hand of the man behind the bar, speaking briefly to him as he passed him the envelope. Gesturing to them both he said, 'Stuart, this is Beth, the new reporter at the paper. Beth meet Stuart, who owns the pub.'

Stuart grinned at her. 'Nice to meet you, Beth.'

'You too. Nice place you've got here.' It was a cosy and welcoming pub, with wooden floors, a mixture of trestle tables and wooden circular tables, which were all adorned with twinkling tea lights.

'Aw, thanks. You two take a seat and I'll bring your drinks over.'

'Thanks mate. Shall we sit by the window?' Alessandro pointed to a small table in the corner.

'Perfect.' Beth sat down and then Stuart brought their drinks over.

'Cheers.' Alessandro clinked his bottle of alcohol-free beer against her glass of wine.

Beth made a mental note not to have any more alcohol after she'd finished her drink. She didn't want to do or say anything she may regret, or give Alessandro the wrong idea, especially as he wasn't drinking.

'Tell me how your week has been.' He fixed his eyes on her face.

'Great. I am loving the job. I mean it's not every day that you get to write about a wooden seal sculpture being washed away and then found on another island.' Clyde the seal was a favourite focal point in the village of Corrie where the sculpture sat on a rock. However, he was washed away in bad weather and eventually turned up on the Isle of Bute, which was further up the Firth of Clyde.

'It must be very different to what you're used to?' he asked with an enquiring look.

'Yes. But different is good. It's what I needed.' She took a sip of wine. 'How about you, how has your week been?'

He sighed. 'Fine. It's been busy over summer and autumn, and now we have a lull before the holidays. I'm due to take some holidays after the New Year, before things start to pick up again around Easter.'

'Have you any plans?' She took another drink of the full-bodied Malbec.

'Some sunshine I think would be good. Sometimes the winters here can feel very long.'

She nodded. 'Yes, I can totally understand that. I had forgotten what Scotland can be like in November. I've been away a long time.'

'Tell me about yourself. What really brought you to Arran?'

She wrapped her fingers around the glass and shrugged. 'I was ready for a change and wanted to get out of London. I had been there a long time.'

'No husband or family?'

She hesitated. Beth was used to being the one asking all the questions and she didn't like how much he was probing. 'Footloose and fancy free,' she said as breezily as she could manage. 'And very happy to stay that way. How about you?'

'Same.'

Neither of them spoke for a moment.

'And where is home for you?' asked Beth.

'Dundee. Despite my name.' He laughed. 'My parents moved from Umbria more than forty years ago. They came to Scotland for work and I was born and raised there.'

'Do you still have family in Italy?'

He nodded. 'Yes. We have a large Italian family there, and here. And you? Where were you brought up?'

She groaned inwardly. This felt like a game of tennis, both of them keen to bat questions back to the other. 'In Glasgow. And I worked summers here when I was a student. Then I moved to London and, well, now I'm back.'

Just then a crowd of guys arrived and the noise level increased. She glanced over at the bar, which was now really busy. Beth was struggling to hear what he was saying and had to lean forward to listen. His eyes didn't stray from hers and it all felt a bit intense.

'Fancy another drink?' She stood up.

'Another beer would be great. Thank you.'

She hoped that one more drink would be ample and they could head back to Brodick. Alessandro was good company but, as she stifled a yawn, she realised that she really did just want to have a hot shower, pull on her pyjamas and lie on the sofa. As she waited to be served, her eyes strayed to the three blokes standing on the other side of the bar, nursing pints. Then she did a double take. It was the same guy who she'd noticed walking his dog the other day. Except now he was closer and she had a much better view. Her mouth gaped open and her heart leaped with a complicated mixture of nausea, fear, sadness and excitement. Was that really *him*? Or were her eyes deceiving her? Her instinct was to run out the door and far away.

But then Stuart took her order and she distracted herself by keeping her eyes fixed on him as he grabbed two more beers from the fridge. By the time she reached Alessandro it was taking her a huge amount of effort not to glance backwards. She managed to focus on listening politely to Alessandro as he shared another humorous story of a very keen hotel customer who had done her best to chat him up. Trying her best to smile and pretend she knew what he was saying, she then felt ashamed that she was so distracted.

She drank her beer in super-quick time. 'Listen, do you mind if we just head off soon? I am so sorry but the red wine has gone to my head and I feel a migraine coming on.'

Alessandro hesitated for a moment and then looked at her sympathetically. 'Yes, of course.' He tipped his head back and finished the rest of his drink.

She was grateful for her own sake that he readily accepted her excuse to leave. As she walked out the pub, Alessandro slipped his hand protectively on the small of her back, and she was convinced that she could feel *his* eyes on her. She knew she shouldn't, but she couldn't resist looking over her shoulder and over at the guy she had recognised. When she did the world seemed to slow down completely. Her eyes locked on his. She saw the surprise, or perhaps it was more confusion, on his face. Then she turned and followed Alessandro out onto the street. She felt dizzy with shock — she didn't dare to look back.

CHAPTER TWENTY

Fergus and Grant were discussing the finer details of a penalty from a European football game that had been on TV last night. He hoped they wouldn't notice that he had zoned out of the conversation. So much for his plan to make the effort to spend more time with guy friends. They wouldn't be asking him back at this rate. He looked across the bar and noticed an extremely handsome guy flashing a smile at the woman he was sitting opposite. Callum was momentarily taken aback by the whiteness of his teeth — he hoped his companion was wearing sunglasses. The woman had her back to Callum and he wondered if she was finding the white teeth a turn on or a bit dazzling. Is that what women found attractive these days? He rubbed his hand over his jaw. He was so out of the dating game that he had no idea.

'Earth to Callum.' Fergus gently nudged his elbow. 'Are you still with us? Or is there somewhere else you need to be?'

'Sorry mate. Just got a bit distracted by the guy over there with the white teeth. He looks like Ross from *Friends*. He could light up a small nation with those gnashers.' He took a sip of beer. 'Is that what women go for these days?'

Grant chuckled. 'Depends on the woman. Some men are really into their grooming and all of that. Fortunately, Thea tells me that nobody likes a man who tries too hard.'

Fergus snorted. 'That's extremely lucky for you then isn't it? Who is he anyway?'

Grant put his pint down on the bar, turned to have a quick look and then nodded. 'It's that guy, Alessandro, from the Brodie Hotel in Brodick.' He glanced over at the bar and frowned. 'He's big mates with Stuart here.' He lowered his voice and tipped his head towards the table. 'He's a bit of a smooth operator and a real ladies' man, if you catch my drift.'

'*Right.*' Callum shrugged. 'Who's up for another drink? Same again?'

Fergus and Grant both nodded with a smile.

Callum glanced over again at the guy in the corner. Even though she had his back to him, he couldn't peel his eyes away from the woman with him.

'What can I get you?' asked the barman. His voice brought Callum's attention back to the moment. He placed his order and kept his eyes fixed on Grant and Fergus. He really needed to get a grip of himself.

'How's Daisy getting on?' asked Grant as Callum handed him his drink. 'Cheers mate.'

Callum took a sip of his pint, focusing on savouring the taste, grateful for the distraction of a question about Daisy. 'Keeping me on my toes. Her latest project has been making vegan cakes . . . she follows that woman on Instagram. You know the one who was here last summer and made them?'

Fergus nodded. 'Aye, Kitty. She's my cousin, you know. She's brilliant, and so are her cakes. She did a roaring trade when she was here and supplied some of the cafés.'

Callum nodded. He was desperate to look over again at the woman, but he didn't dare. 'Um, yes, so Daisy's been following her on Instagram and trying out her recipes.' He winced. 'Let's just say that more practice is required. I think it takes a while to perfect it. Maisie used to teach her to bake when she was younger, and I suggested that she ask her to go over the basics with her again. But Maisie is apparently horrified that she's trying to bake without any eggs, and laughed when Daisy suggested they use the liquid from a can of chick-peas instead.'

Grant chuckled loudly. 'Aye, I don't think you'd be wanting tell Maisie what to do.'

Callum shook his head. 'Indeed. She's a woman who knows her own mind.'

'Being responsible for another human being must be very full on.' Fergus had a look of admiration on his face.

He nodded. 'There's never a dull moment. And I've got parents' night soon, which she's warned me about. I have a feeling there may be some issue she's not telling me.'

'Part of being a teenager, I suppose,' said Grant. 'God, do you remember back in the day, when you would be absolutely bricking it when it was parents' evening. It was such a big deal.'

Fergus nodded. 'I know, right? And my parents always insisted on going together, and I would wait at home praying that the teachers gave me a good report. Otherwise life would be hell.'

Callum was fidgeting, desperate to turn round, but made himself look at Grant.

'Er, changed days now,' said Callum wryly. 'Daisy comes with me, which is just as well, as the school is like a warren. I've no idea where anywhere is anymore. And she sits next to me, keen to hear what the teachers are going to say.' Callum wanted to roll his eyes at himself. He was aware how much of a middle-class yoga mum he sounded. But he was so proud of her, and he'd felt such a sense of relief when Daisy had run out to the car earlier more enthused than he had seen her in a long time.

'The journalist was brilliant,' she'd said. 'She had loads of great advice, and told us about some of the stories that she covered in her younger days. She's offered to come in once a week and help us sort out our newspaper.'

She was so excited, and Callum was just happy that she had found something she was passionate about. She had always loved English, but lately had started to make comments about finding it a bit of a struggle. He turned the conversation back on to Fergus and Grant, asking them what their plans were for the weekend. But the truth was that he couldn't stop his eyes from drifting towards the woman in the corner. They both stood up and were gathering their things to leave. Callum frowned. There was *definitely* something about her. He had seen her somewhere recently. As she flicked back her hair, shock rippled through him when he realised he knew *exactly* who she was. *Bloody hell.*

When she turned round and looked at him, their eyes locked. Her face visibly paled. It was as though time stood still. He had dreamed of seeing her again for years. In fact he didn't think he would ever see her again. Then his world started to spin on its axis. He couldn't believe she was now here, within touching distance.

CHAPTER TWENTY-ONE

Beth was walking up the driveway of Meadowbank Cottage when she spotted Kirsty walking towards the front door of her house.

'Good morning.' Beth waved and smiled.

'Beth,' she said excitedly. 'You remembered where we are then?'

'Yes, though I'm not going to lie. For a moment I thought I'd gotten lost. Then I recognised where I was.'

Kirsty grinned at her. 'Come on in out the cold.' She ushered Beth through the front door. 'I was just over at my dad's making him a coffee.'

'This is lovely.' Beth looked around the bright hallway. 'And something smells incredible.'

'Thank you. Here, let me take your jacket.' Beth shrugged it off her shoulders and Kirsty hung it on one of the pegs by the door. 'I'm not sure if you remember much about it, but it will have changed a lot since you were last here. Steve and I completely gutted it when we moved in. And, of course, the barn over there was totally dilapidated. That's where my dad lives now, and Amy and her partner James live in the studio next door.'

'I have a vague memory of a party in there . . .'

'Oh yes, there were certainly a few when we were younger.' Kirsty laughed. 'Changed days now though. I've made scones. That's about as exciting as it gets these days.'

'That's what the lovely smell is?'

Kirsty nodded. 'Yes, I thought, seeing as you were coming, it was a good excuse to whip up a batch of scones. Steve is out this morning, and with the kids away from home, I guess I don't always bake as much as I used to. It's been nice to have an excuse.'

'They smell wonderful. Thank you.'

'Come on into the kitchen. The fire's on there and it's nice and cosy.' She gestured through to the kitchen and invited Beth to take a seat at the large table. 'Would you like coffee or tea?'

'Coffee would be great thanks.'

Kirsty busied herself, filling a large cafetière with ground coffee and boiling water. She stirred it, plunged the lid down then set it on the table alongside a plate of scones. 'Now, don't be shy. Please do help yourself.'

Beth was a bit nervous, and grateful that Kirsty was being so welcoming. 'Thank you. This is so kind of you Kirsty. I can't actually quite believe I'm here after so long. It is very weird.'

'You are very welcome. It is *so* nice to see you Liz — Beth. Sorry, it will take me a while to get used to calling you that. You were always Elizabeth or Liz or Lizzie.'

Beth shrugged apologetically. 'Beth just kind of stuck when I started working for various reasons. I was quickly told that Elizabeth or Liz Taylor would just be asking for trouble, and I would just be opening myself to all sorts of jokes. And also that I was no movie star either . . .'

'Charming.' Kirsty shook her head in disbelief.

'I got used to that kind of comment.' Beth watched as Kirsty poured the coffee.

'Milk?'

'Just a splash please.'

Kirsty looked at her. 'What brought you back to Arran then? I'm obviously dying to know what you're doing working here now. After all this time.'

Beth sighed. 'I know, I agree it's all quite random. And I had no idea you were still here either, Kirsty. I guess I didn't really think too much about what I was doing when I applied for the job.'

Kirsty nodded encouragingly at her. 'I actually lived in London for a while. That's where Steve and I met and the kids were born.'

'Really?' Beth was surprised. 'Where did you live?'

'In south-east London, a place called Dulwich,' said Kirsty.

'I don't believe that we were so close and we didn't know . . .'

They both sat in silence for a few moments, revisiting their memories.

'I needed a change from London . . .' Beth took a gulp of coffee. 'Life's been a bit challenging for various reasons the past few years. I've been freelancing for a while now, and that all started to dry up just with everyone's money getting squeezed . . . I saw the job advertised and just thought I would go for it. It was a complete leap of faith.'

Kirsty raised an eyebrow. 'You know, sometimes these things happen for a reason. But I am impressed. I do think it was a brave move to make. And it's so good to catch up after all this time.'

CHAPTER TWENTY-TWO

Beth didn't feel brave at all. As she sat there at Kirsty's kitchen table, she felt the absolute opposite. Her heart was practically still thudding from the shock of seeing Callum last night in the pub. She'd frozen when she'd made eye contact with him. If it hadn't been for Alessandro steering her out the door, she would probably still be standing there, stuck to the spot, staring at him in disbelief. Yes, he might look older, but there was no doubt who it was. And from the way he looked at her she knew he recognised her too. The fact her heart had also started to race at the sight of him had put her into a spin. She'd thanked Alessandro for taking her out for the evening, trying to make polite conversation during the car journey home. She wanted to make sure it was clear that she was only interested in him as a friend. She was so glad when she got back to the safety and anonymity of her flat.

'Listen, please don't feel you need to tell me everything though. I know there's a lot to catch up on.'

Kirsty's voice brought Beth back to the here and now. She knew Kirsty was expecting some kind of explanation as to why she was there, and what had happened in her life over the past couple of decades. For a moment she desperately wished she could turn the clock back. She would hate Kirsty to think she deliberately cut her out of her life. Her hands felt clammy and she took another quick gulp of coffee. She wasn't quite sure she could be too evasive with Kirsty. She'd always had a knack of cutting through any bullshit. But, thanks to her journalistic background, Beth was also very used to explaining stories in a series of soundbites. Glancing over at her she smiled. 'How long have you got?'

Kirsty steepled her hands together and leaned forward. 'As long as you need.'

'Well, I'll try and give you a potted version,' she said. 'I guess starting at the beginning is always a good idea.' She crossed her feet under the table. 'When I left here, it was all about the work. I threw myself into it and loved it. I started on newspapers and then moved into magazines. I was lucky enough to travel, I had a really nice lifestyle. Then things changed . . .' She paused, hoping she wasn't obviously skirting over it all too rapidly. 'I had started to freelance by then, and work started to dry up with the way the industry was going. It all started to become a huge amount of effort for little income. I was ready for a change.'

Beth knew she was glossing over things but she wasn't ready to go into the details with anyone, never mind Kirsty. 'I needed a job and, when I saw the one that was being advertised here, I had a feeling I ought to apply. Especially as it meant I would be nearer to my dad. It does all feel like a full-circle moment, as though I'm supposed to be here.' Beth looked around the room, her eyes resting on the large studio-style family photograph that hung on the wall. 'And is this your family?'

Kirsty nodded. 'Yes, that's Becky and Tom, our twins, who are almost twenty. And my husband Steve.'

'I can't believe you have kids that age. I always knew you'd be a mum. And I bet you're a great one too. You always were so patient.'

Kirsty smiled at her. 'Ah, thanks. That's kind of you to say. I'm not sure the kids would necessarily agree with you though.' She giggled. 'How about you? Did you ever settle down?'

Beth felt her stomach twist as she shook her head. The word *family* was unspoken but still hung in the air between them. 'No, I didn't really settle down for long with anyone . . . and I don't have any children. I mean, if it had happened then that would have been great. But it wasn't meant to be. My life was always about work.' Her heart ached that she couldn't just be honest with Kirsty, but she just couldn't go there with anyone yet.

'So, you didn't ever marry or live with someone?' asked Kirsty.

'Nope, I didn't marry. I had a few long-term relationships over the years, but there's no partner now. Just me.' She thought fleetingly of Tim. She'd gotten very used to being evasive over the years. It was easier to continue to be so.

'Oh.' Kirsty sounded surprised. 'When I saw Beth Ferguson in the paper, I wrongly assumed that was your married name.'

Beth shook her head. 'No . . . I never got married. But I decided that my boss was right about my name, Liz Taylor, causing problems, so I just used Beth Ferguson for my by-line and it's stuck ever since. Ferguson was my mum's maiden name.' She also didn't want to add that it suited her to reinvent herself with a brand-new surname too, so she could start again and shake off the past and her broken heart when she had left Arran behind.

Beth was ready to deflect attention away from herself. 'And how about you? How are things in your life? Do you like running your own business?'

'Well, Steve and I moved back here when my mum and dad decided they wanted to downsize. We'd had enough of London life, especially as the kids were so small. We decided that we would buy the house and started running it as a B&B. It's been great fun, and a lot of hard work. But I wouldn't change it.'

'And your sisters? What did they end up doing?' Beth remembered them to say hello to, but they were younger than Kirsty and very shy back then.

'Amy is back here now as well. She teaches yoga in the community centre and also works as a massage therapist. She lived in Canada for quite a while then came home when my sister, Emma, got married. She met her old boyfriend from school when she was back and that was it. They've been together since. It's been great having her here and she's really good with my dad . . . he has dementia, which has been worse since Mum died.'

Beth's hand flew to her mouth. 'I am so sorry Kirsty. I was always so fond of your mum. And I am so sorry about your dad too. That's tough.'

Kirsty nodded. 'It was awful when Mum died. All our friends loved her when we were growing up. She was like a surrogate mum to them all.'

'I'm so sorry for your loss. My mum died too. I don't think anything ever prepares you for it.'

Kirsty reached for the cafetière and topped Beth's mug up with more coffee. 'You are so right. Even though she was ill, and we knew was dying, it was still a massive shock . . . and I'm sorry for your loss too, Beth. It's so hard to exist when you're trying to navigate grief.'

Beth nodded her head in sorrow. 'That must be tough if you're now caring for your dad?' She made a mental note to check in again with her own dad soon, to make sure he'd be visiting at the end of the month.

'It's actually been easier since he was diagnosed. It just means we know what we're dealing with and we've been able to put a support plan in place. I don't know if I would manage if Amy wasn't so nearby though. Her timing of coming back from Canada was perfect.'

'And how about your other sister. Where is she?'

'Emma? She lives in Edinburgh and works as a lawyer. Though not for much longer.' Her eyes widened with excitement. 'She and her husband are quitting the corporate world to open a restaurant in North Berwick. He's a brilliant cook, and running their own business is something they've always wanted to do. She's excited to live by the sea again too, though she'll be at the opposite side of the country to us. She's very good though. She does come back and visit as much as she can, and she and Max got married here a couple of years ago. Anyway, enough of me. How about you and your family?'

'It's just me and Dad now. Mum died five years ago just as they were selling up and downsizing. Dad lives in a retirement complex on the outskirts of Glasgow.' She chuckled. 'It's like a senior version of first year at university. It's all about bring your own bottle, cheese fondue evenings and competitive chess. They're like a bunch of freshers.'

Kirsty burst out laughing. 'Apparently all that socialising is very good for the brain. It sounds like he's got quite the community around him?'

'He certainly does.' She thought of Margaret next door. 'They do all seem to be quite carefree and enjoying life, that's for sure.' Beth noticed the clock on the wall, shocked to realise she'd been there for two hours. The time had flown in. 'Gosh, look at the time. I had better go.'

Kirsty started. 'Wow, where has the time gone? It's just been so nice to catch up.'

'I agree. Thanks so much for having me Kirsty. I've loved seeing you. Do you fancy getting together again soon?'

'I'd really like that. Let's just keep in touch. Maybe text me sometime when you fancy another coffee?'

'Come to the flat next time? Or let me take you to one of the cafés? I'm dying to check them all out. You can recommend the hot spots.'

'That sounds like a deal,' said Kirsty. 'It's been great catching up. Though I feel like we've only just begun and barely scratched the surface.'

Beth made to stand up. 'I'd better get going and leave you to get on with your day.'

Kirsty looked at the sky. 'It looks like it might stay fair. I'll try to get Dad out for some fresh air.'

As they walked towards the door, Beth zipped up her jacket and couldn't resist asking if Kirsty kept in touch with anyone else from their summer gang. 'Do you see anyone from back then?'

A look flitted across Kirsty's face, and she hesitated a little before answering. 'No, not really. Everyone just seemed to go their separate ways. Especially as so many folks had come over from the mainland. I guess we all just drifted apart.'

'As is life, I guess.' Beth wondered if she should just brazenly ask about the one person she was thinking about in particular. She waited for a moment, in case Kirsty added anything else. But, as she bid her farewells and walked back towards the flat, her curiosity was now piqued. Why did neither of them mention his name? Beth couldn't help but think that there was something Kirsty wasn't telling her.

CHAPTER TWENTY-THREE

A few days had passed since seeing her in the pub that night. Callum had been on high alert, in case he bumped into her at the supermarket or happened to see her again when he was out and about doing his errands. But there had been no sign of her, which made him now doubt that it had actually been her in the first place. Was he actually starting to gaslight himself? Had he imagined it? But then he reminded himself that there was no imagining that definite connection when they'd caught sight of each other. Never in his wildest dreams did he expect to see her again. He now assumed, if it was her, that perhaps she had just been visiting, and just happened to be with the guy from the hotel that night. Especially as it sounded like he was a one-night-only type of guy.

Since catching up with Fergus and Grant he had vowed to make more of an effort to keep in touch with them. He'd popped in to see them at the outdoor centre in Lamlash. Daisy seemed to be a bit more settled at school, and was absolutely loving the newspaper project, which was the highlight of her week on a Friday afternoon.

Callum was glad it was finally the end of the week and was looking forward to the weekend. He'd been busy with the online course and had started brainstorming a few ideas, which he hoped might help him with the running of the joinery business. When he'd been doing the banking and admin earlier, he sighed when he realised how chronic things had become. But he knew he wasn't alone in feeling like this. The cost-of-living crisis seemed to be affecting most people he knew.

He was in the kitchen making pizza dough — homemade pizza was a Friday-night tradition for them both — and keeping an eye on the clock, knowing he would have to leave soon to collect Daisy. Callum smiled when his phone buzzed and it was a text from her. His hands were covered in flour, so he quickly washed them in the sink and dried them before picking up his phone.

Hello! We are nearly done. Can Murray have a lift too please?

He typed his reply.

Sure. I will leave in two minutes.

He looked at Ruby, who was curled up and looking very cosy in her bed in the corner of the kitchen. 'I'm just going to go and get Daisy,' he told her. She opened one eye and thumped her tail, making no attempt to jump up and join him. He couldn't blame her. Although the afternoon had been bright, it was now turning dark. And from the way the trees were swaying he knew the wind had picked up.

The school was a ten-minute drive away and one that he was used to doing on autopilot. Shivering, he turned up the heating in the car as he swung into the school car park.

The kids opened the doors and jumped in. 'Hey guys, how was it?'

'Really good thanks.' Daisy's eyes sparkled with excitement. 'It's brilliant that this journalist is helping us. We managed to get loads done today.'

Murray slid into the backseat. 'Thanks for the lift. I strained my ankle at football practice last night, otherwise I would have walked home. Daisy said you wouldn't mind dropping me off.'

'That sounds sore and very frustrating. And it's no problem at all mate. The wind is starting to pick up again anyway. Not so nice for being out in.'

Callum was intrigued to know how they'd got so enthused about this extracurricular activity. He knew Murray's dad, Jim, edited the local paper, and was surprised that Murray wasn't mortified he was coming into the school to help. Maybe it was different for teenage boys and things like that didn't bother them as much.

'Daisy, would you like it if I came in and helped with stuff at school?' He reversed the car out of its space. 'I could run a few joinery or DIY workshops?'

'Um, absolutely no way. That would be like the ultimate embarrassment.'

'Ouch, that hurt. I mean I don't think I'm that embarrassing, am I?'

'Yes, you are.'

'I'm sure that Murray isn't bothered about his dad coming in to help with the newspaper are you, Murray?' Callum looked in the rearview mirror and watched as Murray pulled a face.

He puffed the air in his cheeks. 'There is no danger I would be doing it if *he* came in. That would be mortifying. I mean, it's bad enough that he insists on coming along to watch the football games.'

Callum frowned. 'I'm confused.'

'He comes along supposedly to support the team, but he ends up shouting at the ref.'

Callum burst out laughing. 'To be fair I think I'd be the same. No, I was actually meaning the school paper. I thought he was helping you with that.'

'Honestly,' Daisy shook her head, throwing her hands up in the air, 'you never listen to a word I say, do you?'

Callum was lost now. 'What do you mean?'

'*Urgh*! I told you that the *new reporter* at the paper is helping us. That *she* is helping us. I've told you this *so* many times and you have stood there and nodded your head as you "apparently" listened to what I was saying.'

'Sorry, sorry you're right. I'm getting confused and delusional.' Callum tried to make light of the fact she was right

— he didn't always listen properly when she was telling him something. He really had to do better. It was just tough, as he couldn't always keep up with everything Daisy told him. His mind always seemed to be in a swirl of different stuff. 'You did mention the new reporter and said she was very good.'

'Look.' Daisy pointed out the car window. The rain had now started to fall and Callum flicked on the windscreen wipers.

'What am I looking at?' Callum's eyes were drawn to the woman wearing a red coat, who was metres from his car and battling to put down her umbrella.

'That's her there. The reporter who's been helping us.'

His heart gave a small lurch. 'Um, what's her name again?' He knew fine well what Daisy would say.

CHAPTER TWENTY-FOUR

'Beth,' Daisy said impatiently. 'Beth Ferguson.'

Now he *was* surprised. He wasn't expecting Daisy to say that at all. Maybe she had a doppelganger, and he was mixing her up with someone else.

'She's been brilliant.' Murray sounded equally as smitten. 'Very cool *and* she worked in London for ages. So she knows stuff and she's interviewed loads of famous people. It's way better than having my dad there getting in the way. He is *so* embarrassing.'

'I see.' Callum tried to look in his mirrors, clinging onto any view of this woman they were talking about.

'He says she's great to work with as well. The best colleague he's had in ages. And he's mega old, so that says a lot.'

Callum took a moment to process this. 'Ah, I see. That's good . . .' He wondered how to tease out more information from the kids without sounding creepy.

'She said she'll come to parents' night if anyone's folks want to talk to her about the project, she said she'd be happy to,' said Daisy. 'I think you should. She's really nice. You'll like her.'

It was now dark and Callum was grateful Daisy couldn't see his cheeks colour. He was completely confused as to

114

whether it was her, although if it wasn't then it had to be her long-lost twin. But if it was her, then why did she use a different name? And why had she come to work here? His brain couldn't quite keep up with all the what ifs and whys.

'I am so hungry,' said Murray. 'Can't wait for dinner tonight. It's pizzas.'

'That's what we're having too. I hope?' Daisy turned to Callum.

'Worry not, yes, we are.'

As they pulled into Murray's driveway, Murray shouted his thanks to Callum and said he would call Daisy at the weekend about an assignment they had to finish.

'See you later mate,' said Callum.

'Bye Muz,' Daisy called affectionately as he slammed the door shut. Then she pulled out her phone and scanned it for new messages, the stuff that seemed to feed teenage minds. 'Did you make the pizza dough already?' she asked.

Callum nodded, gave her a smile then focused on the winding roads that would take them home. But he couldn't stop himself from probing for some more details about this reporter, Beth. 'Did she say what brought her to Arran?' It was the best nonchalant tone he could muster.

'What's that?' muttered Daisy.

'The reporter Beth. Why did she come to work here on the island?'

'I know, *right*.' She managed to pull her eyes from her phone and look at Callum. 'We said the same thing to her but she just laughed. She said she used to come here when she was younger and it was a place that she'd never forgotten or something like that. *The most special place in the world.* Sounded like some kind of advert for Visit Scotland. Anyway, you get the idea. It was a bit cringe.' She looked back at her phone, which had just pinged.

Callum tried to shrug casually but felt tingles running up and down his spine. *The most special place in the world . . .* He couldn't believe how just a few words could have such an effect and make the years fall away. As he parked the car outside the cottage, Daisy unclicked her seatbelt and jumped out the car declaring that she was "starving".

'Go and wash your hands,' he tried to sound breezy, 'and I'll roll out the bases.' But when he walked back into the house and was greeted by Ruby — who wagged her tail as though he had been out the country for weeks rather than half an hour — he found he was completely fixated on finding out if it was her. Although, deep in his heart, he knew it must be. He could feel it. But he needed some kind of confirmation.

He pulled out his phone and Googled her name. As her picture appeared multiple times on the search page, he dropped his phone in shock and it clattered onto the kitchen table.

'Everything okay?' Daisy's voice was cheerful but with an impatient edge. She had wandered back into the kitchen wearing her pyjama bottoms and a huge sweatshirt.

'Sorry love. Just coming.' He realised he would have to park the research on Beth for now. Feeding Daisy was the priority, otherwise she would get hangry. 'There's some dip and veggies in the fridge if you want. That should keep you going for a few minutes at least . . .'

'Aw thank you.' Daisy turned from the fridge with all the toppings she wanted to put on her pizza. 'You even got me the vegan mozzarella.'

Callum grunted. 'If that's what you want to call it. I'll be amazed if it even melts.'

'You have no faith.'

He looked at her speculatively for a moment and realised she was fairly spot-on with that statement. He used to have faith, but that was a very long time ago, at a time where his future stretched out before him and his world was full of possibilities and adventures. Until his life was turned upside down in the space of a night and everything changed. Glancing over at Daisy — as she turned on the oven and reached to get out the pizza trays — he realised that her arrival in his life had been another major curveball. He never expected in a million years that being a parent to Daisy was the direction his life would have taken.

'Um, earth to you. You need to roll out the bases.' Daisy pointed at the bowl where the dough sat, then handed him the rolling pin.

He inclined his head slightly and laughed at her. 'Let's get to it.' He rolled up his sleeves and sprinkled flour across the table. But, as he kneaded the dough, he realised that Daisy had anchored him to the world again when he had lost every other ounce of hope. His love for her was so fierce that it threatened to overwhelm him at times. As he rolled the dough into thin bases he knew that, yes, he would definitely have changed the circumstances that led to her living here with him on Arran. The loss of Isla had caused agonising heartache for all of them. But Daisy was like a ray of sunshine, and she had transformed his life in a way that he didn't think would be possible. He owed her absolutely everything.

CHAPTER TWENTY-FIVE

The winter market at the school was an annual extravaganza with stalls, crafts and a food market. It was always held in November, so it didn't clash with the Christmas fair, and Beth was delighted when Jim asked her if she wanted to cover it for the paper. 'I'll be there as well, in a dad capacity, but if you need anything just give me a shout. I'm down on the rota to cover the bottle tombola, which can be an *interesting* gig. Things can get very tense. And a bit physical. You would not believe how enthusiastic folks can get at the thought of winning a bottle of cheap plonk.'

Beth had laughed. This was such new territory for her and she was loving every minute. This week she had been out and about, covering all sorts of events, including a book launch by a local author, a business and civic award ceremony and a fun-run fundraiser for the RNLI. She had watched as the Christmas lights in Brodick had been put up by a team of volunteers, and she couldn't wait to see them switched on. She told herself that she would definitely volunteer to help put them up next year. There had been no sign of Callum since that night at the pub, and she now wondered if it had been a figment of her imagination. Alessandro had asked her out again but she had let him down as kindly as possible, telling him that she was busy with work. The last thing she wanted to do was give him the wrong idea, especially when he had made it clear he was *interested* in her.

It was Saturday morning, the sky was dark and heavy, and Beth wondered if it might even snow. She parked her car at the school and shivered as she got out, glad she had pulled on her winter boots and her thick red coat. It had become really cold these past few days, and she laughed in delight as a few wisps of snow started to fall, landing on her nose. She followed the bustling crowd, making her way through the school's main entrance, then into the sports hall where the market was being held. Jim had warned her it could get really busy, but Beth hadn't expected to see quite so many people. It was as though *everyone* on the island was here. She scanned her eyes across the hall, looking for any familiar faces.

'Beth,' Jim's son Murray tugged at her hand, 'you made it. Come on and buy some raffle tickets.'

'Sure.' She smiled, happy to be pulled along by him. 'Wow, it's busy in here, isn't it?'

'Yes, it's always like this. Right, it's three for a pound or twenty for a fiver.' He had the prowess of a Barras Market stall holder.

'Twenty it is.' She pulled her purse out of her bag, glad that Jim had warned her to make sure she had plenty of cash on her, as the kids were experts at getting everyone to part with it.

'Thanks Beth.'

'Where is your dad's stall? And Rory? I promised I would go and buy some of his cakes.'

Murray pointed in the direction of their stalls and she gently made her way through the throng of bodies, reminding herself to be observant — she'd need to write something for the paper. It was warm in the hall and she pulled off her coat. When she reached the tombola stall she saw a harassed-looking Jim with only a few bottles left on the table.

'It's been crazy,' he said. 'No wonder Freya signed me up instead of her. You take your life in your hands doing this.' He threw his hands up in a gesture of defeat. 'I've only been open an hour and that's the bottles almost finished. I'm going to need a stiff drink by the time I get out of here.'

Beth gave a wry smile, knowing that Jim was actually in his element. Murray had told her that her dad *loved* this kind of thing. 'I do have to admit, I am quite partial to a tombola Jim. I'll take three tickets.'

Jim grinned and held a bucket out to her, giving it a good shake first. Beth put her hand in to the small folded pieces of pastel-coloured paper. She looked at the first number and showed it to Jim. He frowned as he scanned the few bottles of wine that were left — along with a bottle of washing-up liquid, ginger beer and a bottle of Babycham, which looked like it needed a good dust. 'That has to be vintage.' She pointed at the green bottle.

'Do you know what? I think you can still buy it in the shops. But I think this particular bottle has clearly been in the back of someone's cupboard for a while.'

'It looks positively historic.' Beth watched him hopefully as he scanned the tickets on the bottles, trying to match hers up with one of them.

Jim shook his head. 'Sorry, no luck. Try again.'

Beth reached in and was again unlucky with her second ticket.

'Third time lucky?' he asked.

'Sure,' she smiled happily, 'you never know.'

Jim's eyes lit up when he realised she had a winning number. 'You *are* a winner.' He laughed. 'Congratulations Beth. And I hope this comes in useful for all those dishes.' He handed her the bottle of washing-up liquid.

Beth burst out laughing. 'Well, yes, at least it will come in handy. And I'm sure it's far better for my health than a bottle of wine. Thanks Jim.' She slipped it into her handbag. 'I'd better go and see the kids at the baking stall before that sells out too.'

Jim raised his eyebrows. 'You should be okay. Rory and Freya were up late last night, baking. The house was like a cake shop this morning. I was told in no uncertain terms to keep my paws off it all.'

'See you soon.' She gave him a small wave and made her way across to the baking stall. It was crowded, and for a moment Beth was lost in her own thoughts as she waited to be served. Maybe it would be better to come back later? She had also spotted the local cheesemaker's stall, and wanted to buy some of that too. Just as she turned to move away, she stumbled, then felt a strong arm catch her before she fell flat on her face.

'Elizabeth?' asked a voice above her.

With the strong arm still holding her, she looked up to see who it belonged to. Beth was then glued to the spot — speechless — and her legs turned to jelly.

'Callum?' she eventually croaked.

He hadn't let go of her arm and his eyes were full of concern. 'Are you okay? That was quite the tumble.'

She nodded, studying his face, which was older and a bit more lined. He was still as rugged and good-looking as ever. His dark hair was now flecked with grey, and he was standing *very* close to her. 'I'm fine, honestly. Thanks for helping me.' She used as measured a tone as she could, given that her heart was now dancing to its own disco beat.

He shrugged, let her go and took a step back. 'No worries.' He paused and looked at her inquisitively. 'Well, this is a bit of a surprise after all this time . . . What brings you to Arran?'

Beth felt her cheeks flushing. 'I moved over at the start of the month. To work on the local paper.'

His gaze didn't waver from her face. 'Right.' He paused. 'I see. So you're living here now?'

Beth nodded, trying her hardest to stay calm and not show her utter shock at seeing him. Her arm was still tingling from his touch. 'I live in Brodick, near to the office. And you?

121

Are you still near Lamlash?' She tried to sound casual, but her voice was more high-pitched than usual.

'Yes.' He shrugged. 'Family stuff, you know?'

Beth didn't, but she nodded anyway, her cheeks reddening even more. She hated to think what sort of flustered state she must look. *Of course* he was settled with his own family. She had to keep reminding herself that most people her age were. She realised this was her cue to exit. The last thing she wanted was to bump into his wife and brood of kids, especially when he was having *such* an effect on her. She didn't want to be the sad ex-girlfriend who was now having a midlife crisis, and lusting over her old boyfriend who happened to still be as hot as anything.

'Well, it's been really nice seeing you Callum. Thanks for your help. I'll let you get on with your day. Hopefully I'll see you around?'

He looked a bit taken aback. 'Oh. Sure thing.'

Beth's heart sank when she saw his expression. Had she said something wrong? She longed to say something else to break the ice and move the conversation along. She just didn't want to linger if his wife and kids were about to appear. Then, quite unexpectedly, he reached over and gave her a warm hug. Beth had to stop herself from squealing. His firm torso was pressed against hers. He smelt of spice and cinnamon. All the years seemed to melt away as she momentarily hugged him back. Then he stepped away.

'It's really good to see you,' he said. 'Maybe we can catch up sometime?'

Beth stood for a moment, bewildered by his hug and his words. 'Good to see you too Callum. Yes . . . that would be, er, great. See you later.' She smiled and turned away, walking back towards the cake stall as nonchalantly as she could manage. *Cake*, she told herself calmly. That was what she needed. A nice slice of chocolate cake. A sugary treat would be the perfect distraction. She gave herself a shake. Who was she kidding. What she *really* needed was a cold shower. As she looked over her shoulder, she saw Callum standing, watching her. He gave her a small wave, then turned and disappeared. Beth was sure he was off to find his family — she felt a pang of sadness. She would finish up here and head home as soon as she could. Right now, she couldn't face seeing him with anyone else.

CHAPTER TWENTY-SIX

It had been a long week at work, and Beth's concentration had been scattered since seeing Callum at the winter market. She hadn't been able to get him out of her mind. She was glad it was now Thursday, as her dad was due to arrive the following afternoon and stay until Monday. Beth was really looking forward to seeing her dad and genuinely didn't mind if he wanted to bring Margaret along. Especially as Margaret had been so kind as to lend Beth her car. As it was, Margaret had plans with her daughter and granddaughter in Glasgow on Friday night. However, she said she would love to come over and join them on Saturday if that suited. Bill had asked Beth if she could sort a room out somewhere nearby for her, and she had popped by the Brodie Hotel earlier in the week. Somehow, she had managed to avoid Alessandro since that night in the pub. She hadn't been dodging him on purpose. She just hadn't had any reason to be in touch, and her head was still spinning from the trip she'd taken down memory lane this week with Callum.

She'd been walking across the foyer of the hotel, admiring the large Christmas tree in the window, when Alessandro had called out to her cheerfully. 'Hallo stranger.'

Turning round, she saw him coming down the wide, festively decorated stairway towards her. 'Hi Alessandro,' she said. 'The hotel looks good.'

'Yes, we have just literally finished putting up the decorations.' He sounded proud.

'How are you?'

'I'm good thanks. All the better for seeing you.'

She winced. He tried too hard. 'I just wondered if I could book a room with you at the weekend, please?'

'This weekend?' His gaze rested on her mouth. 'Are you tired of the flat already?'

She shook her head and laughed. 'It's not for me. I'm booking for a friend. I need a single room for Saturday and Sunday nights please.'

'Okay.' He went behind the desk and tapped on the computer. He frowned as he scanned the system. 'For one person you said?'

'That's right.' She realised she didn't know Margaret's surname. Not that she supposed that mattered.

'I do indeed. The last single room.' He looked at her and flashed a smile. 'Would you like me to book it?'

Um, yes, she thought. That's why I'm here. She gave herself a shake, not quite sure why she was being so mean-spirited. She couldn't put her finger on what it was, but there was something about him that unsettled her — she felt a knot of tension forming in her stomach. 'Please. If you can put the booking in my name just now that would be great. Thank you.'

'No problem. Will you be wanting to dine with us that evening?'

Beth didn't know. She hadn't thought that far ahead. Maybe it would be nice to try out one of the local pubs?

'It's just that we are quite busy so I would advise that you book a table. Just in case you can't get anywhere else.'

'Oh, okay thanks. Can I book for three please? For 7 p.m.?'

He glanced down at his booking system again and typed for a moment. 'That's it. All sorted.'

'Great, thanks.'

'You have a friend visiting?'

She nodded. 'Yes, my dad and one of his friends are coming over.'

'Great. I look forward to seeing you all then. And do let me know if you fancy a drink sometime soon?'

She didn't, and she thought she had already made that clear. 'I'm really busy with work just now. Sorry Alessandro.' There was something about the way he looked at her that gave her the ick. She was grateful for his kindness since she'd arrived, but it felt a bit loaded. She just wished they could be mates. He wasn't her type. He wasn't *Callum*. He was too groomed, excessively smooth and, from what she could gather — from snippets of what Jim had said — he was a complete ladies' man. Which she knew herself, from when he had slipped his arm around her waist as they'd left the pub that night. She just hoped that nobody, or rather Callum, hadn't noticed and got the wrong idea.

Just then, the office door swung open, which snapped her out of her thoughts and back to the moment. It was Laura, the postwoman, who — as Jim had said she would — doubled as a bit of an oracle. As she knew everything and everyone, Beth had been trying to work out the best way to ask her about Callum. But there was no way to be subtle, despite having racked her brain for ages, trying to think of a tactful approach. But she knew that if she did ask after him then Laura might wonder what was going on. The last thing she wanted to do was draw any attention to her fact-finding mission. Or imply she was some kind of nosy stalker. She knew people were used to journalists asking lots of questions, which Beth had no problem doing if she was working on a legitimate story. That was the problem. This wasn't a story. It was all just so she could satisfy her own curiosity, and try and join some dots together. She had done an online trawl for any information she could find, but he didn't have an online presence, which didn't surprise her at all. He'd always been very unassuming. Beth had worked out some possible questions to pose, and had been watching the clock all morning as she knew Laura would be due to drop their mail at any moment.

As it was, Laura didn't have time to stand and blether. She stuck her head in the door on her way past to the terminal. 'Not much for you today I'm afraid.'

'Do you fancy a coffee?' asked Beth.

'No time just now but thank you. I'm in a bit of a hurry. There's a big delivery coming in any time that I need to go and sort. It always starts to get crazy this time of year.' Laura looked at Jim, who had just come out the kitchen with two mugs of coffee.

'I can't tempt you?' he asked with a grin.

'Sadly no, though I could murder a cup of something hot. It's bloody freezing out there. See you later.' She turned and closed the door behind her.

Jim glanced at his watch. 'Will you remind me that I need to be away sharp for parents' night? I'm so worried that I'll forget. Freya would be raging.'

'You make her out to be some kind of tyrant.'

He raised his eyebrows. 'You have no idea what I have to put up with.' He grinned at his own joke.

Beth picked up her mug and took a sip. 'I doubt that very much. You're forgetting that I'm going along too. There is no chance you'll be late with me.'

He hit his hand against his forehead. 'Of course. So you are. You're giving feedback on the newspaper?'

'Yes, and I can tell you right now that Murray has been a complete superstar. He and his friend Daisy are great. They listen to everything that I say and ask lots of brilliant questions. Honestly, they will go far. It's been such a lovely project to work on.'

'Thanks,' Jim beamed with pride, 'that's great to hear. And I'm grateful you were up for taking this on so quickly.

I wouldn't have had the time or the impact either. Murray would have been mortified.'

'They're a fab bunch, I've loved it. Highlight of my week.'

'I mean, obviously I think my kids are great, but I know that I'm biased. And Daisy is brilliant too.'

'She is a bright cookie. Very creative and curious, with a real maturity about her.'

Jim nodded. 'She's had a lot of challenges to overcome. Her—'

Just then the phone rang and he was cut off, leaving Beth intrigued to know what he had been about to say.

CHAPTER TWENTY-SEVEN

'Good luck with the meetings,' said Beth. They walked into the school's entrance hall, decorated with streamers and tinsel, where lots of parents and carers were waiting. She spotted Freya, who was waiting with Murray, and gave her a wee wave.

'You are actually on time.' Freya was incredulous. 'That is all down to you, Beth. Thank you. I wish you knew how glad I am that you've come into our lives. We are so much happier *and* on time for things. Isn't that right Jim?'

Beth gave a gusty laugh. 'I don't think anyone has ever said that to me before. You're making me blush.' She turned to look at Murray. 'Hope you get a good report from all your teachers. I'm sure you will. I've been telling your dad how much I've enjoyed working with you on the newspaper.'

Murray gave her a small smile, then shrugged his shoulders. She watched as he scuffed his feet following Freya, who had started to march along the corridor. What was it about kids and parents' evenings? They always got so worried and anxious, and she knew Murray had no reason to be. Then she reminded herself that she had been exactly the same at that stage.

'Right I hope your sessions go well too, Beth. I better keep up.' Jim was full of mock horror as he gestured after Freya and Murray. 'I'm sure our paths will cross again.'

'Most definitely. I'm going up to the English department. See you there.' Beth followed the signs that took her down a corridor and to the large classroom. Here she was to take up a small corner with examples of the kids' work they'd produced over the past couple of weeks. It was incredible the amount of progress they had made in such a short space of time. Although she didn't have to be on hand at the parents' evening, as she wasn't a teacher, she had offered in case any of the parents wanted to see and hear about some of the extracurricular work their children had been doing. Beth was extremely proud of what they had achieved with their newspaper. She busied herself, laying out printed copies on a table, along with some laminated photographs of the kids in action at meetings, discussing ideas and typing up their stories.

'Hi Beth,' said a voice behind her. She didn't need to turn around to know who it was.

'Daisy.' Beth was genuinely delighted as she spun round and moved around the table towards her, reaching over for a hug. 'It's so good to see you. I'm glad you came over to say hello. How are you? How's it going?' Beth gave a conspiratorial wink. Daisy had told her last week she was worried she would get a bad report — she tended to talk too much in class.

'Mmm.' Daisy twirled a lock of hair absent-mindedly. 'Okay, I suppose.'

'That sounds a bit ominous.' Beth looked at her in concern.

'It's English that I'm worried about.' Daisy glanced across at a teacher who was on the other side of the room, in full flow with another parent. 'I just find bit a bit of a struggle. It used to be my best subject.'

'How come? I mean, from what I've seen, you have a really good grasp of things when we're working on the paper. What is it you're finding hard?'

Daisy shrugged. 'The reading for understanding bit, which then means I struggle with the analysis and evaluation . . .' She lowered her voice to a whisper. 'I don't think the teacher likes me either.'

'Ah okay.' Beth had met the teacher earlier and she reminded her of teachers she dreaded when she was a kid. She wasn't exactly warm or engaging, so it was fair to say she realised why Daisy was getting stuck. 'You do know that you're doing all that anyway when working on the paper? But I'll let you in on a secret Daisy. I struggled with the way English was taught at school. I could do it, but as soon as they started doing the exam papers, I had a complete blank.'

From the way Daisy was looking up at her, she knew she had struck a chord.

'Would it help if I spent some time going over stuff with you?' Beth asked carefully.

Daisy nodded, smiling in relief as Beth's suggestion. She perched on the table. 'That would be amazing. If you don't mind?'

'Of course I don't. I would love to help you, but we just need to check if it's okay with your parents.'

'It's just me and my—'

'There you are. I've been looking everywhere for you.'

Beth's eyes widened. She took a sharp intake of breath when she turned and saw who was now standing alongside Daisy.

'Hello,' Callum said, his voice gruff. He nodded at Beth and smiled. 'Long time no see. I have been hearing all about the famous reporter who's been helping the kids. You seem to have made *quite* the impression.'

An unexpected frisson of excitement ran down her spine. Beth had no idea what to say. Her heart raced as she looked over at him, his face a mixture of shifting emotions. 'Hi Callum. We meet again.' She groaned inwardly. *Why on earth had she said that?* 'Um, how are you doing?'

Daisy raised an eyebrow curiously. 'Wait a minute, have you two already met? Do you *know* each other?'

Callum gave a small, wry laugh. 'Yes, you could say that. At the winter market last weekend. Though we met a very long time ago before that. Back then you were known as Liz or Lizzie.'

Beth was rendered speechless again, overwhelmed at the way she responded to being up so close and personal to him. Her mouth was dry and her palms felt clammy. She clearly hadn't imagined his magnetic appeal from when she saw him last.

Then she had to shake herself. He was a father now. And his daughter was standing between them, wondering what on earth was going on. She needed to pull herself together before she made an utter fool of herself. Especially if his wife was about to appear. 'Yes, things have changed a bit since then.' *Seriously was that all she could say?*

Daisy cleared her throat loudly. 'Hello? Is anyone going to tell me what's going on? Are you two going to tell me how you know each other?'

CHAPTER TWENTY-EIGHT

'We used to work together. A long, long time ago.' Callum was unable to peel his eyes away from Beth. He still couldn't believe she was here on the island. He hadn't stopped thinking about her since she fell into his arms at the winter market. 'Back in the olden days.'

He could feel Daisy staring at him, wondering what it was he wasn't saying. She was as intuitive as her mother had been, and he knew she would grill him the moment they left the classroom.

'Where did you work?' pushed Daisy.

He could see that Beth's chest was flushed. He remembered from way back that was a sign she was nervous. Some things hadn't changed — he was curious why she should feel that way. Instead of stepping in and answering Daisy, he waited for Beth to reply.

'Oh, just at one of the hotels in Brodick,' Beth said. 'I used to come over during the summer when I was a student, that's where we met. We all kind of got to know each other.'

He held her gaze for a moment — until his phone buzzed and he looked to see Maisie's name flash up on the screen. 'Excuse me, I need to take this.' He stepped aside to answer.

'Hello dear. I'm sorry to call you. I hope I'm not interrupting your dinner. I know you'll be busy cooking just now,' said Maisie.

'That's okay. I'm just at the school with Daisy. It's parents' evening.'

'Sorry of course it is. I totally forgot.'

'Is everything okay?' His brows furrowed as he looked over and saw Daisy and Beth deep in conversation. He didn't like to think what they might be talking about.

'The back door is locked and the key is jammed,' she said. 'I was just wondering if you would mind popping by to have a wee look when you can. No rush though.'

'Of course I will. Give me an hour or so and then I'll be there.'

'Oh thank you Callum,' she said. 'You are so kind. What would I do without you?'

Callum smiled. 'That's okay Maisie. Do you need anything brought in from the shops while we're out?'

She cleared her throat. 'Well, I mean if it's not too much trouble, and you don't mind, if you could bring me a wee bottle of red wine that would be appreciated. I'm running low.'

Callum shook his head and laughed. She was some woman. 'No problem. See you soon. Bye Maisie.' Ending the call, he walked back over to Beth and Daisy.

'Is everything okay?' asked Daisy.

'Yes. It was just Maisie asking if we could do an errand for her.' From the way Beth inclined her head, he could tell she was wondering who Maisie was. He decided he would let her be curious. For now. Yet, despite that, he wanted to know more about her. He wanted to know *everything*. Where had she been and why was she really back on Arran to start with? Callum knew that they needed to get on with their appointments, but he was finding it hard to drag himself away from Beth. He had a flashback of what it felt like to kiss her, the way in which her lips moved on his. It was impossible to ignore the way she was looking at him — the rosy flush on her cheeks and the brightness in her eyes. It was as though she was also having the same flashback, and for a moment they looked into each other's eyes.

Daisy coughed. 'Right, I think we need to go. Mrs Richards is ready to see us. She's staring at us.' Daisy tugged at his arm. 'Come on, I don't need you making things even worse for me than they already are in that class.'

Beth smiled over at her. 'Good luck.' She turned to him. 'That reminds me, I offered Daisy some help with English if she'd like it. I said to check with you first though.'

'That's very kind. Thanks. We'll get back to you on that.' He could smell her perfume from where he was standing and it was unnerving. He didn't want to leave her side.

'You'd better go.' Beth eventually broke the spell. 'Nice to see you again. Maybe we should catch up properly . . .' She sounded unsure, and a bit embarrassed.

Callum nodded his head and tried his very best to sound casual. 'Sure. I'd like that. We will sort something out. See you later. Come on Daisy.' He turned and walked to the other side of the room, taking a seat opposite the teacher. He tried hard to focus on what she was saying, but knowing Beth was just metres away was a huge distraction. All the feelings he once had for her came flooding back. He felt a mixture of love, lust, regret, anger and sadness. He leaned forward, making himself focus and listen to what Mrs Richards had to say. After a few minutes with her he could now understand why Daisy had been feeling so out of sorts with this subject in particular. She reminded him of his old English teacher who hadn't done much to encourage his love of the subject. No wonder Daisy was struggling.

As they left the classroom, he glanced over to steal a look at Beth, but she was engrossed in a conversation with other parents.

'See what I mean.' Daisy's eyes were downcast as they walked along the corridor.

'Mmm,' he said. 'Yes. She's not the most encouraging of teachers, is she?'

'Nope,' mumbled Daisy. 'Can I get Beth to help me then? I think that would make a difference. Plus you two go way back, so technically she's an old friend? Or more than that?' Daisy looked at him and winked.

Callum rolled his eyes. He knew that Beth's offer to help made sense. He had no doubt that Beth would help Daisy with her English, but he just didn't know if he could face allowing her back into his life again. So much had happened since they were last in each other's worlds. But how could he say no to Daisy? 'If you think it will help you with English, then I'm sure we can work something out.' He couldn't believe the impact Beth had on him after all these years. Despite the sadness he felt — when he thought back to how much his heart had been broken in the days after Beth had left to go to London — he now felt something else. A flicker of excitement, a glimmer of hope and, most of all, a longing for the woman who he was head over heels in love with all those years ago.

CHAPTER TWENTY-NINE

The next day, Beth finished up from work early and walked along to the ferry terminal to meet her dad. Jim had worked from home that day, which she was relieved about, as she needed some time to think after seeing Callum last night. All her memories of him were at the forefront of her mind, and she knew she might end up oversharing with Jim. He was the only person she saw on a regular basis at the moment. She was grateful to have the space to try and process how she felt. She realised, with startling clarity, that Callum still had the same effect on her despite the massive time lapse. Deep in thought, as she walked with her eyes fixed on the incoming ferry, she didn't realise someone had been calling her name.

'Beth.' Kirsty put her hand on her arm.

'Oh Kirsty. Sorry I was miles away. How are you?'

Kirsty smiled gently. 'I am wonderfully relaxed. I've just been for a massage and must make a point of going more often. I feel amazing.'

'That does sound nice.' Beth reached to knead the sore muscles on her neck. 'In fact it sounds like something I could do with. Where do you go?'

Kirsty pointed across the road and up the hill. 'Just up there.' She rummaged around in her bag, then pulled out a small business card. 'Here.' She pressed it into Beth's hands. 'I know I should really be recommending Amy. But it's almost impossible to get a slot with her and, when I do, she refuses to charge me. I've started seeing Lyssa on the quiet. She has the hands of an angel. Just don't tell my sister.'

'I will make a point of booking in. Thanks for the recommendation.' Beth glanced over at the ferry as it blasted its horn. 'I'm just meeting my dad. He's visiting for the weekend.'

'How lovely.' Kirsty shivered. 'It's getting cold isn't it. I love this time of year.'

'Me too. It'll be fun to take him to the lights switch-on.'

'Absolutely. I'll maybe see you there?' asked Kirsty. 'I'd better leave you to it and let you get there on time.'

For a fleeting moment she thought about telling Kirsty that she had seen Callum, and asking her what his story was. Then she realised now was not the time or place. 'Thank you. And, Kirsty, I was wondering if you might fancy catching up for a coffee sometime again?'

'Yes of course. I'd love to. How about you text me when your dad is away? Then we can meet up maybe next week?' Kirsty beamed at her.

'Okay. I will. Thanks Kirsty. Take care.' Beth threw her a grateful smile, wondering if she knew how much she appreciated her kindness. Stopping to talk to her on the street may not have been a massive thing, but it meant a lot to Beth. It made her feel a bit more anchored and connected to this community. She was increasingly finding it was small acts of kindness that were making a huge difference to her life. She walked briskly towards the terminal, scouring the passengers making their way off the ferry, looking for her dad. She stood on her tiptoes, anxious and excited to see him. When she spotted him, she waved. 'Dad, over here.'

His face lit up as he walked towards her, pulling his small suitcase. 'Hello dear. I've made it. I tell you what, I'm glad I didn't bring the car over. They were packing them on like sardines.'

Beth chuckled as she took the handle of the bag from her dad. 'You made it. Come on. Let's go home. It's not far from here. I bet you could do with a cuppa?'

Barry nodded. 'That sounds nice.' He linked his arm through hers and they walked the short distance to the flat.

* * *

The following morning, Beth decided that, while it was dry and fine, she would take her dad for a short drive to Lamlash and treat him to coffee at Cèic the café. She'd heard lots of positive things about it from Jim, who raved about their almond croissants in particular. Her dad was on good form as they drove down the hill into the village, as he admired the view of the bay ahead.

'It's been years since I've been here. I forgot about that view.' He pointed at the Holy Isle. 'Your mum and I did a trip over there once. A man in a wee rowing boat took us across.'

She smiled at him.

'It's really nice to be back. Isn't it funny how things sometimes work out. I would probably never have come back if I'm honest. And that's all down to you coming here to work.'

Beth reached a hand over and patted his arm. 'You're welcome, Dad, and hopefully you'll thank me even more once you've been to this café.'

When they arrived it was busy, and she quickly scanned for a free table. There were a couple of free stools over by the window, so she directed her dad towards them. 'Is over there okay, Dad?'

'Yes of course.'

'You go and sit down and I will get the drinks. Would you like something to eat?'

'Just surprise me please.' He chuckled.

As she stood in the queue she grinned when she realised Jim was in the corner with Freya. They both looked up and smiled. Jim then waved at her and mouthed, '*Is that your dad?*', pointing at Barry, who was now perched on a stool.

Beth nodded and watched as Jim stood up and made his way over to introduce himself to her dad. As she looked at the mouth-watering array of goodies on the counter, she decided to order a hot chocolate with marshmallows for her dad, a coffee for herself, an almond croissant and a special Christmas scone with cranberries and cinnamon. They looked as though they were fresh out the oven — a delicious festive scent lingered in the air. After paying, she made her way over to her dad and Jim. They were deep in conversation.

Her attention was focused only on what they might be saying to each other when she walked straight into another customer. 'Oh, I am so sorry.' She looked up and immediately flushed when she realised it was Callum. His eyes widened in surprise. What were the chances? She realised with a jolt that his chest felt solid. She jumped, pulling away as though he was burning hot.

'Hi again.' He raised an eyebrow.

'Hello.' Her voice was squeaky. 'Sorry about that. I seem to be a bit clumsy these days.'

'No problem.' He stood for a moment, his face unreadable, and Beth wondered if he was waiting for her to elaborate.

'It was good to see you the other night. I meant what I said about Daisy. I'm happy to help.' She couldn't help admiring how effortlessly handsome he looked, even though he was dressed in old jeans, trainers and a navy padded coat.

'Thanks. I'll be in touch. She has your number?'

'Yes.' She nodded, wondering if he could *be* any more gorgeous? 'I'll let you get your coffee. My dad is visiting. He's just there.'

He glanced over. 'That's nice. I see Jim has him cornered. There will be no escape.'

Beth smiled. 'I'd better go and rescue him. See you later.' As she walked towards her dad, she tried to take a few deep breaths. She was trying her best to be friendly towards Callum, even though her physical reaction was a very strong desire to pin him against the wall and kiss him passionately. But her head reminded her that he was a family man now. Not to mention the memory of the pain he'd caused all those years ago. She had been head over heels in love with him, and he had ripped her heart in two. She wondered if she would ever find the courage to ask him what went wrong, why he disappeared completely from her life. Or whether she should just leave the past alone.

CHAPTER THIRTY

Beth may only have been on the island for a few weeks, but she was starting to realise that living and working in a real community had softened her. The hard edges she had needed to survive in London were slowly starting to disappear. It was so nice to be able to stop and chat to a friendly face when she nipped to the shops or out to a café. She'd enjoyed showing her dad around, and it had been an added bonus that Jim and Freya had been there at Cèic too. She'd driven round to the high school to show her dad the outside of the building, so he could get a picture in his head of where she was working on the newspaper with the kids. This afternoon, they had picked up Margaret from the ferry and taken her to the hotel, which was looking very festive, a large tree draped with tinsel lighting up the entrance. Fortunately Alessandro had been nowhere to be seen. Beth and her dad promised to let Margaret get settled and "freshen up", and then they would walk back over to meet her for a drink before they had dinner.

When they arrived back at the hotel, Margaret was already in situ at the bar, holding court with Alessandro. Beth felt her heart drop. Who knew what he'd been saying to her. He flashed a dazzling smile at Beth and she was half-expecting him to say, 'Ciao Bella,' just for show.

'Hi lovelies.' Margaret waved them over. 'Don't worry, I've just been on the lemonade until you arrived. I didn't want to be sloshed . . . although the cocktail menu looks very nice indeed.' She gave a hearty laugh. 'I've just been chatting to Alessandro here and telling him about my trip to Italy in the summer.'

'Erm, did you tell Margaret that you're from Dundee?' asked Beth.

'Och away you go,' Margaret said to him, waggling her finger. 'That's you shattered the illusion. I thought you were a proper local. I mean Dundee's not quite the same as Sorrento, is it?'

He gave a gusty laugh. 'Sorry to disappoint.' He winked at Margaret. 'Please take a seat.' He gestured to a table at the window.

The bar was busy, and Beth was surprised the table was free. Then she spotted a reserved sign on it. She felt bad that her immediate reaction on seeing Alessandro had been dread. She had to remind herself that he was very kind. But the voice inside her head was loud and strong. *Just remember that he wants something in return.*

'What would you like? I'll bring it over,' he said.

'How about a bottle of fizz?' Margaret looked very smart in a pair of navy trousers and a cerise pink blouse. 'Seeing as this is a wee celebration. And it's the festive season.'

Beth was glad she'd made an effort and changed into a newer pair of jeans and boots, rather than the old denims and trainers she tended to live in at the weekends.

Beth and her dad nodded in agreement.

'It would be nice to have a wee toast,' her dad said.

'Prosecco would be ideal. You're a wee superstar, Alessandro. Thank you.'

They were soon settled at the window table overlooking the garden and Barry proposed a toast. 'To your new beginning on Arran.'

'Cheers.' Margaret clinked her glass against Beth and Barry's. 'And to all that lies ahead.' She gave Beth a conspiratorial look. 'He can't take his eyes off you love.'

'Who?' asked Beth.

'Your pal Alessandro.'

Beth shook her head. 'I don't think he's got the message yet that I'm not interested.'

'Aye,' she took another sip from her glass, 'something tells me he's not the type who's used to getting a knock-back. You watch yourself love. That type of man is more hassle than he's worth.'

Beth gave her a wry smile. She couldn't agree more.

* * *

The following afternoon, Barry insisted he needed to have a snooze after a morning spent wandering around the gardens at Brodick Castle, which he and Margaret had been particularly enthused about — they had their National Trust for Scotland cards with them.

Margaret was triumphant when they realised they could use them to gain free entrance. 'I told your dad these would be a good investment. And we'll just need to come back again and use them when the actual castle is open. Maybe in the spring, Barry, eh?'

Beth had offered to take Margaret round to Lamlash for the afternoon so she could see the Christmas fair in full swing. Margaret was also desperate to do some Christmas shopping at the gift shop, the Wee Trove, to buy some pottery mugs that she'd heard about when she'd met Edie, the woman who made them, last summer.

'Are you sure you don't want to come and see the lights being switched on, Dad?'

'No, honestly, I will wait till you come back and see them being turned on in Brodick tonight. I'll save my energy.'

As they got ready to leave the flat, Barry pulled his iPad from behind a cushion.

'Now Barry, you must think me and Beth are buttoned up the back or something? A wee nap? Is that right? More

like there's a football game on and you don't want to miss it.'
Margaret pursed her lips together.

Barry yawned, though he did have the grace to look a bit guilty. He'd asked Beth for the Wi-Fi code earlier so he could use his iPad.

'It's okay, Dad. You just sit and relax. I'm sure you'll only watch the first five minutes anyway, and then you'll be fast asleep.'

'Aye, well, that's what football does to me. Sends me straight to sleep. More powerful than any sleeping pills,' muttered Margaret.

'Thanks dear. You both go and enjoy yourself. Don't rush back.' Barry's eyes twinkled.

'It's been a busy weekend for him.' Beth had noticed her dad did seem to be tired. 'He's walked a lot the past few days, and the sea air will be tiring him out. Plus I know he's used to his own space.' Beth opened the car for Margaret. 'It's fine, really, I don't mind. He'd only be bored if we dragged him round the shops.'

'Gives us a chance to have a wander and a proper catch-up I suppose. Gosh, that wind is chilly.' Margaret shivered as she got into the car. 'I hope it doesn't rain. That sky looks a bit threatening.'

Beth turned up the heating in the car, then realised she should ask Margaret if she wanted to drive. It was her car after all.

'Not at all,' she said firmly. 'It's your car just now, and I have no intention of taking over. I quite like being chauffeured about.'

Less than ten minutes later they had luckily managed to find a parking space. The village was busy with final preparations for the Christmas lights being switched on, and the fair that would go on until later that night. Stallholders were adding the final touches to their displays, and Beth stopped to chat to a few people she had met through work events. She waved at Grant from the RNLI and then spotted Freya and introduced her to Margaret.

'I just hope it doesn't rain,' Freya looking upwards, 'otherwise it will be a wash out. I'll let you ladies get on and maybe see you later? I know Jim will be here when the lights are switched on.'

Beth looked at her watch. It was growing darker and darker and she wondered if plans may need to be abandoned due to the weather. 'We better hurry,' she said to Margaret, 'unless you want to get soaked.'

Margaret walked along the road and admired the window of the Wee Trove. She pointed at the mugs set against a backdrop of red and green scarves and sprigs of holly. Beth thought the shop was aptly named. She couldn't wait to get in and have a look at what else was there.

'That must be them there,' said Margaret. 'Shall we go in and see what else they have?'

'Of course. Though I think this could be dangerous. It looks like we may want to buy the whole shop.'

Inside was a treasure trove of beautiful and colourful mugs made by the woman, Edie, who Margaret had mentioned. There were bright canvas paintings, artwork by local artists, and some beautiful sea glass jewellery including earrings, pendants and bracelets.

'Isn't this place great? My Isobel would love that necklace.' Margaret pointed at a silver chain with a bright blue piece of glass. 'In fact I'll just buy it for her, I think. Why not?' She chewed her lip as she thought. 'I'd better get something for Bella. Otherwise she'll feel put out that I didn't get her some jewellery as well. They're like a pair of kids sometimes rather than mother and daughter.' She sighed loudly. 'What do you think about those earrings there Beth?'

Beth leaned towards the cabinet and admired the palest of pink glass earrings that Margaret was pointing at. 'They're beautiful.' She nodded her approval. She helped Margaret choose some of the mugs and then waited while she paid.

'What a lovely shop you have,' she said to the owner, who was busy wrapping Margaret's purchases carefully with layers of tissue paper.

'Och, thanks very much,' said the woman, who had long curly auburn hair and a huge smile. Her eyes were blue and she wore a thick green sweater with purple trousers. Beth knew it wasn't a look that she could have pulled off, but the woman looked effortlessly stylish. 'We do try to stock as much local produce as we can and support local artists. It's good to have things in that are a wee bit different.'

Beth was well used to counting her pennies and was quite relaxed about going into shops and not buying anything. She was an expert window shopper, and had told herself to think of it all as stuff. There wasn't anything that she desperately needed, although she couldn't pull her eyes off the mugs in every colour of the rainbow. They would brighten up the flat and make drinking coffee extra special. Maybe when she was next paid . . . That would be her treat to herself.

'I was here in the summer at the Brodick Games . . . and I met Edie very briefly,' Margaret told the woman. 'It wasn't until later on I realised she was the person who made the lovely mugs I'd been admiring at a friend's cottage,' said Margaret.

'Edie's our local star. And, that's such a shame,' the woman shook her head, 'you have literally just missed her. She was here five minutes ago to drop off more stock. But . . . I think she was heading to the café that overlooks the bay, you know Cèic? If you go there next then you might just catch her. Then you can tell her yourself. I'm sure she would *love* that.' The woman beamed, and then said knowingly, 'I really don't think she realises just how talented she is. Edie is *very* unassuming.'

Margaret grinned at her. 'That sounds a splendid idea. Thank you. It would be nice to say hello to her again. What's your name? I'll tell her you sent us chasing after her. Just in case she thinks we're weird stalker fans or something.'

She gave a hearty laugh. 'I'm Thea. Tell her I sent you. But she'll be so pleased to see you and hear you've bought some of her mugs.'

'Well thank you Thea.' Margaret picked up the paper shopping bag. Then she paused. 'Just in case I don't recognise her straight away, do you remember what she's wearing?'

'She's wearing a red coat and has her dog, Molly, with her, she's a spaniel. You'll recognise her when you see her. Our Edie is one of a kind. Once you've met her you never forget her.'

Margaret chuckled. 'That sounds like a jingle. Well I for one am glad we've been able to come here this time. Thank you. Right, Beth. I think we need a cuppa. I don't know about you but I'm gasping. Let's go and check out the café and see if we can catch Edie.'

'Great idea. And this time it's my shout. I insist.' Beth was starting to feel a bit anxious about the number of times her dad and Margaret had insisted on paying for things, including dinner last night and coffee and scones that morning.

Margaret raised an eyebrow. 'Well, okay, but on one condition.'

'What's that?'

'That you also throw in a bit of cake.'

Beth laughed. 'I can do that.'

'Their cake is amazing,' added Thea. 'You'll love it.'

'Then that's a deal,' said Margaret. 'Let's go. We better hurry up as well. It looks like the heavens are about to open.'

CHAPTER THIRTY-ONE

They arrived at the café just as the rain began to bounce off the pavements and batter against the windows.

'Oh no,' groaned Beth. 'I hope it passes quickly. Otherwise it will be a washout for all those poor stallholders.'

As soon as they walked in, Margaret identified Edie and made a beeline for her. Edie was sat at a table in the corner, nursing a cappuccino, her dog curled up on the floor next to her. Beth watched as she looked up at Margaret in surprise — then she beamed when she evidently recognised her. She jumped up and the women hugged, with Margaret excitedly telling her she'd finally managed to buy some of her coveted mugs. Beth lingered a few metres away while she wondered whether to go and order, but just then Margaret turned round and beckoned her over.

'This is *the* famous Edie,' she said.

Beth smiled. 'Hi Edie. I've heard a *lot* about you, and the excitement of buying your mugs has been the most animated I've seen Margaret all weekend.'

Edie chuckled, her eyes twinkling with amusement.

'I'm Beth.' She reached out her hand.

'Sorry love, me and my lack of manners. Beth is a friend and she moved here not long ago. I'm just over visiting for the weekend with her dad.'

Edie looked beyond them. Beth wondered if she was expecting him to appear.

'He's at home having a nap and watching the football.' Margaret rolled her eyes. 'We're out doing some Christmas shopping.'

'Well it's lovely to see you again Margaret, and to meet you, Beth. How are you settling in?'

'I'm loving it thanks. I'm working with the paper in Brodick.'

'Ah, I see.' She nodded. 'That makes sense. I saw a new by-line in the paper and wondered who it was. It's really nice to put a face to the name. I do hope you enjoy working and living here.'

'Thank you. That's really kind.' Beth glanced at Margaret. 'Listen, I'm just going to order some coffee. Can I get you another, Edie?'

She shook her head. 'Thank you, that's really kind, but no. I was just having a quick caffeine fix on my way home. It's always much nicer when someone else makes it for you, and Cano makes such brilliant coffee. Hopefully that rain will go off soon so I can make a dash for it.'

'No problem,' said Beth. 'Hopefully I'll see you again, Edie. Really nice to meet you.'

'Do say hello if you pass me again,' said Edie.

'I will.'

While Margaret and Edie said their goodbyes, Beth walked over to the counter to look at the cake selection.

Moments later she was joined by Margaret, whose eyes widened. 'Will you look at those cakes. I'd like to stick my fork in them all.'

Beth nodded. 'They do all look delicious. But I think we might get chucked out if you start doing that.' She laughed. 'How about we get two different ones and share?'

'Aye love, that sounds like a very good idea.'

'You go and take a seat and I'll order it. Anything you fancy in particular?'

'No, I will eat anything. Thanks love. I could do with a wee rest myself now. All this shopping is *exhausting*.'

Beth couldn't help but chuckle at Margaret. She was very easy company — Beth was glad she'd come over to visit. As she stood there trying to decide which cakes to choose, she became aware of someone standing next to her.

'The carrot cake and the chocolate cake are both very good,' he said.

Beth looked up. Her cheeks flushed when she realised it was Callum. Honestly, twice in two days? You couldn't make this up. He would think she was totally following him. Her whole body felt like jelly as his elbow brushed against hers. *So much for female empowerment*, she said to herself crossly, willing herself to try and act normally.

'You're becoming quite the regular in here,' he said pointedly.

She shrugged. 'Erm, not really. This is only the second time that I've been in. Could say the same for you. Or is this your usual haunt?' Beth was struggling to pull her eyes away from his very kissable mouth. She could tell Margaret's eyes were lasered in on her — she'd be taking in every little detail of this interaction.

'Must just be a coincidence,' he said.

'What can I get you?' asked Cano the owner.

'Um, a piece of the chocolate and carrot cakes please, and two lattes.'

'No bother. I'll bring it over,' he said. 'You take a seat.'

'Thank you.' She smiled, then she turned to Callum. 'Nice seeing you.' She spoke as slowly and nonchalantly as she could.

'Same time tomorrow?' His eyes twinkled in amusement.

Neither of them spoke for a moment. When she saw Margaret waving at her she took that as her cue to move. 'Okay see you.'

'Beth,' he rested his hand on her arm, 'if it's okay, I'll take you up on that offer to help Daisy. I'll be in touch.'

She gave a small nod. 'Of course. Enjoy your coffee.' Then she turned to walk towards Margaret as casually as possible.

Beth sat down and did all she could to avoid Margaret's penetrating stare. She was relieved when the waitress arrived with the cake and coffee. It was only when she looked over at Margaret, offering her some chocolate cake, that she saw she was still looking at her with a smile on her lips.

Margaret leaned towards her. 'Are you going to tell me who that hunk is? And what is going on there?' She lowered her voice. 'I mean you could cut the sexual tension with a knife. The air was practically fizzing.' She sat back and gave her a knowing look.

Now Beth felt completely flustered. 'Oh, that was just an old friend from my student days.' She spoke quickly — but actually wanted the ground to swallow her up. She knew that Margaret wouldn't let this lie.

Spreading a napkin on her lap, Margaret took a forkful of chocolate cake. 'Delicious — a bit like your man over there. I mean he has certainly aged very well indeed. And he looks like someone famous. He's like that doctor off the television. Do you know who I mean?'

Beth sighed, wondering which direction Margaret was going to go with this. 'Which one?'

'You know that programme?' Margaret clicked her fingers in frustration.

'Casualty? ER?' Beth desperately tried to fire off the medical programmes she knew.

'No, no. You *know* the one I mean. That Scottish actor is in it too. The one off *Trainspotting*.'

'What, Ewan McGregor? I didn't know he was in a medical drama.'

'Not him. Honestly,' she threw up her hands in exasperation, 'you're meant to be a journalist and know this stuff.'

Beth frowned. '*Trainspotting*? Robert Carlyle?' Though she didn't think he had been in a medical drama either.

'*Tsk*,' she said. 'He's got red hair.'

Suddenly it dawned on her. 'Ah, you mean Kevin McKidd?'

Margaret clapped her hands together. 'That's the one.'

'You think he looks like him?' Her voice had dropped to a whisper, wondering if Margaret was actually *okay*? Or perhaps colour-blind, given that the actor she was referring to had red hair. Callum's hair was most definitely dark brown, albeit now threaded with a few silver strands.

'*Honestly*. Would you have a bit of cake, Beth. I think your blood sugar has gone all funny. You're making no sense.'

'Um, same could be said for you . . .'

'No I don't mean him obviously. I mean he's in the same show as McDreamy or McSteamy.' She was practically shouting and a few customers looked over. Beth also clocked Callum glancing across curiously. 'Sorry love. I didn't mean to be quite that loud.' Margaret quickly dropped her voice to a whisper. 'I was just pleased I remembered.' She gave her another of her looks. 'You know that guy that played McDreamy on *Greys Anatomy*? That was the programme.'

'Do you mean Patrick Dempsey?'

'Aye,' she stabbed her fork into the carrot cake in triumph, 'that's him. I knew we'd get there eventually. Anyway he looks a bit like your fella over there.'

Beth hadn't really made the comparison before, and now didn't dare turn and look at Callum, in case he thought she was checking him out. Which she totally would be.

'He is *very* good-looking, dear, and in a much more rugged way than that Alessandro chap from the hotel.' She took a sip of her latte.

Beth gulped her coffee so she didn't say anything she would regret.

'Besides anything else,' continued Margaret, 'he hasn't been able to take his eyes off you from the moment he sidled up to you in the queue. I'm good at noticing these things you know.'

'Maybe,' hissed Beth, 'he's not been able to stop turning round because you keep shouting random actors' names so

153

loudly. Everyone in the café has been looking over. Or maybe he's looking out the window to see if the rain has stopped.'

'You mark my words love. I have a spidey-sense about these things. You two are *destined* to be together.'

Beth quickly took a forkful of carrot cake just at the moment Callum walked past with his takeaway coffee. He gave her a small smile as he passed — she had to raise her hand to wave when she realised her mouth was full of cake.

Margaret sat back and crossed her arms. 'See what I mean? He's got it *bad*. Now then. Are you going to tell me what the story is?'

CHAPTER THIRTY-TWO

Beth looked outside and was relieved to see the rain had now gone off. Callum could make a quick getaway with the rest of the customers who'd been waiting, apprehensively looking at the sky. She looked across at Margaret. 'Um, are you sure you really want to know?'

Margaret burst out laughing. 'Of course I do. I want all the juicy details.' But she was looking at her with such kindness and warmth that Beth found herself opening up to Margaret in a way that she hadn't to anyone in a *very* long time. She smiled faintly as she thought back to those heady days of being young and carefree. 'Where to begin?' She scrunched up her nose. 'It was a long time ago.'

'Well, just start at the beginning. Tell me how you met.' Margaret took a forkful of the carrot cake.

Beth nodded in agreement and studied Margaret's face thoughtfully for a moment. Then she began to tell her about how she met Callum. She told Margaret about the summers she had spent working at the Brodie Hotel when she was a student.

'I absolutely loved it. Everyone was so friendly and welcoming and we all got on brilliantly. Some people I worked

155

with already lived on the island. Then there were a few others like me who had come over from the mainland to work for the summer. I loved it and couldn't wait for the season to start. It always felt like a bit of a haven, and the rest of the world felt like it was a million miles away.'

'Aye, I can imagine,' said Margaret. 'Must have felt like time stood still.'

'Exactly.' Beth smiled at Margaret. 'That was exactly how it felt. Like a really special time with endless summer days and nights. And funnily enough my memories are that it was *always* sunny.'

Margaret laughed. 'The sun always shines in happy times.'

That was so true. When she looked back, she thought of sunshine and fun — the rain didn't feature at all. The work at the hotel wasn't difficult. There was plenty of free time to laze on the beach, swim, play tennis and hang out with friends. However, it was her final and third summer on the island that was the happiest few months of bliss. That's when she and Callum met for the first time. He worked two jobs, pulling pints behind the bar of the hotel in the evenings, and for his father's joinery business during the day. They would snatch any time they could together, which was hard given their conflicting schedules. Beth would spend most of her evenings off nursing a drink in the bar until he finished his shift, then they would go for late-night walks and sit on the beach talking until the sun came up. Then they would grab a few hours' sleep before Beth started her housekeeping shift and Callum had to be back at the joinery workshop just outside Lamlash. It was handy that he could drive and had his own car. The rare nights off that Callum did have they would go to the local pub and listen to live music with the other staff from the hotel, including Kirsty. Beth sometimes wondered how they had managed to actually sustain a relationship when they were both so busy. But the connection between them had been magnetic. They had been young and in love. Or so she had thought.

'It sounded like it was a very special time.' Margaret smiled at her.

'It was,' she said wistfully. 'I mean, I knew it wouldn't last forever, and that life would go back to some kind of normal. I guess it had to. But then I had the offer of a job in London, and it seemed natural that he would also come. He was really up for doing something different, and I knew he would pick up work in a pub or as a joiner, as he'd finished his apprenticeship with his dad.' Beth took a sip of her coffee. 'It's strange to think I was also offered a job on *The Arran Times* then. But I turned it down. I desperately wanted to be in London, where all the action happened.'

Margaret inclined her head to one side. 'What happened to Callum?'

'Well, I went back home to Glasgow for a couple of weeks before moving. I needed to get myself organised. Callum and I were going to take the train to London, and we spoke on the phone right up until a couple of days before we were due to leave.' Beth poked at a piece of cake with her fork, then placed it back on the plate. 'We arranged to meet on the platform at Central Station. I kept looking at my watch, wondering where he was. I thought I'd got the meeting point wrong and I checked everywhere. I was running about the station like a headless chicken.' She shook her head sadly as she remembered. 'We didn't have mobile phones then and I didn't have any coins or even time to use the phone box. But I knew he wasn't coming . . . I'd always told him that he didn't have to, and that if he didn't show up then I would know he had changed his mind and that was okay. He needed to do what was right for him. But I was devastated when he didn't show. I had really fallen in love with him . . . and I thought he felt the same way too. But it just wasn't meant to be. I'd got it all so very wrong.'

Margaret placed a hand on her heart. 'Oh Beth. That's so sad. You must have been bawling when you get on that train. I don't know if I would have managed it. That would have taken a fair amount of strength. It's like a scene from a movie.'

Beth felt her eyes glistening as she remembered how upset she'd been as the train chugged out of the station. She had managed to hold it together until she got to her seat. She had sunk into it and gazed out the window as the train went over the bridge and across the River Clyde. Only then did she let the tears start to fall — she sobbed on and off for the next few hours. Her heart felt as though it had been smashed into smithereens. She had been grateful that her mum had given her some tissues to take with her. She had used every single one.

'That must have been so tough,' said Margaret.

'It was. But I just had to get on with things. There was nothing else for it.'

'And did you keep in touch with anyone else from the hotel?'

Beth felt a pang of guilt as she thought about Kirsty. Her shoulders sagged. 'No, I didn't. I had planned to, but I just threw myself into work and building a life for myself in London. I worked all the time, and I guess I wanted to forget it all and try and move on. I felt as though I'd made a bit of a fool of myself. But I did bump into an old friend from back then quite recently. She lives here now, she invited me for a coffee.'

'Ah,' said Margaret, 'that's interesting. Did she shed any light on your fella?'

Beth blushed. 'I didn't want to ask after so long. And he's not my fella, Margaret. Anyway, it's all water under the bridge now. It doesn't matter. It all happened in another lifetime.'

'But do you have any plans to see this friend again?' Margaret clasped her hands together on the table, leaning towards her.

Beth nodded. 'Do you know, it was actually really lovely seeing her. She's called Kirsty. Turns out she lived in London for a while and then moved back here with her husband and children. We're going to catch up again soon.' She paused. 'I guess I feel bad about missed opportunities with people. If I'd known that she was in London maybe we could have been in each other's lives down there. But I guess it wasn't meant to be.'

Margaret reached her hand out and patted Beth's arm. 'I'm a great believer in fate you know. What's for you won't go by you and all that. Things happen for a reason.'

'I suppose so . . .'

'So you never did find out why he didn't come with you?'

'No. I just assumed he'd changed his mind.'

'Did you ever think that something might have happened?' She shook her head. 'What do you mean?'

'Something may have happened to stop him from coming.'

'Nope. I was so young back then. And our arrangement had been to meet at the train station at a certain time. If he wasn't there I would know that he wasn't coming. I just thought it wasn't meant to be. Until . . .'

'Hmm?' Margaret waited for Beth to elaborate.

Beth waved her hand dismissively. 'It might sound daft, but when I first saw him in the pub a few weeks ago I couldn't believe it. I felt like a teenager again. My heart was racing and it felt as though there was still a connection across that crowded bar. I mean how stupid does that sound? Decades have passed and we haven't had a proper conversation . . .'

If truth be told, Beth hadn't been able to push away thoughts of Callum since seeing him that night.

'Did *he* ever try to get in touch with you back then?' asked Margaret.

'No, but it was very different back then. We didn't have social media in the way people use it to connect now. And I changed my name.'

Margaret nodded. 'Yes, your dad explained that to me. Not sure I would have agreed to do that. I mean Elizabeth Taylor is a splendid name.'

'I know. I wouldn't do it now. I was young and thought I had to do what I was told if I wanted to get ahead.'

'I understand that. Changed days now, thank God. What are you going to do?'

Beth shrugged. 'I'm not sure there is much I can do. I can hardly ask him. That would be weird. Anyway, his life has moved on.'

'Well everyone's life has moved on since then, Beth . . . It was a long time ago. I mean, I'm sure you've had plenty of men in your life since. For all he knows you could have been married and divorced three times.' Margaret looked at her inquisitively.

Beth nodded. Her heart hammered as she wondered if this was the time to tell Margaret about Tim. He was a whole other story though. Perhaps she would share that another day. 'Well things have changed for everyone, but most certainly things have changed for him. He has definitely moved on.'

'What do you mean?'

'He's a dad now. He has a daughter.'

'Ah, I see,' said Margaret. 'Though not unexpected at your ages and stages of life. Most people have baggage. And is he married? Does he have a partner?'

'I have no idea,' said Beth. 'It would be a bit weird if that was my opening question to him.'

Margaret leaned towards her. 'I have been around the block a bit my love. It's called growing older. But I can tell you, the way he was looking at you would suggest to me that he is a man who is unattached.'

Beth smiled without conviction. 'I've got no idea about his personal life.'

'It sounds like you could do with asking your friend Kirsty a few questions.'

'That would be weird and stalkery though.'

'Rubbish. There's always a way. I think the first thing you should do is see Kirsty for a coffee and ask her.'

'I don't think I can.'

'Of course you can, you're a journalist. You ask people questions for a living.'

'What would I say?'

'Just ask if anything happened that summer after you left and see what she says. She may be able to shed some light on what stopped Callum from making that train.' She raised an eyebrow. 'But more importantly she might be able to tell you a bit more about his current circumstances.'

Beth looked at her watch. 'If we're quick we'll catch the lights being switched on.'

'Stop trying to change the subject young lady . . . But I agree. Let's go out and join the party. We might even bump into your fella again if we're lucky. Then you can introduce us properly.'

CHAPTER THIRTY-THREE

Callum sat in the car with his takeaway coffee staring straight ahead at the sea. He couldn't think straight and he knew why. Elizabeth. He couldn't take his eyes off her in the café. Even though he had seen her yesterday, somehow she had managed to take his breath away again. She was wearing jeans, trainers and a red sweater, and with her hair swept up in a ponytail she looked as fresh-faced and beautiful as ever. She had *always* had that effect on him, and he couldn't believe she was still having such a profound impact on him a couple of decades on.

He had felt a sudden quiver of excitement when she'd walked into him yesterday and he'd felt her against his chest. What he wanted to do was hold her tight and kiss her the way that he used to. Did she also feel the connection? Surely she must and it wasn't him just imagining it? Lately he seemed to be questioning his own judgement on things. Maybe it was all in his head? Maybe she thought he *was* stalking her. He had never been into the café two days in a row in his entire life. What were the chances of her literally bumping into him both times? He had planned to go to the Christmas lights switch-on with Daisy. But he assumed that was why she was in Lamlash. If he went that would be really creepy, and she might think he was stalking her. He shook his head. Now he was totally over-analysing things.

Callum had spent so long regretting the day he hadn't gone to meet her at the train station. Even now, as he thought back, he could feel that visceral pain in his heart. They had spent such an incredible summer together. From the moment they met, Callum couldn't take his eyes off her. It didn't matter that she was dressed in her work cleaning outfit — drab grey trousers and a tunic — she could have been wearing a bin bag and he would still have thought her the most beautiful girl he'd ever seen. Whenever she saw him, a bright smile lit up her face and he only ever had eyes for her. He would always look back on that summer with fond memories — he had fallen head over heels in love and they had planned a future together. But fate had intervened and called a halt to those plans. The truth was, what happened next was out of Callum's control and he wasn't to blame. Something *had* happened that prevented him from catching the ferry to the mainland that morning, and then the train into Glasgow. Something huge, which had turned his life upside down completely.

He took a sip of his coffee as he thought back to those final few days before he was due to leave Arran. He had been all set to go and had planned so meticulously for this adventure. His bags were ready and sat by the door, having been packed and repacked several times. It was as though he was about to set off on the most incredible adventure with the love of his life. His parents were sad that he was leaving, but totally supported his decision to follow his heart and do what he wanted to do, rather than what he felt everyone else expected him to do, which was continue working with his dad. He closed his eyes and let out a long slow breath as he thought about his dad, who had worked so hard to provide for his family, and then had passed on his trade to his son. He adored his kids and his wife and was loved by everyone who he'd ever done some joinery work for. His dad had been the kind of man he'd always aspired to be then, and now. The night before Callum was due to leave, his mother had made a special roast dinner with all the trimmings in his honour.

'Just let me treat you for one more night,' she'd said. 'It's not often we're all here together.' His sister had just arrived home from a summer job working as an au pair in France, and having a family meal together was a bit of a rarity. 'You never quite know when we'll get the chance to do this again,' his mum had said. 'Or where your next meal will be coming from. Especially in London. Everything will cost a fortune.'

Callum had laughed. 'I'm not sure it's all that bad.'

His mum had ladled extras of everything onto his plate. 'You need to keep your strength up.'

After they had eaten his dad had groaned, 'I've eaten too much. My eyes are bigger than my stomach. It'll be back to the bread and water tomorrow.'

'I'll remind you of that then will I?' His mum had laughed.

His father stood up and stretched, then made his apologies. 'That was delicious. But I'm so full. I need to move from the table. I'm just going to go and have a soft seat by the window.'

Callum could still clearly remember hearing him pad across the flagstone tiles of the kitchen and the familiar creak of the chair when he sank into it. He could still hear the background chatter of his mum and sister as they clattered the plates into the sink, the whistle of the kettle as his mum waited for it to boil. He glanced over at his dad, whose head was slumped down, his chin pointing towards his chest. It hadn't taken him long to nod off. It never did. His dad had a knack for grabbing a twenty-minute nap when he could.

'Here's your tea love.' His mother had placed the mug on a nest of tables next to Dad's armchair and lightly tapped his arm.

Callum had started to help with the drying of the dishes, but looking over he'd seen the anxious expression on his mum's face. It was like watching something unfold in slow motion — he could do nothing to stop the tsunami of a wave that was about to hit his family. His mum was now on her knees and gently shaking his dad. His sister ran over and looked up at Callum, her eyes wide and willing him to fix things.

'Dad,' she wailed. 'Wake up. Help Callum. Do something.'

But Callum couldn't do a thing. He couldn't manage to fix or save his dad. In the fog that followed, the medics kept telling him afterwards that nobody could have done anything to change the outcome. His dad had had a massive heart attack as he sat down in that chair and had died immediately and peacefully. In the weeks that followed, Callum felt a sense of duty to honour his dad and step up and make the decisions. Callum had to organise his funeral, and all that went with that, and then deal with the trail of administration that his father had left behind. All his plans were cancelled as he took over the running of his dad's joinery. He knew that's what his dad would have wanted him to do. Leaving the island was impossible. How could he abandon his mum and sister when they were all so absorbed in grief? Several times, he thought vaguely about trying to contact Beth. But what difference would it have made? She had already gone and would be very settled in her new life. He was glad that she'd always said there was never any pressure to be at the station. He hoped she would assume that he'd changed his mind and move on. The last thing he wanted was for her to feel saddled with him, or so guilty about being away that she should return to Arran.

His phone started to ring, pulling him back into the present. It was Daisy, who had spent the afternoon with a friend.

'Hi. It's me. Can you pick me up now please?'

'Course I will.' Callum immediately wondered if she was okay — she sounded quite subdued. 'I just stopped at the café to get myself a coffee. I will be with you in five minutes. Are we still going to see the lights being switched on?'

'No. I just want to go home.' Her voice was flat.

Callum frowned. 'Okay I'll be there soon.' He wondered what was on her mind. Maybe it was something to do with school, though it couldn't be English, as they had chatted about that and agreed that enlisting Beth's help in the first instance would be a huge help. Then they could take it from there. He knew Beth would have drawn her own conclusions from being at parents' evening the other night. But he could hardly start getting into big conversations about his role as a single parent when all they seemed to do was have stilted and brief chats in the café or school.

He shook his head, wondering if Daisy maybe had the Sunday blues as she thought about going to school the next day. He also knew, by the time he collected her, that her mood could have changed completely. He was somehow slowly becoming more used to the ways of a teenage girl. He wiped away a tear that had rolled down his cheek. How he missed Isla.

Clearing his throat, he started the engine. It didn't matter what had been thrown in his path, his world had somehow kept going. He'd long ago decided that he needed to treat each day as an adventure. He had to always remind himself to have hope. That had kept him going. Well, just about. Maybe Beth was just the next curveball in his path and, as Isla had always told him, it was better to be open to all of life's possibilities. How he wished she was here so he could ask her what to do now.

CHAPTER THIRTY-FOUR

Beth was sad to say farewell to her dad and Margaret at the start of the week. She wasn't sure if she could get away from the office to walk them to the terminal — a hang up from her early workdays when you would be labelled a shirker for stepping away from your screen even to go to the toilet. However, as she was slowly learning, that world of work was not one she existed in anymore. Jim was a brilliant boss.

'Of course you can go. No problem at all. Take your time,' he'd said. It had been a fresh but sunny morning and she'd enjoyed walking at their slow pace towards the incoming ferry.

Beth's arm was linked through Margaret's. 'It's been just brilliant.'

'It's good to picture where you are now Beth. Means I can picture where you're living and working.' Her dad's voice was warm. 'Thanks for having us and showing us your haunts. We'll see you at Christmas then?'

Beth felt her eyes fill with tears. 'Of course you will. I'm looking forward to it, Dad. I can't believe it's just a few weeks away.' She hadn't failed to notice that her dad had started to slow down. She needed to make more of an effort to see him now she was living closer.

'We'll definitely be back over when it gets warmer too,' said Margaret. 'The Highland Games was *quite* the experience.'

'Thanks for putting me up,' said her dad, 'and showing me the sights. It's been grand.'

Once they arrived at the terminal Beth gave them both a warm hug. It felt so good to have them on her side. They accepted her and supported her for who she was rather than what she could do for them. She now realised that had been the case with many of the people in her London life. They wanted to be friends with her because of the free tickets to parties or the favours she could do for them. When she'd needed those friends, the silence had been telling.

'I'll see you in a few weeks,' Beth added.

'Great dear.' Her dad hugged her again tightly.

'Be good.' Margaret winked at her. 'And remember, do your job and ask *lots* of questions.'

It was clear what Margaret meant and Beth smiled at her. 'You'll be glad to know that I'm seeing Kirsty later in the week. I will keep you informed.'

'Good girl.'

Margaret and her dad waved as they headed upstairs to wait in the passengers' lounge.

As Beth had walked back to the office, she realised she felt content, but also curious. She was ready to find out a bit more about Callum.

* * *

Beth and Kirsty met in a café in Brodick on Saturday morning. Beth was there early and sat reading the news on her phone, glancing up and keeping an eye on the door. When Kirsty arrived, she made her way towards Beth.

'Good to see you,' said Kirsty.

'You too. Thanks for this. I've been looking forward to catching up again.'

'How was the visit from your dad and his friend?'

'All good thanks. It was actually really nice showing them around. It's been years since Dad was here. Margaret was over in the summer for the Highland games, and she was determined to track down some mugs by Edie . . .'

Kirsty burst out laughing. 'I know the very ones. I've got some in my kitchen too. I think many folk do.'

'I'm not surprised. They're lovely. In fact, Margaret bought a couple for my flat too. They make coffee very pleasurable.' Beth had been touched when she'd got back to the flat after waving them off on their ferry, to find a package that Margaret had left. It was a pair of bright orange mugs from the Wee Trove.

'How has your week been?' Beth asked. 'Is Amy back now?'

Kirsty nodded. 'Yes, thank goodness.'

Beth raised an eyebrow in surprise.

'Oh, that sounds terrible, doesn't it? I don't mean it like that. I just realised how much I've come to rely on her when she's here. Especially with Dad.'

'It's not terrible at all, just honest. It sounds like it can all be quite full on, especially with running the guest house too.'

'I think it's just that stage in life when I feel like I'm being stretched in loads of different directions. And feel permanently knackered. Anyway, I'm sure once we get into January things will slow down after the Christmas and New Year rush. We are fully booked as of next week. Everyone seems to want to get away.'

Beth looked at her with sympathy. 'Well, it looks like you're doing an amazing job of juggling a lot, Kirsty. Be a bit kinder to yourself.'

Kirsty waved her hand dismissively. 'Ignore me. I'm fine. Sorry, I didn't come here to offload.'

'That's okay. And anytime. That's what friends are for.' The waiter arrived at their table with a very enthusiastic grin. 'What would you like Kirsty? This is my treat.'

'A large Americano with some hot milk would be great thanks.'

'I'll have the same.' Beth sat up straighter in her chair, practically hearing Margaret's voice in her ear. *Ask the questions.* 'You'll never guess who I've bumped into a few times since I last saw you.'

'Who?' Kirsty frowned.

'Callum. From way back.'

'Ah.' Kirsty nodded slowly. 'I wondered if you might come across each other.'

'Yes. Turns out I've been helping his daughter on the school newspaper.'

'His daughter?' Kirsty sounded surprised.

Just then their coffees arrived. Beth watched as Kirsty picked up her teaspoon and stirred her coffee. There was something she knew and wasn't telling her.

'Yes,' said Beth. 'Daisy.'

'Mmm.' Kirsty smiled faintly.

Beth looked at her quizzically. 'Is there something I'm missing?'

'Look, I don't really want to be the one telling you. I think this is a conversation you should be having with Callum.'

'What do you mean?'

Kirsty took a sip of her coffee and looked at Beth thoughtfully. 'It's easy to jump to conclusions . . .'

'You might have to spell it out to me.' Beth really didn't understand what she was getting at.

'I don't like gossiping about folk, but I think you should know that Daisy isn't Callum's daughter. Daisy is Callum's niece.'

CHAPTER THIRTY-FIVE

Beth was stunned into silence. She hadn't expected Kirsty to say that. 'I had no idea.'

'It's easy to make assumptions. We all do it,' said Kirsty kindly.

'But how . . . why . . .'

Kirsty fidgeted with the napkin in front of her. 'Look, I'm not really at liberty to say anything else. It's not my story to share. It's something you should talk to Callum about. I would say you both have a lot of catching up to do.'

Beth sat back in her chair. 'You're right. I think we do need to have a chat. Isn't it funny how our minds quickly create stories around people? I was convinced he was married with a squad of kids.'

Kirsty smiled. 'We all do it. I'm as guilty as anyone else for making up narratives and getting it completely wrong. But, I can confirm that he is not married, nor does he have a big team of kids. It's just him and Daisy.' Kirsty frowned, looking as though she was about to say something else.

'What is it?' Beth leaned towards her.

'Beth . . . I'm just going to come right out and say this. I have the feeling you've been badly hurt in the past. I know

I'm now the one making assumptions, so please correct me if I'm wrong. But what I will say is that it's okay to give Callum a chance. He's one of the good guys. Don't let the past ruin your future.'

Beth was thoughtful for a moment. She realised that she'd missed having good and dependable girlfriends. She had pushed everyone away after what had happened with Tim. After their relationship had broken down, she vowed never to get involved with a man again. She promised herself she would remain single forever. Tim had reduced her thoughts of love and romance to ash. Until she bumped into Callum, she never thought anyone would spark that fire again. She wrapped her arms tightly around her body, trying to make sense of the maelstrom of thoughts whirring around her head.

Beth had tried so hard to hold things together over the past couple of years. She didn't want to let the house of cards she'd so carefully constructed to collapse. Yet she knew she had changed since she'd arrived on Arran. She looked at Kirsty and took a deep breath. 'Can I tell you what happened to me, Kirsty? Do you have time?'

Kirsty's eyes widened and she reached for Beth's hand, grasping it. 'Of course I do Beth. I'm here and I'm listening.' She smiled and tilted her head. 'But before you start, would you like another coffee?'

Beth could have hugged her. 'Yes please. I certainly need one.' While they waited for their coffees to arrive they made small talk about Christmas and the weather. Then, once they were settled with their coffees, Beth began to tell her about Tim.

She shuddered as she thought back to when she met him — a sophisticated and extremely handsome entrepreneur, on an online dating site, not long after her mother had died. 'He was a good listener, attentive, and came across as very caring and supportive. Things moved slowly to begin with as we were both busy with work. But after a year he had moved in with me and I thought we were both happy and in love.'

Beth had Kirsty's full attention as she told her about Tim's work interests abroad, how he would often fly to Switzerland and Dubai where he had business interests. Beth thought this was glamourous and brought more excitement to their relationship. Especially when their reunions were passionate and he would shower her with gifts. Looking back, because hindsight was such a handy thing, she wasn't quite sure when she started to question his commitment, or started to see the little cracks. It might have been when he started to borrow money for yet another new start-up he was involved with.

'I mean, to start with I was completely unsuspecting. Why would I question him when I trusted him?' Beth sighed loudly. 'And being the supportive and generous girlfriend that I was, I was always happy to help . . . Until his requests started to be for bigger chunks of cash, which I didn't have.' She paused and took a breath. Kirsty nodded reassuringly at her. 'Whenever I questioned him, which was ironically what I did for a living after all, he always confidently reassured me, dispelling any fears I had.'

He was always able to explain and rationalise, and she soon learned to ignore any doubts she had. She didn't want to be alone, especially as she had invested several years of her life in their relationship. She blinked hard to stop any tears falling as she told Kirsty how, even when they started to explore the adoption process, he had failed to get his DBS check. He had told her that he couldn't have children himself and had suggested adoption. It was something that Beth was very happy to consider especially as she would have been happy to take an older child. But even when Beth had received her DBS and reminded him about his, he claimed it must have been held up in the system. Her mind rationalised his behaviour. Especially when he said he thought they should take a break from talking about adoption as they needed to focus on each other for a while. 'His final parting gift was when he persuaded me to remortgage my flat as he was having "cash flow" problems. Then he abruptly ended our relationship and vanished. Along with all the money I had lent him.'

Kirsty's eyes widened in horror. 'Oh Beth. That's horrific.'

She shook her head. 'Even then, I thought something awful had happened to him. Meanwhile my own finances were in a complete mess and I couldn't afford to pay the huge mortgage repayments. That's when I was forced to put my beloved home on the market. I was mortified, too embarrassed to tell anyone what had happened, especially my dad and my friends, most of whom I lost touch with anyway. I knew they would just think I'd been foolish. I was supposed to be an intelligent woman. What a mug, eh?'

Kirsty shook her head sadly. 'It sounded like he knew exactly what he was doing. What happened next?'

'Are you sure you want me to go on?'

'Of course. As long as it's helping you to talk about it.'

Beth exhaled loudly. 'Sharing all of this is tough. But it's actually good to say it all out loud.'

Kirsty nodded.

'One night, after watching a documentary on television about romance scammers, the penny finally began to drop. I felt totally humiliated, embarrassed and ashamed over what had happened. I'm a *journalist*. I kept telling myself that I should have seen the signs, I should have been savvier and known what was happening. When I was commissioned to write an article on romance fraud for a women's magazine it was cathartic. That was when I finally realised and accepted what Tim had done, and realised that it wasn't my fault. Interviewing other woman for case studies, I realised I wasn't alone. It's sadly quite common, and the target is usually women, often vulnerable for a mix of reasons, who are successful and own their own property or business. I also learned that Tim probably wasn't his real name. Not long after that I spoke to the police about him. They told me that his real name is Zander Evans. He was known as a conman, and there were multiple complaints and reports against him.'

'This is horrendous Beth. Did they catch him?'

'Yes. He was eventually caught and sentenced to a ten-year prison term for defrauding two women, but I wasn't able to recover all the cash I had lost. By then I had started renting a room in Deptford and begun to piece my life back together. I knew that things could have been worse. Some of the women I'd interviewed, their lives had been completely devastated. Their confidence had been shattered to the point they couldn't leave their houses, and one woman contemplated suicide. Even at my lowest point, I kept holding on to the tiny positives I could find every day. I got a job working at a café, which gave me a focus and a purpose.' Beth was just beginning to realise now how grateful she was to Frankie for reaching out and giving her that lifeline.

'I'm not surprised that you feel wary about any new relationships, Beth. That's a lot to go through.'

Beth was grateful that Kirsty hadn't fled the scene, that she'd stayed and listened. For too long it had all felt too raw to share. But sitting here now, she realised how much she'd needed to. 'Thank you for listening Kirsty. It has really helped.'

'Beth, I am sorry that you had to go through all of that. Thanks for telling me, and thanks for trusting me. I can see now why all the stuff with Callum has thrown you.'

It was true. Her feelings for Callum had surprised her. Being with him had given her a sense of hope, which was something she'd lost after Tim. And Callum was different, she told herself.

'Speak to him,' said Kirsty softly. 'Speak to Callum.'

Beth frowned. She and Callum were connected through their past. Surely that had to count for something.

CHAPTER THIRTY-SIX

A couple of days later Callum pulled into the driveway of Edie's house. Two large pieces of driftwood framed the door of the whitewashed building, and above it hung a little sign: *Welcome to Coorie Cottage.* A stylish Christmas wreath was hung on the door. As he knocked and stepped back to wait, he wondered if she would mind if he had a wee peek at the shepherd's hut she had at the bottom of her garden. Fergus had told her all about Coorie Cabin, and he was intrigued to have a proper look. He knew she'd had it brought over a couple of years ago and now rented it out to visitors.

'Hello Callum,' said Edie, swinging the door open. 'Lovely to see you. Come on in.' She closed the door behind him, ushering him through to the bright living room at the back of the house. 'Just watch these boxes. They are a bit of a hazard, which is why I need your help.'

He was welcomed by Molly the dog, who immediately ran over to him, wagging her tail and sniffing his hands. Rubbing her ears, he was rewarded with a lick.

'Honestly Molly, what are you like?' asked Edie. 'She's always liked the men. She's exactly the same with Fergus.'

Callum laughed. 'Well, I don't mind. In fact I'm flattered.' He looked around and immediately felt at home. The cottage was warm, with cushions and throws and a log burner ablaze in the centre of the room. There was a small Christmas tree in the window that twinkled with fairy lights.

'Now, first thing's first. Can I get you a cup of tea?' asked Edie.

Callum always made a point of declining tea, otherwise he would never get any work done. But something about the way Edie was smiling at him made him want to make an exception. 'That would be lovely please. Though only if you're making it.'

'The kettle's just boiled. I am gasping for a cuppa.'

'Great, thank you, and I take it with just a splash of milk.'

'Back in a moment. You take a seat and I'll be with you shortly.'

Callum sat down. His eyes flicked around the brightly coloured framed prints and canvases on the walls. Then his eyes rested on the orange flames of the log fire. Molly settled at his feet. When he felt his phone buzz in his pocket, he realised that he was very tempted to ignore it. But he knew he should answer it in case it was the school or another customer. It was a number he didn't recognise and, when he answered it, he realised it was Beth.

'Hi Callum, I thought I would give you a quick call to check it's still okay to see Daisy later tonight? About her English?'

'Erm, yes, that's fine.' Daisy had failed to mention anything to him about it. 'Did you make an arrangement with her?'

'She said she was happy to take the bus over to Brodick after school and come to the office. Is that okay with you? Sorry, I thought you knew.'

'Yes, that's fine. What time will she be finished? I'll be there to collect her.'

'We should be done by six o'clock.'

'Okay.' He looked up at Edie as she walked towards him and placed a mug on the small table next to him. 'Thanks. I'll see you then.' He ended the call and hoped he hadn't sounded too curt, but she'd caught him off guard. He had been meaning to call her to arrange to meet up. But he was nervous. He didn't want to mess things up.

'Everything okay?' Edie looked at him quizzically.

'All good thanks. Now tell me about these shelves.' He reached for his tea and took a sip. 'I have a few ideas, but you tell me if there's something specific that you'd like.'

'Well, you'll have seen the boxes in the hallway. I'm surprised I've not broken my leg yet as I keep walking into them. I've been wondering about making the best use of space in the hallway, but also in the wee room at the front of the house.' She stood up. 'Come on, bring your tea and I can show you.'

As they walked back into the hallway, Callum felt the unfamiliar excitement of a challenge. This was going to be interesting — there were lots of nooks and crannies in this type of old cottage — but he was confident he could give Edie what she wanted. Although he had originally trained as a joiner with his dad, and the majority of his work focused on DIY jobs, the thing he absolutely loved doing most was woodwork and traditional craftsmanship, whether it was making bespoke bookcases like Edie had asked for or a special piece of furniture. Unfortunately there wasn't such a high demand for work like that, so it was a treat when he was commissioned for a job like this.

Edie showed him into the room at the front. He frowned as he looked around, thinking about the best ways of maximising the space. 'I can absolutely do this for you Edie. There are plenty of spaces I can work with to fit in shelves and get your books all organised.'

'Oh good,' she said. 'I'd hoped you could help. I know the sizing of these old houses can be a bit tricky, they have all sorts of anomalies. You have free rein to do what you think will work.'

Callum smiled. 'That's what makes me happy. I love a challenge. Did you have any thoughts on the type of wood you might like?'

She waved her hands, her orange-beaded bracelets clinking together. 'Not really. If you can just make them look pretty,' she chuckled, 'and maybe tone in with the flooring?'

'Of course. I'll take some measurements now and source the wood. I'll be back to show you some options and give you a price.' He pulled a tape measure from his pocket and a small notepad and pen.

'Righto,' said Edie. 'I'll leave you in peace. Just give me a shout if you need anything.'

As he busied himself measuring the space and working out dimensions, he thought about the years after his dad had died. How his focus had been to keep the family business running, which he had managed to do when friends of his dad had also stepped in to help. It was only several years later, when he felt able to take some time away from the island to travel, at his mum's insistence, that he had discovered his love of woodwork after enrolling in some workshops in Malaysia. When he'd returned home, he'd started experimenting — first with the kitchen table at home, then with coffee tables and cheese boards, which were beautiful, with their attention to design and intricate detail. He had even started selling some of them at the local craft markets. But then Isla had died and he'd become responsible for Daisy, and life had changed for him again. He had to clear away any potential dangers, including knives and saws, from the cottage. It was a health-and-safety disaster zone for a young child. He always meant to pick things up again and start crafting in the joinery workshop, but so far it hadn't happened. That was very much a functional space for the day-to-day jobs. He had tried to teach Daisy a few basic skills over the years, and her DIY skills were fairly impressive for a teenager. But she'd lost interest in learning any more. Which reminded him that he still hadn't been able to get to the bottom of what was going on with her. She'd perked up a bit over the past few days, but she still wasn't her usual happy self and he didn't quite know what to do. He hoped it was just her hormones and age and that it would pass. Maybe seeing Beth would help her. He knew it was good for her to have positive female role models in her life. Hopefully Beth would live up to the task. Although he knew he could call his mum and ask her advice he didn't want to worry her. She'd had enough of that to last her a few lifetimes. Sometimes he wished she still lived on the island, but he understood her reasons for leaving. Although she'd tried her best following the death of his dad, she found that being surrounded by the memories was all too painful. Eventually Callum and Isla encouraged her to move, to be closer to her sister who lived in the small town of Crieff. The fresh start seemed to have been good for her. She'd managed to build a life for herself, which had stood her in good stead for what happened next.

'Callum, there's another cup of tea for you.' Edie had arrived with a fresh mug and a chocolate biscuit. 'I've just remembered that I need to collect something from the post office before it shuts. I'm going to have to love you and leave you. There's a key there, if you lock up and put it through the letterbox.'

'Thanks Edie.' He was grateful for her kindness. 'I can't remember the last time someone made me a cup of tea, never mind two.' He laughed.

'Well, yes, I can imagine you're the one doing all the running around after your niece.'

'Indeed,' he said. 'Look, I shouldn't be too much longer to be honest. Once the measurements are all done, I'll drop off the quote and a sample of pale oak, which I think will look good. We can take it from there?'

'Wonderful,' said Edie. 'Thanks again for coming by. I appreciate it. And there's no rush. I know this is always a busy time of year for tradesmen.'

'No problem at all.' He stopped to take a gulp of tea. 'I'm glad you asked. Things have been a bit quiet lately, so you've asked me at a very good time. If I can make a start on this for you before Christmas then I will.'

Callum finished up the measurements and enjoyed the rest of his tea, then took his mug through to Edie's kitchen where he carefully rinsed it out in the sink and left it on the rack to dry. His eyes were drawn to a photo in the window ledge of Edie and a man smiling. He wondered if it was her husband. Molly had followed him through to the kitchen and sat, watching and waiting.

'I'll go now Molly. But Edie will be back soon.'

She looked at him, then slinked over to the sofa, jumped up and curled into a tight ball.

'I'm not sure if you're allowed to do that.'

She looked at him with sad eyes.

'But it's okay, I won't tell.' He walked over to her, patted her head and she thumped her tail. He sighed. A dog's life wasn't bad at all.

CHAPTER THIRTY-SEVEN

Callum decided to head home to work on Edie's quote straight-away, as he'd left the rest of the afternoon clear for admin. He'd left Ruby behind and wanted to take her for a quick walk before he went to collect Daisy. When he opened the fridge door, he realised they were out of milk, which confused him — he was the only one meant to be drinking it. Then, when he realised they needed a few other groceries, he made a mental note to stop at the shops before he collected Daisy.

It was just after half past five when he arrived in Brodick, intending to do a quick sweep around the supermarket. He quickly grabbed everything that was in his rough list and, as he paid on the self-service till, which he was amazed had actually worked for a change, he glanced up and saw a woman standing watching him. Realising it was Kirsty he grinned. 'Long time no see.' He lifted his bag of shopping and walked over to her. 'How are things?'

'I know,' she said. 'It does feel like it's been ages since I saw you. It's not often you're round in these parts. What's made you venture out of Lamlash?' She laughed.

'I'm picking up Daisy,' he said. 'She's having some tutor-ing . . .'

'How is she?' asked Kirsty. 'She must be about fourteen or so now?'

'Spot on, yes. Just at that tricky stage, or so I'm told.'

Kirsty smiled. 'Yes, the teenage years can be trickier than the toddler years. Anything in particular?'

Callum set his bag down at his feet. 'You name it. I keep buying the wrong shampoo, which is tantamount to some kind of horrendous crime, I don't cook the correct things. She's decided to go vegan.'

'Ah, the normal teenage stuff then. No drugs or alcohol yet?'

Callum was horrified. 'Don't say that. I don't think I could cope.'

'I'm joking. Well, kind of. Hopefully that will all pass her by.'

'She's been a bit quiet lately.'

'The moody hormonal phase?' Kirsty looked at him in sympathy. 'It can't be easy when she doesn't have her mum.'

Callum nodded. 'I know. I do wonder if that's on her mind.'

'Just ask her Callum. Remember she's not a wee girl anymore. Just talk to her like she's a grown-up. You might be surprised.'

Callum realised she was right. 'Thanks. I will. I don't like mentioning Isla to her in case it upsets her. But you're right. Maybe talking about her mum will help.' He glanced at his watch. 'Sorry Kirsty I need to go and collect her. I don't want to be late. Are you all well?'

Kirsty nodded. 'Yes, we are all fine thanks.' She paused. 'Who's the tutor?'

Callum felt his cheeks redden. 'You're not going to believe it but . . .' His voice trailed away when he realised Kirsty already knew.

'If you're about to tell me that Lizzie — I mean Beth — is here, I know. I've seen her, Callum, and I think you two actually need to have a proper catch-up. That's all I'm going to say.'

He frowned. 'Right, well, okay. Thanks for the advice. Hopefully see you soon.' He picked up his shopping and walked briskly to the car, wondering what Kirsty meant. A minute later he'd parked outside the newspaper office and saw Daisy waiting at the window. He gave her a wee wave and smiled. He was about to get out the car to thank Beth. But before he got the chance Daisy had jumped in.

'I was going to come in and say thanks,' he said.

'I'm not eight, you know,' she said.

'How was it?' He glanced at the window of the office, looking for Beth.

'Amazing,' she said. 'She has been such a help. Honestly, what an amazing person she is. A lifesaver. It's all starting to make sense.'

Callum was glad things were starting to make sense for Daisy. But his mind was now more jumbled than ever. What had Kirsty meant? And should he just ask Beth for a coffee sometime? Maybe getting everything out in the open would be a good thing.

'I'll be back in a minute.' He got out of the car before Daisy had a chance to protest. Callum strode into the office where Beth was packing up her bag.

Beth seemed surprised. 'Oh hi. Did Daisy forget something?'

'No, I just wanted to say thank you.' She was wearing a red blouse, her hair pulled back in a loose bun. It dawned on him that she would still look lovely wearing a bin bag.

'You are very welcome. She's brilliant. A real credit to you Callum.'

'Oh.' He had not expected her to say that. 'Thanks . . . Er, look, I wondered if you wanted to catch up properly sometime? It would be good to hear a bit more about Daisy and how she's doing. And, well, just catch up on other stuff.'

Beth nodded. 'Sure.' Her mouth twitched into an almost smile. 'Do you mean a date?'

He felt his cheeks redden. 'Um, sure.'

Beth smiled. 'Just give me a call and let me know when suits.'

CHAPTER THIRTY-EIGHT

Beth was rushed off her feet at work. Poor Jim had been floored with a nasty flu, and she'd insisted that he didn't even bother trying to work from home. 'Just rest and get better,' she'd told him on the phone. 'I will handle things here, please don't worry.'

'Thanks Beth,' he said gratefully. 'I'll be in touch when I'm out the other side.'

She was pleased that she could step in and hold the fort, and that she felt confident enough to do so. That was a feeling that had been unfamiliar to her for a long time. But she was starting to remember that she was more than capable — that she was good at her job. She was starting to make more connections with the locals and felt like she belonged.

Ever since Callum had walked into the office the other day, she had been keeping a close eye on her phone just in case he texted her to arrange their *date*. She knew it was none of her business, but she couldn't help feeling in awe of him for stepping in to raise his niece, and she was still curious as to what had happened to Callum's sister, Daisy's mum. She was due to see Daisy later on that day, to go over some English with her, and she was looking forward to it. Not just because of the Callum connection, but because she was genuinely very fond of the girl. She didn't know all the circumstances and what had happened to her mum — she would let Callum tell her that in his own time — but she knew it couldn't be easy for her. She didn't know how she would have coped without her mum during her teenage years, which were not the easiest.

'Hey Beth,' said Laura. 'Here's your post. Urgh it is horrible out there.' She grimaced as her eyes flicked around the office. 'Is Jim still off?'

'Yes, seems to have it bad.'

'That is so unlike him. I don't ever remember him being ill before or taking a day off sick. Mind you, it's a good day — or week — to be in bed.' She shivered. 'It's set to get worse. I think the ferries are going to be cancelled from about two o'clock.'

'I wonder if people ever get used to that.' Beth had been working on a campaign the newspaper had been running to try and improve the ferry service for the islanders. 'Coffee?' she asked, holding up a mug.

'Aye, please, thanks. I'll have a quick one to warm me up. And I think they're just resigned.' Laura shrugged. 'What do you do about it? It's part and parcel of living on an island. Though I don't remember it being as bad as this when I was younger. You could always get on and off the island, no matter what. But maybe that's me looking back with rose-tinted spectacles.'

Beth had walked into the kitchen to make their drinks and poked her head back out, laughing. 'Yup. I've got a pair of them as well. I just hope the weather gets better for Christmas.'

Beth placed the cup of coffee on the desk next to Laura. 'Here you are.'

'Well, cheers. Don't tell Jim, but you make nicer coffee than he does.'

'That's because I insisted that we get a cafetière for the office. I don't like instant stuff.' Beth smiled.

'Well what a difference. Now you know why I always turn him down when he offers me one.'

'Yes, he'll just use that big jar of instant that's been in the cupboard for God knows how long. He seems resistant to change. Aside from that, he's a breath of fresh air to work with.'

Laura nodded thoughtfully. 'He's a good guy. I just hope he bounces back soon.'

'Hopefully another few days and he'll be fine,' said Beth.

'And how are you getting on?'

'Great,' said Beth. 'I love it.'

'That's good. It's a big change, not everyone can hack it. Especially at this time of year when it's dark and bleak. But the fact you're loving it now is a good sign.'

Laura drained the rest of her coffee, then pulled up the zip on her jacket. 'Right, thanks for that Beth, but I'd better go. I want to get my rounds done so I can get home and hole up before the weather gets worse.'

'Nice to see you, take care. Hope you get home soon.' Beth looked out at the grey sludgy sea. 'I wouldn't like to be out on that.'

Beth took the empty cups and washed them in the sink. When she got back to her desk a message had pinged on her phone. It was from Daisy.

Really sorry Beth but I don't feel well. Can we put off our study session today please? XX

What a shame, thought Beth. Sounds like the flu is doing the rounds. She looked outside, shuddering when she saw the huge swells in the sea and the rain that was lashing against the window. She typed a reply.

Aw of course. What a shame Daisy. Take care and rest up and get in touch when you're feeling better. Stay cosy it's horrid out there. X

Beth glanced at the clock. She had a quick job to do at the RNLI station in Lamlash. Two of the crew were receiving long-service awards and she needed to get a couple of photos and some words from them. She sincerely hoped that they wouldn't get called out in this weather. The conditions looked horrific, and Laura had been right, all the ferries were cancelled until later the following day at the earliest. She quickly printed out some information she thought would be handy for Daisy, pulled on her coat and then ran upstairs to the flat, raiding her emergency chocolate stash. Then she made the journey round to Lamlash, her windscreen wipers barely clearing the rain as it battered down. There was a reason that the roads were empty. Everyone was staying indoors, which was what she should have done too. Just as she drove down the hill towards the village, her phone rang.

'Hey Beth, it's Grant from the RNLI.'

'I'm just on my way round Grant. Should be there in a few minutes.'

'Ah, sorry Beth. I was calling to ask if we can postpone. George can't get down, the road from his cottage is flooded. I'm sorry if you're already on the way. We were looking forward to meeting you in person.'

'Of course. Don't worry. I've another errand to do anyway. I'll call you and rearrange?'

'Ideal,' said Grant. 'Don't stay out too long though. It's only set to get worse.'

'I won't. Thanks Grant.'

'Cheers,' he said ending the call.

Beth shrugged. She was out anyway, so she may as well do what she had planned to. Then she could get back to the flat and hibernate.

CHAPTER THIRTY-NINE

Beth knocked on the large red door of the cottage, realising her knuckles were sore and frozen with the cold wind. As she admired the large Christmas wreath on the door, she felt herself shaking slightly. She wasn't sure if it was nerves or if she was getting a chill. The road through Lamlash had been fairly treacherous — she'd almost turned back. She could hear a dog bark, and then a few moments later Callum opened the door, a look of surprise on his face.

'Beth . . . what are you doing here? Is everything okay?' He looked beyond her, as though looking for someone else. 'I was going to head over sooner rather than later before the weather got any worse.'

Beth looked at him confused. 'I hope you don't mind, but I just wanted to drop of some bits and pieces for Daisy.' Now she wondered if this had been such a good idea. 'I was out in the area anyway and passing . . .'

He frowned, shaking his head. 'But I don't understand, Daisy should be with you at the office studying. Why are you here? And where is she?'

That caught her completely unaware — she hesitated, unsure what to say. She felt herself tremble when she saw the worry etched on his face. Much as she didn't want to land Daisy in trouble if she had just wanted to skive off their study session, she had to tell him the truth. What *was* Daisy up to? Where was she?

'She texted me a couple of hours ago to say she wasn't feeling well and she wouldn't make it to our session, asked if we could do it another time. I just assumed she had the flu that's been doing the rounds.'

'Look come on in,' he said. 'It's Baltic out there. I don't want you to freeze.' He ushered her into a hallway that was littered with shoes. 'Let me try and get to the bottom of this.'

She carefully removed her mud-splattered wellies at the door, then he led her through to the kitchen with a huge oak table and white painted walls. Beth patted the beautiful Labrador who slowly got out of her bed by the fire and greeted with her a wag of her tail.

'This is Ruby,' said Callum distractedly. He was looking at the clock and had his mobile clamped to his ear. 'It's just going to her answer machine.'

'If she was leaving school she would have left by now?'

He nodded. 'Yes, the bus would have dropped her off at the end of the road.'

'And she's been at school all day?'

'Yes, she went away this morning quite the thing, though she didn't eat much of her breakfast now that I think about it.' He ran his hand over his jaw. 'This isn't like her. The thought of her being out in that . . .' he gestured to the window '. . . it isn't good at all.' He exhaled loudly. 'What time did she text you?'

Beth looked at her phone and showed him the message. 'Just after one.'

'Think,' he said, more to himself than Beth. 'Where would she be?'

'Any friends you could try?' Beth watched as he found the contacts on his phone and pressed call. 'Damn,' he said angrily. 'There's no reception. Honestly, this bloody weather.'

Beth winced and pulling out her phone, saw she had a couple of bars. 'Here, let's try mine. Tell me the number.' She

190

quickly typed as he spoke, waited for it to connect, then shook her head. 'It's switched off. Who is it?'

'Her friend Zola.'

'Any others?'

He looked desperate as his eyes widened with worry. 'She's been a bit out of sorts lately. I should have made more effort to find out what's been up with her.'

'I'm sure there's a simple explanation,' said Beth as calmly as she could. 'She's a teenage girl. She can't be far away.'

'Unless she's run away? Left the island.' Callum sounded like he was beginning to panic.

'The ferries are now off and it's highly unlikely she would have done that. Unless she's done it before and went this morning?' She tried to rationalise what a teenage girl might do.

He shook his head vigorously. 'No, never.'

'And if she had missed school earlier then I assume they would need to let you know.'

He nodded.

'Okay. Where else might she be? Just take your time and think. Any neighbours?'

'Of course, Maisie, she lives in the wee house next door.' He tried his phone again. 'It's no use, I'll be quicker running and asking.' Within seconds he run out the front door, banging it shut behind him.

Beth stood anxiously in the kitchen as Ruby started to whimper. 'It's okay.' She patted the dog's head. 'He won't be long.' Beth watched out the window as the rain lashed against the glass. It was difficult to see anything or anyone.

A few minutes later he burst through the door, soaked to the skin. She could see the fear in his eyes as he desperately raked his hands through his hair. 'She wasn't there. Maisie hasn't seen her all day. Where is she? What if something's happened to her?'

Beth had never seen him so emotional. She longed to reach for him and tell him that everything would be okay. But she had a nagging sense of unease. Where on earth could Daisy be?

CHAPTER FORTY

Callum, soaked to the skin, had started pacing around the kitchen. 'What if someone's taken her?' he shrieked. 'Or if she's got lost or hurt herself and is out there?'

Beth winced. He looked so lost and deflated, but she couldn't blame him. Those were her usual lines of thought for a missing child. But this was different, surely? Even so, she wasn't quite sure what to say. She knew she had to calm Callum down and reassure him, but it was all so surreal. What she wanted to do was put a comforting arm around him, but she didn't think that would be appropriate.

'Okay,' she said slowly. 'Let's stay calm and think about her other friends. Who else would she usually hang out with aside from Zola? Are there any other numbers we could try?'

Callum scrolled through his mobile. Then he grabbed the phone handset on the kitchen counter. 'I don't believe it.' He slammed it down in frustration. 'The bloody landline is down too.'

Beth moved about the room, holding up her phone. She could have wept with relief when she saw that her mobile still had some reception if she stood in the far corner of the kitchen. 'What about Murray? Shall I try him?'

'Jim's son?' Callum's head suddenly snapped up. 'Of course. Why didn't I think of that?' His dark brows were drawn together.

'I'll try their landline first,' she said. He looked subdued as she dialled the number on her mobile and waited to see if the call would connect. She gave him the thumbs up. 'Hey Freya. It's Beth. Sorry to bother you. But . . . no, don't worry, I don't need to speak to Jim. It's just that I'm with Callum and he's trying to get hold of Daisy.' There was a pause and Beth put a hand on her heart. Callum moved closer to Beth. 'Oh that's great.' She felt the worry seep from her. 'I'm *so* glad she's okay.' She put her hand over the phone and looked at Callum. 'She's with them and she's safe.'

'Oh thank God.' He was visibly relieved. He put his hand on Beth's shoulder and squeezed it gratefully. Giving him a small smile, she turned her attention back to Freya who was still talking. 'Ah, I see, well, listen, shall I put Callum on? It sounds like there's been a bit of a misunderstanding. But as long as she is safe and okay that's the main thing. Tell Jim I hope he feels better soon and I'll be in touch. Here's Callum.'

Callum took his hand off her to take the phone, but he stayed standing close. 'Shall we put her on speakerphone?'

'Good thinking,' said Beth.

'Freya, what's happening?' he asked. 'We should both be able to hear you. I've put you on speakerphone.'

'Hi Callum. I was just saying to Beth that the kids came home at lunchtime and Daisy wasn't feeling well. I know she was trying to call you but couldn't get through. Did you get the text from the school saying they were closing early because of the weather?'

'No,' he said. 'But I've got no reception on my phone and the landline is down.'

'No wonder you were worried. I know I would have been frantic. She said she had let Beth know she wasn't feeling well and couldn't see her after school. She did say she had texted you and that she couldn't get through on the house phone.

But the poor soul's been fast asleep for the past couple of hours. I thought that was the best thing for her. I'm so sorry. I just assumed you knew.'

Beth watched as Callum's shoulders sagged with relief and exhaustion. She could only imagine how horrendous this had been for him, not knowing where Daisy was.

'I'm just glad she's okay and that she's safe. She was probably wondering why I didn't reply to her text, poor wee thing. I'll head over to get her now, Freya, and thank you. I can't tell you how glad I am that she's with you . . .' There was a catch in the back of his throat.

'You would do the same for me Callum if it was Murray,' said Freya. 'No need to thank me. You know how fond of her I am. But I don't think it's a good idea to go out in this. Please, will you wait until the weather is more settled? It's horrendous over here. The road out of Lamlash is flooded now. You won't get to us anyway. The last thing you want to do is get stuck . . . Beth I hope you're hearing me too.'

Callum pulled up the zip on his jacket and grabbed his beanie from the back of the chair.

'Yes, I'm still here Freya.'

'Beth, I don't think it's a good idea for anyone to be out. Please tell Callum. I know what he's like. He's probably got his jacket on already and is sitting in the car. Tell him that Daisy is safe with us. She's tucked up in the spare room and cosy.'

Beth was now struggling to hear everything that Freya was saying — her voice was breaking up. 'Okay. I hope you can hear me. But we will stay put. Thanks Freya. Take care.' She ended the call.

'I need to go,' he said to Beth.

'You can't,' she said, pleadingly. 'You heard her. Freya said the road is flooded and that Daisy is tucked up in bed. It would be crazy to go out there. In fact just stupid.'

Callum sighed in frustration. He pulled off his wet sweater and threw it onto the ground. Ruby, sensing that something was amiss, barked and jumped up on him, placing both paws on his chest. 'Down girl,' he said sharply. Immediately her tail went between her legs and she started to whimper.

'There,' said Beth, 'that's her also trying to tell you that she thinks you're a plonker for wanting to go out in the storm. She's telling you that she doesn't want you to leave. She's trying to protect you. Stop being so stubborn.'

He looked at her incredulously. 'Are you joking?'

'Not at all.' She realised that she had maybe said too much. Her comments clearly hadn't landed well from the way he was now glaring at her. 'Anyway, the main thing is that Daisy is okay.'

'Yes,' he said, his voice softening a bit. 'That is true.'

'Right,' she said, feeling a shift in the energy of the room. 'Now we know Daisy is okay, I would really like to get home. But I'm worried about the road. Is there another route?'

'And you've just accused me of being stubborn? You heard Freya. It's flooded. And going the long way round would be plain silly. I think you're just going to have to sit this one out with me.'

Beth felt her heart skip a beat — she felt lightheaded. Was being stuck here with Callum a good idea? Especially as all she could now focus on were his muscles, outlined very clearly through the long-sleeved wet top that clung to him.

'Are you warm enough?' He threw another log on the fire. 'Here, why don't you take your coat off and I'll lend you a dry jumper.' A sweatshirt lay over the back of one of the kitchen chairs and he threw it to her. She pulled it on and breathed the scent of him on it.

'I'll go and get changed.' He pointed at his wet clothes.

Beth had imagined them catching up over a drink or a coffee. Not holed up in his cottage in the middle of nowhere. It was a very lovely kitchen though, and she gazed at the lights on the Christmas tree in the corner of the room. She could smell the scent of the pine needles and felt incredibly relaxed. She smiled, a bit embarrassed, and felt her cheeks redden when he walked back into the kitchen wearing dry clothes and towelling his hair.

'We've got lots to catch up on,' he said.

'I guess so. This isn't quite how I imagined it though. I was imagining we might meet at the pub.'

'No time like the present.' His gaze was on her face. 'Anyway, it's not like we can go anywhere else, so we may as well make the most of this. Unless you fancy a game of Scrabble?'

Beth shrugged. 'Or Monopoly?' She'd suddenly remembered it was a game he'd always detested.

He chuckled. 'I still hate that game.'

Beth sighed.

'Shall I put the kettle on?' Callum asked. And right at that moment all the lights went out.

CHAPTER FORTY-ONE

'I don't believe this is happening,' said Callum in exasperation.

'Just as I was thinking that the day couldn't get any better,' said Beth. 'I'm assuming you're prepared for this though. I hope so.' She laughed nervously.

Callum struck a match and began to light the candles that were already sitting in holders. 'Daisy likes to light candles to create the right *ambience* when she's baking. We've got her to thank for being so organised and leaving these out for us. But no, it's not the first time we've had a power cut. And it won't be the last. It's fair to say we're prepared.' His eyes adjusted, and he could see Beth looking slightly worried. 'Don't panic, just give me a minute and I'll get the torches too. Are you warm enough Beth? You look like you're shivering.'

'I'm not going to lie. I am a bit cold.' Then she sneezed and pulled a tissue from her pocket.

Now he was worried that she was coming down with something. When she had arrived at the door, she'd been fairly sodden. 'Okay, aside from your jacket, is anything else wet?'

'My jeans are a bit damp,' she said hesitantly. 'And my socks.'

'Right, just take them off and I'll give you some dry stuff to wear. Give me a minute to fetch some things and stand by the fire. The boiler will have gone off with the power cut, but at least we have the wood burner.'

Callum strode through to his bedroom and found a pair of jogging bottoms and another fleece, along with a pair of thick woollen socks. 'Here you go Beth. Put these on and I'll nip over to see Maisie, let her know what's happening and check she's okay.'

'Thank you for this.' She sniffed.

'It's no bother. Just sorry you won't get that cuppa for the moment. I'll be back soon.' Callum closed the door behind him and went out to the hall, where he pulled on a dry anorak and his waterproof trousers. There were lots to choose from on the peg — he was used to going in and out in all weather. He realised Ruby hadn't followed. He couldn't blame her. He would rather be indoors too. His thoughts were still lingering on Beth. The dog was obviously quite taken with her, she hadn't left her side since she'd arrived. Calum pulled up his hood and tied the toggles as tightly as possible, then opened the front door and made a dash for it. He jogged lightly up the drive towards Maisie's small cottage, which was also in darkness aside from a small, warm orange glow in the front room.

He rapped the door and went straight in. 'Hey Maisie, checking you're okay and have enough to keep you warm.'

Maisie was sitting in her batwing chair by the fire, looking very content with her knitting. 'It's like you've got ants in your pants tonight dearie.' She looked up over the frame of her glasses.

He laughed. 'I wanted to let you know that the panic is over and Daisy is okay. She's over at her friend's house not feeling well and is staying there tonight.'

'That's a relief. I did think it was a bit unlike her not to tell you where she was. But I had a feeling she would be fine. She's not daft you know.'

'All just a case of crossed wires. Now, do you need anything with the power off?'

'Stop fretting about me,' she said sagely. 'It's just a wee bit of wind. It's not like we've not had any storms before.'

Callum looked at her in the dim light. 'Can you see properly though?'

'Away with you,' she said. 'I can knit with my eyes shut. I don't need bright lights. But enough about me. I think *you* should be focusing your attentions on that lady friend who you've left at the cottage.'

Callum felt his cheeks redden. 'Yes, it would seem that she's stuck with me. The road to Lamlash is shut.'

Maisie chuckled at him. 'You're like a knight in shining armour.'

'I don't know about that,' he muttered. 'I'm sure you're far more competent and able to cope in a storm than I am, Maisie.'

'True.' She smiled. 'The electricity will be back on before we know it. I'll probably head to my bed soon anyway. So don't be worrying about me. If I need you, I'll send you a sign. A smoke signal or something like that.' She chuckled again.

'Likewise. I'll do the same if I decide I need you to come to my rescue,' he said wryly.

'Enjoy your night,' she said. 'Perfect romantic conditions for it too with the log fire. Especially as she's stranded and the wind is blowing a hoolie. Even if she wanted to leave, she can't.'

'Oh for goodness' sake,' said Callum. 'It's not like that.'

'Of course not.'

'Bye Maisie.' He shook his head. She had a frustrating way of reading his mind.

Even though the cottage was only about fifty metres away, by the time he reached the front door he was weary and cold. He hoped Beth was cosy and dry now. He pulled off his wet things and shivered. Ruby had slinked through to greet him briefly, then disappeared again into the kitchen when she realised how cold it was in the hallway. When he walked through, he was glad to see that Beth had curled up on the sofa next to the fire. It was only when he leaned in closer that he realised she was fast asleep. He pulled a blanket over her and sat down at the opposite end of the couch, with Ruby in between.

He sat for a while watching her and, before long, he too became drowsy and also fell asleep.

CHAPTER FORTY-TWO

When Beth woke up, she opened her eyes and looked around. She could see pale grey walls and a painting of sunflowers on the wall opposite. She was lying in an unfamiliar bed in a room that she didn't recognise, completely disorientated. Yet she felt comfortable and warm. She knew she should get up, but she had no energy — her body was heavy and lethargic. The thought of even trying to throw off the fleecy blanket that covered her was too much of an effort. There was a gentle knock at the door and it opened, squeaking on its hinges. Callum tentatively walked in, followed closely by Ruby.

'Good afternoon.' He hovered beside her. 'How are you feeling?' His eyes were full of concern.

Beth was aware of Ruby resting her chin next to her on the bed. But when she tried to sit herself up, she found she couldn't. She collapsed back into the pillows.

'It's okay Beth,' he said. 'You don't need to rush to get up. You've obviously caught the bug that's doing the rounds.'

'But why am I here?' She felt so confused.

'Do you remember last night and the storm?'

She nodded as she thought back, the details starting to trickle back into her mind. It felt like days ago that she had driven to Callum's cottage to drop things off for Daisy.

'You looked quite pale last night and were shivering when I went off to check on Maisie. You sat down on the sofa and have been out for the count since then.'

She vaguely remembered him going to see if his neighbour was okay. 'But what time is it now?'

'It's after two . . .'

Beth was horrified. 'I really *do* need to get up.' She tried again to prop herself up. 'I *never* sleep in, and I have to get to work. Especially with Jim off too. We can't both be out of action. The storm is a big news story for the island. It needs to be covered.'

'It's okay.' Callum perched at the foot of the bed.

Beth couldn't help but feel reassured by his genuine warmth as he smiled kindly at her.

'The road is still shut, nobody can get in or out. It sounds like it will be like that for at least another day. Daisy is still with Freya and Jim. I managed to get reception earlier and rang them to check in. Jim is feeling much better and said under no circumstances are you to move or even try to get to work. He said people have already shared loads of pictures from last night and he's on it in terms of coverage so you've not to worry. His words.'

Beth managed a weak smile. 'And Daisy? How is she?'

'Daisy is feeling a bit better, I spoke to her too, and she said Freya is doing a great job of looking after her. She also said they've got Sky Movies which we don't have, so she's making the most of that. Let's just say she's not in a rush to come home. She seems to be okay being collected tomorrow.'

Beth's eyes widened. 'But I can't stay here. I need to get back to the flat.'

'Look, why don't I make you some tea and toast? You must be famished. Then you can see how you feel.'

Beth shrugged, trying to work out how on earth she could have been so out for the count that she had slept that long. 'But how did I get to bed? I don't understand. I've *never* slept right through like that before.'

Callum blushed. 'I carried you through. It's what I used to do with Daisy when she was young, if she fell asleep in front of the television. I did try to wake you but you were dead to the world.' He paused and looked at her curiously. 'Maybe you needed to rest, Beth. Sometimes the body tells us when we need to stop.'

'Well,' she mumbled, 'sometimes you just have to get on with things.' She was aware of the searching way Callum was looking at her, almost like he was waiting for her to share more information. Feeling exposed and vulnerable, she blushed.

'I'll go and make that tea for you.' He stood up to leave. Just then Ruby jumped onto the bed, curling up in the crook of Beth's knees. He laughed. 'Looks like you've got yourself your very own nurse there.'

Beth reached her hand out and patted the dog. 'I don't mind. She's very sweet.'

'I'll be back soon.' He rubbed his hand over his chin. 'Do you still take it with a splash of milk and half a teaspoon of sugar?'

As he smiled, Beth couldn't help but notice how much it lit up his face. Even in her fevered state she was still checking him out. *This is so surreal*, she said to herself. 'Gosh, I can't believe you remember that. But just the milk please. I gave the sugar up a while ago.'

A look flitted across his face and he gave her a slight nod. As she waited for him to return, Beth couldn't help thinking how much things had changed over the years, but also how much had remained the same. Most of all she felt comfortable with Callum. Which was just as well — she was in a completely dishevelled state. She hated to think what she looked like. But then she sighed and closed her eyes again, realising she was too tired to be all that bothered, and relieved that she had grown out of the need to impress a man.

CHAPTER FORTY-THREE

It was later on that night Beth started to feel a bit more like herself. After enjoying her cup of tea, which she'd told Callum was the best she'd ever tasted, and some thick toasted pan loaf with butter, she had a nap and woke feeling a bit more rested. She realised that her dad had sent several texts checking that she was okay. She replied quickly to let him know she was safe and that she would call him the following day. She decided to ignore the missed calls from Alessandro. Beth realised she wasn't quite ready to leave this safe and warm bubble that Callum had created. He had left her some clean pyjamas and a towel on the armchair next to the bed.

'Just use the bathroom whenever you're ready and give me a shout if you need anything.'

'Thanks,' she'd said. 'I really do appreciate this. Especially the spare jammies and the toothbrush.'

'We've always got extra toothbrushes in the house in case one of Daisy's friends stays over. I quickly learned it was good to have a supply. And the pyjamas are my mum's.' He rolled his eyes. 'She has a little drawer of stuff here so she can travel light when she comes to visit.'

After Beth had showered and changed, she felt tired again, but not enough to go back to bed. Instead she padded through to the kitchen, where she could hear Callum moving about.

'Hey there.' He gave her a lazy smile. 'Do you feel better now?'

'Loads,' she said. 'It's amazing what a warm shower can do.'

He nodded. 'I know. I'm just glad that the electricity is back on. Otherwise it would have been the full Wim Hof cold shower experience. And although it was atmospheric last night, I didn't fancy another night in candlelight.' He gestured to the sofa. 'Have a seat and I'll get you some more tea.'

Beth curled up on the sofa and Ruby moved closer to her. Beth looked at the display of Christmas cards on the mantelpiece, then watched Callum as he moved around the kitchen, preparing the tea. It was quite weird observing him now, as a man, compared to the boy she had fallen in love with. He was more confident and assured, yet an air of weariness seemed to follow him around. Tears sprang in her eyes as she thought about how kind he'd been to her the last couple of days. She knew his intentions were genuine and not loaded in any way with expectation. She couldn't help comparing him to Tim and the years she had wasted with him. As she had finally acknowledged to herself many times this past year, he had effectively destroyed what had been her life.

'There you go Beth. I've got some soup on too for when you feel like it.' He handed her a large earthenware mug. 'You've got to keep your strength up.'

She took a deep breath. 'Thanks Callum. I'm not sure that I will ever stop saying that to you.' She gave him an apologetic smile.

'Don't be silly. That's what friends are for.' He held her gaze for a moment, then looked away.

'I know . . . but I still think all of this is quite weird.'

He looked surprised. 'What do you mean?'

'Us being together like this after such a long time, and we don't really know what either of us have done with our lives. We are effectively two strangers.'

He looked a bit caught off guard and took a sharp breath in. 'I'm just sorry that we lost touch . . .' she added uncertainly.

Callum sat down next to her on the sofa. He paused before starting to speak. 'I always planned to come with you, Beth.' He stared at her and smiled sadly. 'To London.'

'You did?' She couldn't believe what she was hearing.

He nodded. 'My bags were packed and I was all set to go. Then the night before I was due to leave, my dad died very suddenly, and everything changed in an instant. My world was turned upside down.'

'But . . .' She was at a loss for words. *Oh Callum,* she thought, suddenly feeling overwhelmingly sad. 'I am so sorry. I really am. I don't know what to say.' A combination of emotions rippled through her. 'Why didn't you tell me?'

He took a sip from his mug and gazed at the fire. 'We were so young, Beth. That night, when my dad died, everything changed so fast. I didn't want to hold you back. I had responsibilities here. I just hoped you would think I'd changed my mind and that I didn't want to come with you. Most of all I just wanted you to get on with your life and do what you dreamed of. I made Kirsty promise not to tell you if you got in touch to ask what had happened. I didn't want you to change your plans for me.'

Beth sighed inwardly and wondered what she would have done if she had known. She had never bothered to get in touch with anyone. She had been so upset. She glanced at him. Would she have stayed if she had known the truth? 'Yes, I did think that you'd changed your mind.'

'And I'm really glad that you did think that and that you lived your life and made the most of London. I knew how important that was to you. I would have hated to hold you back.'

She felt a solitary tear slide down her cheek. Callum reached over and brushed it away.

'Here.' He handed her a tissue. 'Don't cry.' He looked at her for a moment. 'Life is very strange. You can't always plan things the way you want to. But at least you got to live your dream. Am I right?'

It was a question she didn't want to answer, so she just nodded vaguely. Her mind was full of images of what might have been, what could have been, if only she had known the truth about why Callum didn't meet her.

'After Dad died, I became the man of the house and had to help run the joinery. Of course I would much rather have been with you. But I had to push that all to the side. I had to do what was right for my family at the time.'

Beth reached for his hand and clasped it. 'Did you ever leave? Like later on?' It seemed sad to think of Callum never having the chance to do some of the things that he had dreamed of.

He smiled. 'Yes, when I got older, I went off travelling and did my own thing for a while. I'd always wanted to go to Malaysia to learn more about woodwork. That was incredible.' His face became animated as he remembered. 'And when Daisy was born, she gave Mum a new focus, so I felt I had a bit more freedom to explore and do my own thing for a while, especially as the business was doing well and I could trust someone else to run it for me. By then Isla lived in Manchester and I'd go down and visit too.' He looked completely bereft, his eyes tormented, as he sat in deep contemplation.

Beth eyed him for a moment. She could tell speaking about his sister wasn't at all easy, but she had to ask him. 'Callum,' she began gently. He stared at her blankly for a moment. 'What happened to her? What happened to Isla?'

CHAPTER FORTY-FOUR

Callum took a huge breath and exhaled through his mouth, puffing his cheeks out. He leaned forward, his elbows on his knees, his hands clasped in front of him. Beth's voice was full of kindness, and he knew he needed to tell her the truth, but it was always such a hard story to tell. It never got any easier.

'Isla died. She died when Daisy was just four . . .' He felt sick as he said the words out loud. He had buried this heartache away for years. Even though Daisy reminded him of his sister every day, he could somehow cope with that. What he found hard were the circumstances that led Daisy to be with him. Everyone who needed to know already knew, and there was no reason for it to be discussed. Until now.

'Oh Callum. I am sorry. That must have been awful,' Beth said in a whisper.

He felt a surge of sadness as he remembered how horrific it had been.

'Do you mind if I ask what happened?' said Beth.

There was a short silence and he shook his head. 'No, I don't mind at all. But I just find it hard to talk about, because . . .' He could feel Beth's eyes on him as his heart began to flutter.

'It's okay Callum. You don't need to tell me or say anything.'

'I find it hard to talk about. Because I completely blame myself for what happened.' He surprised himself with the force in his voice.

Beth's gaze didn't waver from his face and she gave him a small, encouraging nod.

'I spoke to Isla the night before she died. Not for very long. She was tired and she'd only just managed to get Daisy to sleep. She said she was about to go to bed as she was so tired. She'd had a headache all day, which had got worse, and she felt a bit dizzy. She insisted that a good night's sleep was all that she needed . . . the thing was Isla never made a fuss. She was very stoic and just got on with things. In the same way that she'd raised Daisy single-handedly.'

'Was Daisy's dad ever on the scene?'

He shook his head. 'No, Isla never told us who he was, and he was never named on the birth certificate. As far as she was concerned, she was the only parent that Daisy needed . . .' He had to choke back a sob as he thought about Daisy, the trauma she had gone through at such a young age. 'Isla went to bed and never woke up.'

Beth's face fell in shock.

Ruby slipped from the sofa and sat between Callum's feet. He tickled her ears as she pushed closer into him, as though sensing this was hard for him. 'She failed to mention that she'd fallen off her bike the previous day and banged her head. That explained the headache and the dizziness. But I blame myself. I could have done more . . . if only I had known, I could have helped her and saved her life.'

Beth looked taken aback. 'What do you mean Callum? Why would you blame yourself?'

'I'm her big brother. I should have looked after her, especially when she started talking about headaches that night and feeling dizzy. If I hadn't let her ring off in such a hurry I would have found out about the fall from her bike, and then

I would have told her to go and speak to her GP or get herself to A and E. Instead she went to bed that night and she never woke up. Turns out that she had a brain injury from her fall, the headaches and dizziness were both signs of head trauma.'

Beth's voice was kind. 'Do you think you saying that would have made the slightest bit of difference? I mean, it sounds like Isla was fairly determined and knew her own mind.'

Callum smiled as he thought about the number of stand-offs they'd had as kids. Isla was always so stubborn — she did not like being told what to do. A bit like Daisy. 'I know. I've been through this in my head millions of times over the years. There is nothing I can do to change what happened. It took me a while to stop blaming myself as much. But I think that's part of the grieving process. You replay everything in your head, you over analyse it until you drive yourself to the brink. At one point I felt as though I was on the verge of a break-down. Her loss consumed me, but eventually Mum reminded me that we had to focus on doing the best thing for Isla, and that meant looking after Daisy.'

Callum hadn't opened up like this to anyone in years. She'd moved closer to him and he could smell the vanilla scent of the shower gel that she must have used. Then she pressed her hand on his arm and he felt something good amidst the sadness. He sighed. 'I don't know what I would have done without Daisy to focus on. She saved my life.' Callum thought about how much easier it would have been if Daisy had gone to live with her gran in Crieff. However, that wasn't an option. His mum had reminded him how much he'd loved growing up on Arran, and that Isla would have liked it if Daisy had the same carefree childhood as them.

Beth took a deep breath. 'You have done an incredible and selfless thing for Daisy. Your sister would be proud of you Callum. She's a wonderful young woman.'

He frowned and shrugged. 'I've done my best. Not sure that she would agree, but she's the most important thing in

my life.' Ruby thumped her tail on the floor. 'You too Ruby.'
He looked at Beth, neither of them speaking for a moment.
He realised how tired he was, and Beth's pale face was now
white.

'Do you mind if we just sit here for a while?' he asked.

Beth moved closer to him and put her arm around his
shoulders. 'I don't mind at all.'

As they sat there together, it was as though the clock had
been paused. They were in their own little private cocoon,
sharing their stories of heartache and grief and loss.

CHAPTER FORTY-FIVE

Beth had hardly slept. She'd lain awake all night thinking about Callum, the huge amount of heartache and grief he had suffered over the years. It seemed so unfair that his family had been rocked by two huge tragedies. She couldn't even begin to imagine how difficult it was for him, losing his father, then his sister, then stepping in to raise Daisy. It made her admire him even more than she already did.

Her phone had been pinging with updates from Jim telling her that the road was now open which was earlier than expected. There was also *another* voicemail from Alessandro checking in. She had replied to let him know she was fine and was staying with a friend near Lamlash. He didn't need to know any more details. It was none of his business. Beth knew that she should really get dressed and make her way back to Brodick. She smiled, looking at the cosy room that had become a haven to her. When she went through to tell Callum that she would make a move, he looked a bit deflated.

'Yes, I heard it's open again. I told Daisy I would be over to get her later and she sounded *very* disappointed. Apparently, life with Freya and Jim is much more attractive than living with your middle-aged uncle. Mind you, I can't say I blame her,' he said with a forlorn smile.

'Yes, when you're a teenager the grass is always greener.' Beth nodded. 'Everywhere is always better than where you live. I was exactly the same, Callum. Don't take it personally. You're great with her. She'll be fine when you get her home and she's settled.'

'Let's hope you're right,' he said. 'Can I get you anything before you go?'

'You have done more than enough,' she said. 'You looked after me, you've made me more cups of tea than anyone ever has. And you make a good slice of toast too. The soup wasn't bad either.'

He laughed. 'Next time, I will try something a bit more adventurous. Maybe make you a proper meal.'

Neither of them spoke — the silence began to feel charged. Beth felt her heart start to race as she thought about his words, *the next time.* He wanted to see her again. She took a breath. 'I would like that.'

He didn't reply, but levelled his eyes on hers.

'Right,' she wasn't quite sure what to do, 'I'll head off. I hope Daisy is okay and . . . well, yes. Hopefully I will see you soon. That's if I haven't scared you off and you've had enough of me to last you a while.' She looked around for her jacket, desperately willing herself to stop talking.

'By the door, on the peg.' He pointed outside to the hallway.

Beth nodded, walking to the back door where she pulled on her wellies and coat. It felt like days ago that she'd removed them. 'It's certainly a fresh start after the storm. Look at that beautiful blue sky.' She peered out the door.

'Blue but still fresh,' he said.

'At least it's dry.' She opened the car door and put her bag in the passenger seat. Turning round she was surprised to see Callum right behind her. She was about to say something else, when he leaned down and kissed her very gently on her lips.

She felt a tingling sensation at his mouth against hers. After years of disconnect, it reminded her of what else could perhaps follow.

But then he stepped back and smiled briefly at her. 'Drive safely. And I will be in touch . . .'

'Will do.' She gave him a quizzical glance. She wondered if she should take the initiative and kiss him back. But she felt stuck and lost for words. What should she say? *Let's do this again sometime. About that date? Or do you fancy a coffee soon. Come to mine for dinner?* It all sounded so contrite.

Instead she managed to say, 'Give Daisy my love, tell her I hope she feels much better and I'll see her soon.' Then she jumped into the car and started the engine. As she drove away, she glanced in her rearview mirror and could see him watching her. She could still feel the sensation of his mouths on hers, and for a moment she considered going back. Until she realised he had turned and walked back into the cottage.

* * *

For the rest of the day Beth was in a bit of a daze. She spent the afternoon catching up with a bit of work from the comfort of the flat. She spoke briefly to Jim, who insisted that she wasn't to do anything. However, Beth had always found it really difficult to switch off from work, so she caught up with some emails in her inbox. Fortunately her journey home had been fine — much of the storm damage had been cleared up. There was no need to visit the shops as she had all the supplies she needed. When the rain started to fall again, she was glad she was in her own cosy space.

Feeling a bit lightheaded and not yet herself, she had dozed on the sofa only to be woken in the dark by the sound of the flat buzzer ringing. Her first thought was that it could be Callum. Jumping up, she stumbled over to the door to answer. 'Hello.'

'Beth, it's me,' said Alessandro.

Her stomach sank.

'I wanted to check you are okay?'

'I'm fine thanks.'

'Can I come up?'

She groaned silently. 'I'm not feeling great.'

There was a pause. 'Just for a minute.'

She really wasn't in the mood to make small talk with Alessandro, but she reminded herself that he was just being friendly, and it was kind of him to check in on her.

'Okay.' She pressed the button to let him in the building. Beth opened the flat door a few inches, and moments later he had bounded up the flight of stairs. He was dressed in black, with boots and an overcoat, and an overpowering layer of aftershave. The same one that Tim used to wear. The smell made her recoil.

'Beth, I have been so worried,' he said. 'You haven't been answering your phone. And then it started going straight to voicemail. I thought something had happened. Can I come in?' He didn't wait for an answer and pushed the door open for him to enter.

'I was sleeping.' She was still a bit bewildered as she followed him into the sitting room. Then she saw her phone sitting on the coffee table, picked it up and realised the battery was flat. 'That's why I wasn't picking up. It's out of charge.' She felt awkward in her joggers and sweatshirt, and wished she hadn't let him in. A voice in her head reminded her that she hadn't let him in. He had pushed his way in. His eyes lingered on her as he continued to stand there, a bit too close for comfort.

'Have you been okay?' he asked. 'You said you were staying with a friend?' He raised an eyebrow.

'I got stuck with the weather and didn't feel well so, yes, stayed with my friend.' *This is none of your business*, she wanted to yell.

'I could have come to collect you. You just needed to call me,' he said with a bit of an accusing tone. 'Can I get you anything? You do look a bit pale.'

She shook her head. 'No, thank you. I'm fine,' she snapped, 'I just need to rest and catch up with sleep.' Then she felt guilty when she saw the look of hurt in his eyes.

'But I can make you some tea or bring you some dinner?'

Beth couldn't at that moment think of anything worse. She just wanted him out of her space. 'It's late and I know you mean well,' she said firmly. 'But I really am fine. I don't need anything.'

'Oh Beth.' He took a step towards her, with a strange smile on his lips. She took a step back in surprise, and found herself backed into a corner of the sitting room. *What the hell was he doing?*

CHAPTER FORTY-SIX

Beth could have cried with relief when the entrance buzzer suddenly rang again. She pushed past Alessandro and ran into the hallway, snatching up the phone.

'Hello?' She tried to remain calm, even though her mind was in turmoil.

'Beth, it's me, Kirsty. I was passing and saw your light was on.'

'Come on up.' She willed Kirsty to hurry, opening the door for her. She sensed Alessandro lingering in the door of the sitting room, and she turned round to face him. 'I think it's time you left, Alessandro,' she said sharply. 'I'm not sure why you think I would be interested in you. I have made it *more* than clear that I don't like you in that way.'

'I'm just going,' he said smoothly. 'I obviously misread the situation.'

'No shit,' said Beth, her voice clipped. His expression was now blank. Beth felt herself wondering if she'd imagined what had just happened.

'Oh.' Kirsty had reached the top of the stairs and hovered by the doorway. 'Alessandro, what a surprise.' Her tone was curt, and Beth knew she was looking at her, wondering why he was there.

'He's just leaving.' Beth hoped Kirsty would pick up on the edge to her voice.

'Goodbye ladies. See you around.' He pulled his hat down over his ears. 'Call me anytime Beth,' he called over his shoulder.

She didn't reply, instead ushering Kirsty into the flat and closing the door, making sure it was locked behind her.

'Come on in,' she said.

Kirsty kicked off her shoes, then followed Beth through and sat on the sofa next to her. Kirsty's eyes were wide and she was clearly taken aback by his presence. 'What on earth was *he* doing here? Please tell me there's nothing going on with him?'

Beth shook her head and grimaced. The scent of his aftershave still lingered in the air. 'Absolutely not. He's tried to take me under his wing, so to speak, since I arrived, and clearly wants more. But I'm not interested, and he's clearly not used to getting knocked back. I had to make that very clear tonight. Just because I've been for a drink with him doesn't mean I'm into him, does it?'

'No.' Kirsty pursed her lips. 'He is, to put it politely, a complete and utter arse. He was the last person I expected to find here.'

'I didn't invite him round. He was just chancing it,' said Beth. 'I know him as he's friends with my boss and they play golf together.'

'Of course they do,' Kirsty said in disdain. 'I'm surprised Jim didn't warn you about him. He's a total womaniser, and very good at turning the charm on when suits. Just watch yourself Beth.' Kirsty sighed in exasperation, pulling off her hat. 'Gosh it's warm in here when you come in from the cold. Look, I was passing and saw the light on in your flat and wanted to check you were okay after the storm. I sent you a text earlier.'

'My phone's out of charge,' said Beth. She also thought about what Kirsty had just said. Her words about Alessandro had shocked her, but made sense, and she was now wondering whether Jim warned her about him? Maybe he had, but she hadn't really noticed or listened or thought she needed to worry. She could feel tears of frustration welling in her eyes.

'Are you okay?' asked Kirsty.

'Yes. I am. Just knackered, and glad you arrived when you did.' She couldn't tell Kirsty the real reason she wanted to cry.

Kirsty smiled kindly at her. 'If you ever want to talk Beth, please know you can trust me.'

'Thanks,' said Beth quickly, keen to move the conversation away from her. 'I appreciate it. Anyway, how are you? Was everything okay at your cottage with the storm?'

'Fortunately, yes, we were lucky. We had a couple of trees taken down in the autumn thanks to Tom and his forestry expertise. Otherwise it could have been disastrous. I'd always worried they were a bit too close to the cottage, and Tom advised us to have them chopped down. I'm feeling very grateful for having a son who is so into trees.' She laughed.

'Yes, that sounds like it could have been a nightmare,' agreed Beth. 'I'm so sorry I haven't even offered you a cup of tea or a drink.'

Kirsty waved her hand. 'No need at all. I'm fine thanks. Just glad you're okay. Did you end up being out and about reporting on the lovely weather?'

Beth gave a coy smile. 'Kind of. It has certainly been a strange few days, and I don't think you'll believe me when I tell you where I've been.'

'Try me,' said Kirsty.

'I've been stranded with Callum at his cottage for the past two days.'

Kirsty gasped. 'I was not expecting you to say that. I am shocked. Tell me *all* the details.'

Beth gave her a brief overview of what had happened, and how she now knew what had happened with his dad and sister. 'I know he made you promise not to tell me about his dad dying.'

Kirsty's face flushed. 'That was a very hard ask, Beth, and I'm sorry I didn't tell you. We were all so young back then, and I thought I should respect Callum's wishes. He was devastated. I often wonder if I did the right thing.'

'Kirsty, there is no need to apologise,' Beth said firmly. 'I completely understand. It's all in the past. There's no point looking back with regret now. Maybe if I'd been in touch with you, then you might have told me. But who knows what I would have done if I'd known.'

Kirsty smiled sadly. 'When I didn't hear from you, I took the easy option. It was just easier to let things slide rather than try and track you down when Callum had sworn me to secrecy. He's had quite the time of it over the years. Yet he's remained so positive and stoic for Daisy's sake. I hope you didn't mind me not telling you the whole truth about Isla and Daisy,' said Kirsty. 'But I felt really strongly that it wasn't for me to share or gossip about. I'm glad that Callum told you himself in his own time.'

Beth nodded, a glimmer of a smile on her lips as she thought about how she felt in his company. 'In a way I'm glad I was stuck there. It gave us time to *really* talk properly.'

'And what's next? Any plans to catch up again?' asked Kirsty.

'Nope, no plans yet.' She was a bit too breezy when it was all she'd thought about since leaving Callum earlier.

As though reading her thoughts, Kirsty let out a small sigh. 'Oh Beth. I can tell from the dreamy look on your face that you've got it bad. Maybe *you* need to take the initiative. Call him and ask him out.'

Beth gasped. 'I'm not sure I can do that. Honestly,' she wailed with frustration, 'I feel like I'm fifteen again. This romance stuff doesn't get any easier with age.'

Kirsty raised an eyebrow. 'Except you're not fifteen anymore and you are both free and single and clearly attracted to each other. What have you got to lose?'

Beth didn't reply.

'Come on Beth. I'm happy to place a bet on this. I'm very confident I know what his answer will be.'

CHAPTER FORTY-SEVEN

Callum had now been floored with the virus everyone else had. Yet it seemed to hit him harder than Daisy and Beth, and he'd been in bed for several days.

'That's because you're a man,' said Daisy witheringly. 'You always have to get man flu rather than just a wee virus. Murray's dad was exactly the same.'

Despite her teasing him, Callum was grateful that Daisy was around to help. All the strength seemed to have seeped from his body. He had barely been able to move these past couple of days. Daisy let Ruby out, even though she was loathe to leave her master's side. She had also taken over the feeding of the chickens, and went up and down to Maisie's cottage to check she had all she needed. Fortunately, Maisie had dodged being ill, which she told Daisy was down to her daily cold showers and glasses of red wine.

This morning was the third day that he'd been in bed. Daisy brought him through a cup of tea and a bowl of porridge. He began to protest that he wasn't hungry.

'You need to feed a cold.'

'Thank you, Daisy. And for looking after me.'

She looked at him thoughtfully as she sat at the bottom of his bed. 'It's the very least I can do. I guess I never really thought about it until recently. But you've done so much for me, and I probably haven't ever said thank you.'

Callum's mind was blank and he didn't know what to say. He was choked up as it was — he hoped she wouldn't see the tear that slipped down his cheek.

She frowned. 'Are you okay?'

He nodded. 'You don't need to thank me. I wouldn't have had it any other way.'

'But I know it was the *only* option.'

'What do you mean?' he asked.

'Someone asked me at school why I hadn't gone to live with my gran, as she's still alive, and it got me thinking . . .'

Callum's stomach was knotted as he waited for her to continue.

'I did ask Gran when I saw her at half-term, and she told me, very nicely of course, that living with her was never an option. She said she couldn't have done it as she's a pensioner. Though she's not really that old, is she? I mean, she's had her ears pierced three times and she likes Taylor Swift.'

Callum chuckled. His mum certainly was youthful for her age.

'I guess I've been thinking about it and it made me think that she hadn't wanted me. I know it's silly, but it's been on my mind for a while now.'

He nodded and thought carefully before he spoke. 'Gran was devastated after your mum died. She took it really badly. I mean we both did. But she's older and she'd already lost her husband suddenly. To then lose her daughter in the way she did was horrendous for her. She wouldn't have coped with a young child, and she knew that wasn't fair on you. She said she couldn't look after you because she loves you and she wanted what was best for you.'

Daisy nodded. 'I understand that now I've had a chance to think about it. I spoke to Freya about it too, when I was staying there, and that helped.'

'Good. I'm glad it makes sense to you, Daisy. Life is never straightforward. Gran loves you with all her heart, and she felt awful that she couldn't take you. But it would have been awful for you both. Anyway,' he grinned, 'would you have wanted to live in Crieff?'

Daisy shrugged her shoulders. 'True. If I had to choose the location it would always be here. I love Arran, and I love that it's where Mum grew up. It helps me feel closer to her being here.'

Callum nodded again. 'She would be so proud of you Daisy. As we all are.' He didn't speak for a moment. 'But I think your tea-making skills could be improved. You have put one of your weird vegan milks in my cup.'

She chuckled. 'I wondered if you'd notice. We're out of normal milk so it's actually quite handy we have my long-life stuff in the cupboard.'

Callum pulled a face as she stood up.

'By the way, I've let Beth know that you're in bed with man flu.' She gave a small smile. 'I thought she might like to know. Is there anything you want to tell me?'

There was silence as he drank the strange-tasting tea, buying himself some time. 'Um . . .'

She placed her hands on her hips and stared at him. 'Um? What does that mean?'

'We're just getting to know each other again.'

'Rubbish. I can tell you're totally keen. And if you want my advice—'

'I don't think I do.'

She gave him a *look*. 'Ask her out on a proper date. Or invite her for Christmas.'

Callum closed his eyes. 'That would be totally weird. Anyway, she's going to visit her dad at Christmas.'

'I was joking about the Christmas bit actually. I just wanted to check you were listening to me. Ask her out on a date.'

He didn't want to tell Daisy that he'd not been able to stop thinking about Beth since she'd been here. That memories of her dominated his thoughts. They had exchanged a

222

couple of brief texts when she'd left, but they were polite and perfunctory. He wasn't quite sure what to do next or what to say to her. Yawning, he pulled the covers up around him.

Then he remembered that she'd been in the pub with that guy from the hotel. 'I don't even know if she's single.'

Daisy raised her eyebrows. 'Seriously? She was here for two days and you didn't ask her if she was single?'

'No.'

'Leave that to me. I'll leave you to your dreams.' Daisy chuckled. 'No prizes for guessing who's the main guest.'

Callum didn't have the energy to challenge her. What she said was spot-on, but he didn't want to make a fool of himself and muck things up again. He had once seen a future with her, but fate had intervened, and that life just wasn't meant to be. Just then his phone buzzed. It was a text from Beth.

About that drink . . . let me know when you feel better and want to meet. Beth x

Could he allow himself to imagine and hope that the universe was giving them this second chance?

CHAPTER FORTY-EIGHT

After the drama of the storm, Beth was glad to settle back into a quiet and uncomplicated routine, although now life felt as though it had added sparkle to it. She and Jim were both back to full strength, as busy as ever back at work, especially as Christmas was ten days away. She realised how much she appreciated having work to focus on. It reminded her of working at the café, where her role gave her purpose and stability. She was grateful that she had a job here that she loved. How many people could say that? She and Kirsty were growing closer, and Freya had reached out and met her several times for coffee, and encouraged her to go to Pilates class with her. She had lots to be thankful for. And she was due to visit her dad very soon. She was genuinely looking forward to seeing him, and had promised to take him over some of the local cheese that he loved. It was strange to think it would be the first time she'd left Arran since she'd arrived at the start of November.

This morning, Jim had offered to go out and get them coffees from the bakery. When he'd arrived back with buns to go with the drinks, she turned her attention away from her screen and had a proper break. She'd been meaning to raise what had happened with Alessandro. However, the timing hadn't been right until now.

'Thanks.' She sighed as she bit into the icing that was drizzled over the top of the bun. 'This is just what I needed.'

'Freya would be horrified, so don't tell her. I'm supposed to be fasting till noon but, well, what's a secret between friends?' He grinned as he sunk his teeth into the pastry.

'Talking of which,' said Beth cautiously, 'I've been meaning to ask you about Alessandro.'

He looked at her. 'What about him?'

Beth took a sip of coffee. 'He thinks, because I went for a drink with him one night, that I'm fair game. He came round to the flat the other night and I had to spell it out to him.'

Jim shook his head. 'I'm sorry Beth. I had no idea he was like that. I only know him from playing golf. And now I feel awful.'

'It's not your fault. I'm sure he's a nice enough chap, but that's not the way to behave around women. You can't really get away with that anymore. I'd hate to think that was his modus operandi.'

Jim's mouth was set in a tight line. 'Leave it with me. He's chosen the wrong person to offend. I'm sorry.'

'Stop apologising for him. I'm just letting you know what happened, in case you wondered. I don't think he'll be popping in as much as he has been. I made it quite clear that I wasn't interested. There's no need for you to say anything else.'

Jim's mobile rang, which cut their conversation short. As Beth finished off her coffee and pastry her thoughts wandered to Callum. Again. They had finally made plans to meet later that night for a drink. She hadn't seen him since the storm and she couldn't wait for the evening. Although Daisy had been for a study session since then, Callum had still been recovering from his virus and hadn't left the car. Daisy had seemed much happier and more settled than she'd been previously and Beth was glad. She'd grown very fond of her and knew that, whatever happened with Callum, she wouldn't let that affect her relationship with Daisy. She really enjoyed their sessions together, and Daisy's curious questions kept her on her toes.

She smiled to herself, feeling a warm glow as she thought about the last time she'd seen Callum — leaving his house last week, the feel of his soft lips on hers. Then her phone buzzed, interrupting her daydream, to remind her of an appointment round in Lamlash. She had managed to reschedule the job at the RNLI station which was cancelled on the day of the storm. She pulled on her jacket and gathered her things together, then mouthed a goodbye to Jim who was still deep in conversation. He glanced up and gave her a small wave.

* * *

After being at the lifeboat station, Beth was making her way back to her car when she saw Edie walking past with her dog.

'Hi Edie,' she called.

Edie, who was wearing a bright orange jacket and red jeans, looked over. It took her a moment or two to realise it was Beth calling — she frowned as she tried to place her.

Beth walked closer. 'I'm Beth from the paper. We met in the café a couple of weeks ago, when Margaret visited?'

'Of course,' she said. 'I am sorry dear. My mind was elsewhere. It's lovely to see you. How are you getting on?'

Beth grinned at her. 'Great, thank you. Well, apart from the weather. The storm was awful, wasn't it? But otherwise I'm loving being here.'

Edie nodded. 'The storm was terrible, but fortunately we don't get many of them.' She looked at the sky. 'But, you know, I think there might be snow on the way.'

Beth bent down to pat the dog.

'Oh honestly,' said Edie. 'When I take Molly for a walk it's like being out with a celebrity. She gets so much attention.'

'She's a beauty. It's no wonder everyone wants to stop and talk.' Beth laughed as Molly wagged her tail.

'What brings you to Lamlash?'

'I've just been to the lifeboat station to do a story there.'

'Well, it's lovely to see you, and thanks for saying hello,' said Edie. 'I just nipped out to post a couple of letters and get

226

a pint of milk. I've got a joiner in just now and I was a bit mortified I couldn't offer him a cup of tea.'

Beth's interest was piqued at the mention of a joiner. She momentarily wondered if it might be Callum. She was about to ask when her phone started to ring. It was a number she didn't recognise.

'Sorry Edie, I'd better take this . . . Hello?' She felt bad cutting their conversation short, especially if it was just a cold caller.

'Beth love, it's Margaret.'

'Oh, hi Margaret. How are you? This is a surprise. Is everything okay?' It dawned on her that Margaret didn't sound her cheery self. There must be a reason she was calling. *Dad.* She felt her legs turn to jelly, and she was glad that Edie was still standing there next to her.

'It's your dad,' said Margaret, her voice wobbling.

CHAPTER FORTY-NINE

'What is it? What's happened?' Beth asked in a panic.

'He's been taken to hospital. They think he's had a heart attack.'

'Oh God, is he okay?' Beth's mind was spinning, her heart was racing. Could she be on the next ferry? How long would it take to get there? Her eyes were darting around as she tried to remember where she'd parked the car.

'He's okay love. But he's in hospital just now and they're keeping an eye on him. He said I wasn't to make a fuss and not to ring you. But I knew you would want to know. I would want my Isobel to know if it was me.'

'Thank you, Margaret. You did the right thing.' She took a breath to steady herself. 'I'll be over as soon as I can. I just need to check the ferries, then I'll get on the next one.' Beth was aware that Edie was still standing there, watching her in concern. She pulled a face.

'He may never talk to me again, but I know I would want my family with me if I was in hospital,' said Margaret. 'I mean, the staff are nice and all that but it's not exactly homely, with all the comings and goings. It's a wonder anyone gets any sleep with the racket they all make. Anyway, I knew you would want to know.'

She nodded. 'I'll be there as soon as I can Margaret. Which hospital is he in?'

'The Queen Elizabeth. I know you'll be in a tizz love so don't worry, you just focus on getting yourself over when you can, and I will text you the number of the ward he's in. I'll be here waiting until you get here.'

'Thank you.' Her voice was about to break. 'I really appreciate this.'

'Take care my love, I'll see you when you're here. And take your time. Your dad will want you here in one piece.'

'Thanks.'

She ended the call. Then she promptly burst into tears.

'Oh, Beth, my dear,' said Edie. She pulled out a tissue from her pocket and handed it to her.

'Sorry.' Beth dabbed her eyes. 'I've just had a bit of a shock.'

'What's happened?'

'It's my dad. He's had a heart attack. He's in hospital.'

Edie placed her hand on Beth's shoulder. 'I am so sorry.'

Beth took another shuddering sob and pointed in the direction of her car. 'I need to go and get the ferry.'

Edie glanced at her watch. 'Take a few breaths dear. There's no rush. You still have plenty of time to get the one just after four.'

Reassured, Beth pulled out her phone. 'Okay. Please let this work.' She quickly opened the ferry app, praying that technology wouldn't let her down, that there would be space for her car.

Edie watched her anxiously, clearly thinking the same thing. 'All sorted?' she asked hopefully when Beth looked up at her.

'Amazingly yes. Thanks Edie. Knowing the time of the next one really helped. I completely panicked there and didn't know where to start.'

'Okay,' said Edie firmly. 'You are booked on the ferry. What do you need to do now?'

Beth nodded, thankful that Edie was there and asking her about the practical details. Her head was spinning, she was too wound up to think about what she needed to do next. *Think*,

Beth. 'Er, I need to go back and grab some things from the flat. And let Jim know.'

'Now make sure you take it easy dear, and don't be speeding back to Brodick. You have plenty of time. The priority is to get to the terminal. Once you're parked and waiting, then you can call Jim. I know he'll want you to put your dad first. Okay?'

'Thank you, Edie. I'm so glad I bumped into you. I would probably be wailing on that bench,' she pointed to the seating area on the grass, 'not sure what to do or where to start.'

'That's okay dear. I just hope your dad is okay. First things first though, get your overnight bag, then take it from there.'

Beth nodded. Edie leaned in and gave her a quick hug.

Then she steeled herself and walked quickly to her car. As she drove back round to the flat, she tried to keep her mind distracted with the things she needed: her laptop, chargers, toothbrush, pyjamas and a few changes of clothes, in case she needed to stay for a few days. She bit her lip as she thought of her dad, vulnerable and lying in a hospital ward. He had always hated anything to do with hospitals, and she knew he'd be scared. The sooner she got to him, the better.

CHAPTER FIFTY

Callum was at Edie's house working on the shelves while Molly sat patiently, watching him.

'If Ruby could see you now,' he said, 'she would *not* be very happy.' He walked over to her and patted her silky ears. He'd really enjoyed this job, especially as Edie had told him to be as creative as he wanted with the design.

Edie appeared with a cup of tea. 'I must say, you're doing a wonderful job. Sorry for the delay. I can't believe I ran out of milk. I hope the wait was worth it.' She placed the mug next to him on the floor.

Callum noticed that Edie had already started to unpack some books onto the shelves he had completed. 'Aw, thanks Edie. I'm glad you like them. And thank you for the tea. Good timing.'

'I even got you some chocolate biscuits.' She offered him one from her vintage tea caddy, which now doubled as a biscuit tin.

'Thanks.' He reached for one, then pointed at the window. 'It looks a bit ominous out there, as though it might snow.'

'Yes, it feels very wintery. It was very quiet this afternoon. Everyone must be staying warm indoors. Mind you, I bumped into the new reporter from the paper.'

Callum was immediately interested. 'Oh . . . Beth.' He unwrapped a biscuit.

'That's right. I've met her before. Lovely girl. Anyway, she was in a bit of a tizz. She took a call from someone telling her that her dad had been rushed to hospital.'

'Oh no.' Callum was shocked, putting down his mug of tea. 'I know Beth. She'll be so worried. She's very close to her dad. It's just the two of them.' That night of the storm, Beth had told him how she was glad she lived nearer her dad, how she felt guilty that she hadn't seen much of him these past few years. 'Where is she now? I should call her.'

Edie raised an eyebrow and gave him a knowing look. Then he remembered what Fergus had once told him about Edie. She seemingly had a bit of a knack of noticing things, and was very intuitive. Perhaps she could tell from the expression on his face that he was genuinely concerned about Beth.

'It seems as though he's had a heart attack. She's going over on the next ferry to see him.'

Callum automatically glanced at his watch. The boat was leaving in half an hour. But he could hardly race round there to the terminal and offer to go with her. That would be weird, wouldn't it?

A glimmer of a smile passed across Edie's lips. 'I was thinking, if you wouldn't mind, if you could nip to the hardware shop in Brodick, I could do with a new torch.'

Callum looked at her in confusion.

'If you go now,' she explained patiently, 'hopefully you will get there before it closes. You might even have time to check in on Beth, if you're passing and she's in the queue. She's taking her car over. I'm sure she would appreciate seeing a friendly face.'

Callum realised what she was suggesting and abandoned his tea and biscuit.

'I'll get on with unpacking some of these boxes,' said Edie innocently. 'Take your time.'

'Okay.' Callum grabbed his keys and headed for the door. 'See you soon. Thanks Edie.' He drove as fast as the speed limit allowed. He should have made more of an effort to catch up with her after the storm. If only he hadn't been ill. Yes, they'd planned to meet tonight, but he needed to see her now and let her know that he cared for her and that she wasn't alone. Poor Beth.

Thanks to Daisy's intervention, he knew that she was definitely single. Not that it mattered one jot. Regardless of whether she was single or not, Callum realised that he *needed* to be in her life, one way or another.

'Don't worry,' Daisy had reassured him. 'I didn't make it obvious that I was fishing for information. I just talked about boys in general and how annoying they are. Well, apart from Murray. And you. Though I did say that you had your moments. Anyway, I said I was never getting married or having children. When I asked her if she ever married, she said no.'

His curiosity had been piqued.

'She said she agreed that guys could be more hassle than they were worth, and she recommended being single.'

Callum remembered that he had felt relieved and pleased when Daisy had told him. *Anyway*, he thought, giving himself a shake as he neared the parking bays at the ferry terminal, *there's no point in dwelling on that now*. He just wanted to check in on her and make sure she was okay. As a friend at the very least. He parked the car and jumped out, turning to the queuing cars and scanning to find hers. He was glad she drove a red car — it stood out amongst all the white and grey that was lined up and waiting to board the ferry. Striding over, he saw her sitting in the driver's seat, head dipped. Tapping on the window she looked up in surprise.

She opened the window. 'Callum, I was about to message you. What are you doing here?'

'Oh Beth, I heard about your dad.'

Her face was pale. 'How?'

'Edie.'

'Ah, that would make sense. She said she had a joiner doing some work at the house.' She paused. 'She was great.

Calmed me down when I got the call. If it wasn't for her, I would still be running around like a headless chicken, not sure what to do or where to start.' She sighed.

'I'm sorry Beth. Will you be okay?'

She smiled weakly at him. 'I'm sure I'll be fine. Thank you. It was a bit of a shock, but I'll feel better once I'm there and can actually see him.'

'If there's anything I can do?' He wanted to reach into the car and give her a hug. Anything to take away the look of worry and sadness in her eyes. 'Just let me know. Please.'

Beth unclipped her seatbelt. 'I'll get out. There's a few minutes till we start boarding.' She pointed at the waiting ferry.

Callum stepped aside to let her open the door.

'I just hope he's okay.' She stood next to him, stubbing her foot against the ground.

'He's in the best place.' He reached for her hand. 'Think positively.'

Tears were glistening in Beth's eyes and she took a shaky breath. 'I know. You're right. Thank you. And thanks for coming to check on me. I really appreciate it. I'm sorry that I won't make tonight.'

Just then, huge snowdrops started to fall from the sky. 'Edie was right. She thought it would snow,' said Beth.

She looked so vulnerable that Callum couldn't help but reach for her and gather her in his arms. He felt her soften against him for a moment or two. Then he could hear people starting to turn on their engines. 'I think you've got a good excuse,' he said softly. 'Looks like they're starting to load you on.' He reluctantly let her go.

Beth forced a weak smile. 'Thank you. I suppose I should get going.' She looked at him for a moment, her hair now sprinkled with snow.

In that moment, Callum decided to take a chance. He reached down and kissed her gently on the lips. He was relieved when she didn't move away. 'Keep in touch. Let me know when you're there safely. And drive carefully . . . I'm here for you Beth. I'll be waiting.'

Her cheeks were pink — she nodded. 'I'd better go.' She turned and opened the car door.

He watched as she drove onto the ferry. It wasn't until her car had disappeared from sight that he turned and walked away. He was glad he'd managed to catch her. It felt like the natural thing to do. And he'd meant what he'd said. He would be there waiting for her. No matter how long it took.

CHAPTER FIFTY-ONE

Beth somehow managed to make the journey to the hospital on autopilot, barely remembering much about the ferry crossing or the drive to Glasgow. Seeing Callum had given her a lift that had kept her going. The memory of him coming to see her at the terminal was like a precious little glimmer of joy — she'd tucked it away and would savour it later, once she knew her dad was okay.

When she arrived at the hospital, she texted Margaret to let her know she was on the way to the coronary care unit. Running to the lifts, she barely noticed the Christmas decorations in the huge entrance. She waited impatiently — typically, only one was working, and there was a huge queue of people waiting. So she took the stairs, panting after several flights. As she opened the door from the stairwell, she spotted Margaret lingering by the lift.

'Margaret,' she called.

'Oh Beth, I'm glad you're here.'

Beth ran towards her, hugging her tightly. 'How is he?'

'Resting just now, but you can go in and say hello.'

Beth stepped back and noticed the dark rings under Margaret's eyes. 'You look shattered.'

She stifled a yawn. 'Aye, it's been a long day. But I couldn't have let him go in the ambulance on his own. He was apologising to the paramedics and insisting there was nothing wrong with him, of course.'

Beth sighed and shook her head. 'That sounds like my dad. Thank you for looking after him and staying with him. But I'm here now. I think you should go and get some rest.'

'Yes, I will. Isobel is going to come and collect me.'

'Your car is downstairs in the carpark if you want to take it.'

Margaret shook her head and yawned again. 'Thanks love, but I'm knackered and not roadworthy especially with that snow out there. I would be a danger to others. Isobel can pick me up at the entrance and will have me home soon. Keep in touch, let me know how he gets on.'

'Of course, I will.' She reached over and hugged her again. 'And thank you.' Beth watched Margaret walk wearily down the corridor. Then she turned towards the door of her dad's room. A tear rolled down her face and she wiped it away, taking a few deep breaths. Walking into the room, she saw her dad asleep on the bed, looking small and vulnerable, wearing a hospital gown and attached to various monitors.

'Hi Dad,' she whispered, clutching his hand. 'It's just me. Beth.' He flickered his eyes open, and she saw the trace of a smile on his lips. She was sure she could feel him squeeze her hand back.

It was a long night. Beth dozed in the chair as the nurses came in and out, checking her dad's statistics. They offered her a cup of tea and a blanket, which she was grateful for, as the room had cooled since she'd arrived. She had messaged Jim and Callum to let them both know she was there okay.

Callum was the first to reply.

Thanks for letting me know Beth. Glad you made it. How is your dad?

Her fingers felt like thumbs as she tried to compose a response.

Thank you. I will get a better idea when I talk to the doctor. But I am with him just now. I will keep you posted. Thanks again Callum. I really appreciate your message.

Honestly, she said to herself. There was no need for her to type such a formal response. She deleted it and started again.

Thanks Callum. At hospital with him now. Will keep you posted. X

She always added an X to the end of her messages, and it felt natural to send one to him. When she let herself think about him, she felt quietly excited. She knew it was weird when she was sat next to her dad in hospital. But the thought of their brief encounter earlier was keeping her going.

Beth managed to nod off for a while during the night — she didn't move from her dad's side. The nurse had told her that he was very settled, and that the cardiologist would talk to her in the morning. She hoped they'd have positive news. Her neck had a crick, from the way she had been sitting in the chair. As the morning routine commenced, the ward was a hive of activity. The nurses continued with their rounds and the auxiliaries began dispensing breakfast. She was desperate to go to the loo, and so made a quick dash for it while she could, before the doctors started their rounds. When she saw her reflection in the mirror, a pale face looked back. She splashed some cold water on her cheeks and quickly brushed her teeth. That was one thing she'd remembered to shove in her handbag rather than her travel bag, which was in the boot of the car.

When she got back to her dad's room he was sitting up, looking a bit groggy. 'Hello dear.'

'Dad, you're awake!' She ran over to give him a hug. 'How are you feeling?'

He grimaced. 'A bit sore and very tired. But I'm okay. I'm still here.'

'Do you remember what happened?' Beth pulled her chair closer to him.

His brows knitted together as he thought about it. 'Not really. I just remember I'd eaten a bacon roll. And the next thing was I had a pain. It was a bit like indigestion. Margaret was brilliant. She called the ambulance.' He started to sound a bit breathless. And then coughed. 'Oh dear. I'm so sorry for all this fuss. I'm sure that I'll be fine.'

'Well, it sounds like she did the right thing. She might have even saved your life, Dad.'

'She's been a good friend to me,' he admitted. 'I'm very glad she's my neighbour.'

'Me too.' Beth squeezed his hand.

'Thanks for coming dear. I'm so glad that you're here.'

At that moment, Beth realised there was nowhere she would rather be.

CHAPTER FIFTY-TWO

After a few days in the hospital's cardiac ward, Barry was allowed to return home. Beth had stayed by his side throughout, going back to his flat every night before returning to the hospital, where she liaised with doctors and nurses to find out what the next steps would be. Fortunately there hadn't been too much damage to his heart muscle, and after assessing him they were satisfied that he was well enough to go home. They had both sighed in relief. Barry was desperate to get home, and Beth thought if she never saw inside a multi-storey car park again she would be very happy. She wouldn't miss the daily hunt for a parking space when all she wanted to do was abandon the car and see her dad. Despite the tinsel and glitzy decorations in the hospital it didn't feel at all like Christmas. The big day was just a week away, and Beth insisted that she would stay with him for as long as he needed her, until she was happy that he could be left alone. She knew that he was surrounded by good neighbours and friends, but she wanted to do this for her dad. To let him know that she was there for him and that he wasn't alone. Someone had spoken to him about cardiac rehabilitation, letting him know about specialist exercise classes and walking groups he could join in his area.

He seemed genuinely keen to do so — Beth was relieved. She'd been so worried about him, and whether or not he'd have lost his confidence after the heart attack. Several of the pensioners in the complex had popped get-well cards through his door, and Beth and Margaret were policing the number of visitors, claiming they didn't want to tire him out.

'I'm fine. Stop fussing,' said Barry that afternoon. Margaret had just arrived with another pot of scotch broth. 'There's only so much soup a man can take.'

'Aye, well, you can just stop your moaning Barry. Beth will agree with me that it's lots of fibre and vegetables you need right now for your heart. The days of bacon rolls are over. You need to look after that ticker of yours.' She'd ladled up a bowl of soup for him. He'd silently tucked into it.

Beth chuckled. Despite his protests she thought her dad was actually quite enjoying the attention. Especially from Margaret. Barry had been home for a few days now and Beth was starting to feel like a bit of a spare part. Margaret seemed to have everything under control. She had also insisted that Barry get out for a short walk every day. 'Some fresh air will do you the world of good. And that's the snow melted now so you can't use that as an excuse either. Now come on. Let's get going.'

Beth was amused that Barry didn't try and object. Whereas when she'd suggested it, he had been less than keen. However, Margaret, with her steely glare, really wasn't the sort of woman to take no for an answer.

As she waited for Barry to pull on his shoes and coat, Margaret had taken Beth aside. 'Look love, if you want to head back to Arran for a few days then please do that. I think your dad will be okay, and I promise I'll call you if anything changes or he doesn't do as he's told.' She smiled. 'Aside from anything else, I'm sure you want to get back over to see that fella of yours.'

Beth felt her cheeks flush. Callum had been texting her every day, checking in with her about her dad, but also asking how she was. It would be a lie to say she wasn't looking

241

forward to seeing him. But she was torn — she didn't want to leave her dad until she knew he felt less vulnerable. Though now, as she watched him waiting patiently by the door, he looked the picture of health. It was hard to believe he was the same man who lay in a hospital bed a few days ago.

'Your dad would want you to get on with things,' Margaret whispered. 'And you have a life over there. And a possible love.' She winked.

Beth shook her head. She was used to Margaret's ways now — she was more like a mischievous teenager than a woman in her seventies. There was nothing *elderly* about her. In fact, Beth felt like the adult in the house at times. Fortunately, Jim had been brilliant about her having to abandon the office and be at the hospital. It was a far cry from her early reporting days when you would be sacked if you took a sick day — HR wasn't a big deal back then — as your job always came before your family. No matter what. She now realised why so many marriages had failed in the world of journalism. She'd still managed to do some bits and pieces remotely, but she was keen to get back to her life on Arran, even for a night or two before Christmas. What Margaret said also rang true. She was desperate to see Callum in person. Especially as he'd been a tower of strength to her this past week.

'Okay,' she said slowly. 'Let's see how he is in a couple of days and take it from there.'

'Okay love.' Margaret paused longer on the "O" and sang the rest of the word out. 'You can still be back for Christmas. I checked the weather, it looks like it's going to be fair, so you don't need to worry about the ferries being cancelled either. This is one year that I hope we *don't* have a white Christmas.'

When she took her dad through his cup of tea the following morning, he announced that he wanted to try and get on with things himself. 'The longer you're here, the less I feel able to get on my own two feet.'

He added quickly, 'I have loved you being here Beth. But I'm worried I'll get too dependent on you and become one of these old guys who can't do anything for himself, because he gets so used to everyone else doing it for him . . .' He shrugged. 'I mean, I would love to have everyone else doing stuff for me all the time. But then it's a slippery slope, and I won't want you to end up one of those women who's seventy and who's been stuck living at home with her dad and no life of her own.'

The thought made her shudder. Her dad laughed when he saw the expression on her face.

'See,' he said. 'You'd become the feature of a magazine article. Like those ones that Margaret reads.'

Beth didn't know whether to be pleased or insulted. She'd seen the variety of magazines on Margaret's coffee table, which ranged from *Hello* to *Woman and Home* to *Take a Break*. She had everything covered.

'Okay Dad, let me have a think about what to do and I'll chat with Margaret. I might pop back for a couple of nights, but then I'll be back for Christmas, as planned.' She patted his hand, left him to drink his tea and went back to her room, checking the ferry times and making a plan to return to the island.

CHAPTER FIFTY-THREE

The next day, knowing her dad wholeheartedly supported her decision to go back, Beth caught the early ferry back to Brodick. She stood on the deck and breathed in the salty air, feeling so much more relaxed than she did on this journey only a few months ago. The thought of seeing Callum again, even if it was just briefly, filled her with resolve. She felt as though she was going home.

An hour later, having dumped her bag at the flat, she went for a walk along the promenade by the sea. There was a soft breeze — and she enjoyed the feel of it on her face. It felt as though a lot had happened in the space of a few days. She smiled as she noticed a wee boy walking past on the opposite side of the road wearing a Santa hat. It was Saturday, and she was relieved that she didn't have to go into the office straightaway. They would be closing soon for the Christmas break, and Jim had insisted that he would be on hand to cover anything urgent.

Most of all she was desperate to see Callum. She'd let him know that she would be heading back this morning, though hadn't specified which ferry she'd be catching. She didn't want him to feel any pressure to be there to meet her. Instead she'd texted him from the flat to let him know that she'd arrived.

Kirsty had also kept in touch, kindly asking after her dad, and making sure she was okay too. Beth was looking forward to catching up with her soon. She had missed work, and was grateful Jim had been so understanding. Beth thought about her routine of going into the office and seeing the kids at school — she realised how important that part of her week had become to her. For the first time she was actually looking forward to the New Year and her new routine. As long as her dad was okay, then she would be too.

It was still quiet and as she walked past the bakery. She decided to get a takeaway cup of tea to enjoy in the winter sunshine. She settled herself on a bench overlooking the sea and pulled her hat over ears. Aside from a few dog walkers, it was peaceful. She enjoyed listening to the sound of the lapping waves. Putting her face up to the sunshine, enjoying the feel of gentle warmth on her face, she felt contented and calm. She was grateful to have a bit of space to reflect on all that had happened since she'd taken that call from Margaret, telling her about her dad. She knew the next day would give her a chance to recharge her batteries before she went back to the mainland on Christmas Eve.

A few minutes later she happened to look up and saw a familiar figure coming out of the bakery. It was Alessandro. It was too late for her to pretend that she hadn't seen him. He was making his way straight towards her. She sighed. He really was the last person she wanted to see.

'Good morning,' he said. 'How are you?'

She frowned. 'Fine, thanks.'

He didn't sit down, instead lingered next to her. 'I thought I would come over and say goodbye. Just in case I don't see you again.' His voice was strained.

Beth was surprised. 'Where are you off to?'

'I'm leaving the hotel after Christmas.' He shrugged. 'I have been offered a new job in Edinburgh. It's time for a change.'

Beth almost felt sorry for him. He seemed to have lost his swagger and bravado. Then she remembered how out of line he'd been that night in her flat. 'I hope it goes well. Good luck.' She tried to hide her discomfort and longing for him to leave.

'And to you. I hope this new beginning has been everything that you wanted.'

Beth was distracted by the person walking along the path towards her. She grinned when she realised who it was, jumping up from the bench. 'Thanks Alessandro. Good luck, and I hope it's a fresh start for you too.' She gave him a tight smile, then strode away from him.

'Hi,' she said. His eyes lit up when he saw her.

'You're really here,' said Callum in delight. 'I'm so pleased to see you.' He reached down to hug her. His hands lingered on her shoulders, then he looked over and frowned when he saw Alessandro. He looked questioningly at her.

Beth shook her head and rolled her eyes. 'He's leaving to go to a new job in Edinburgh. He just came over to say goodbye.' She couldn't take her eyes off Callum.

'Ah, I see.' He looked delighted to hear that Alessandro was going away. 'It's good to see you.' He focused his eyes on her.

Excitement fizzed in her stomach as she leaned towards him. 'You too.'

'Listen,' he smiled cheekily, 'if you're not doing anything then I know this great wee place that does coffee. Can I take you there?'

'Do you mean like on a date?' asked Beth coyly.

He grinned. 'That's exactly what I mean.'

At that moment Beth would have followed him anywhere. 'Sounds great.'

'Shall we?' Chewing his bottom lip, he held out his hand.

Beth slipped her hand easily through his — he gripped it. She liked the feel of his skin against hers. Holding hands felt like the most natural thing in the world. It was like coming home. She looked up at him and caught his gaze. Dipping his head towards her, he grazed her lips with his — lightly, then more firmly. She could feel the delicious anticipation of what else was to come.

'Welcome home,' he said.

CHAPTER FIFTY-FOUR

It felt amazing to be sitting next to Callum, to be with him in person after almost a week of phone calls and messages that had grown in intensity. Something between them had shifted, and she felt their connection more strongly than ever. His foot brushed against hers as, under the table, he tapped it in time to Mariah Carey's *All I Want for Christmas is You*, which was playing in the background.

'Like this song, do you?' She smiled.

He grinned lazily. 'I was just thinking how apt the lyrics are.'

That made Beth smile. Normally she hated Christmas songs that played for weeks on end, it made her want to scream. But somehow this year she didn't mind. There was something quite magical about them.

'How long do I have you for?' He reached over to clasp her hands.

She blushed. 'Well, I'm booked to go back on the first ferry on Christmas Eve, and I don't have any other plans. So . . .'

He raised an eyebrow. 'We'd better make the most of our time then.'

'When does your mum arrive?'

'Christmas Eve. And I am *very* organised. In fact I think I've done it all. The food shopping and the present wrapping. Daisy is at Zola's today, and tonight actually. A sleepover.' He blushed. 'She did want to come and see you, but then decided she would let me have some time with you. She even insisted on taking Ruby with her. Apparently the girls are taking her for a long walk, which is a first.'

Beth felt a flutter of excitement at the thought of having an uninterrupted bubble of time with Callum where they could just be together. They didn't need to think about hospital visits or school runs or anyone else. Just them. 'I would like to see her before I go, if there's time.'

'And you can tomorrow. But I'm going to insist that I have you to myself for as long as you'll let me today.' He finished his coffee and set down his mug. 'What do you fancy doing now?'

She couldn't stop herself from grinning. 'I can think of a few things.' She stood up and pulled on her jacket, smiling playfully at him. 'Shall we?'

He caught her hand and pulled her to him, kissing her firmly on the lips. 'Oh Beth, I'm so glad you're here.'

'Me too. I can hardly believe it.' Her lips were tingling from his kiss. She knew that he was waiting for her to invite him back to her flat. But she was determined to make their time together last. That meant drawing out the anticipation of what would happen next.

They opened the door and stood outside in the fresh breeze. 'What now? What do you fancy doing first?' He rubbed his hands together. 'It's chilly, isn't it?'

She chuckled as she looked at the longing in his eyes. There was nothing more she was looking forward to than spending the rest of the day curled up with him in the warmth of her flat.

'I have a feeling that I know what *you* want to do Callum Thompson.'

He held up his hands and laughed. 'I am at your beck and call and will do whatever you want me to.'

He brushed his hand against her waist, and it took all of her willpower not to succumb to the way he was looking at her.

'Okay then. This way.' She pointed at the row of shops along the road. 'Shopping. I need to do some Christmas shopping. And then I'll show you my flat.'

He groaned and kissed her again. Then she grabbed his hand and pulled him towards the shops.

* * *

The following day Beth had to reluctantly drag herself away from Callum's side. They'd had an intense twenty-four hours making up for lost time, and she couldn't remember when she last felt so light and free and happy. He really was the best Christmas gift she could ever have dreamed of.

They had collected Daisy and Ruby from Zola's at lunchtime, then spent the afternoon walking on the beach. There had even been another flurry of snow which seemed extra special so close to Christmas. There was just enough to leave a white and sparkling dusting on the sand. Beth looked up at the hills which were blanketed in snow from the heavier fall last week. It all felt quite magical. Then they had gone back to the cottage where Callum had lit the fire and turned on the Christmas lights. He insisted on cooking dinner for her before she left, and she'd watched him as he put the finishing touches on the table. It was scattered with tea lights, and each setting had a cracker.

Daisy sat down at the table. 'It really feels like Christmas, doesn't it? Did you see the snow earlier? Do you think we'll have a white Christmas?'

It was lovely to hear her so excited about Christmas and Beth smiled fondly at her. 'Maybe . . .'

'I'm so excited that Gran is coming tomorrow. It's just a shame that you won't be here too Beth.'

Beth nodded. 'I know. But hopefully I'll be back before too long, and I can meet her another time.'

Callum checked his watch. 'It's just about ready.'

'It smells amazing,' said Beth.

'Well, it's not quite standard festive food, but at least we have a fancy table and everything else is Christmassy.'

'What are we having?' asked Beth.

Callum walked over from the stove and set a huge pot down on the table. 'Vegan chilli.'

'Oh.' Daisy's face flushed.

Beth glanced over and caught the girl's eye. 'Are you okay?'

'Um . . . Uncle Callum . . .' Daisy began.

'Yes?' Callum furrowed his brow as he started spooning rice into bowls.

'This is lovely. Thank you. But the thing is . . . are we having turkey at Christmas?'

He looked up at her. 'Well Gran and I will be, but I have a special nut roast thing for you.'

'Oh . . . Do you think that . . .'

Beth understood what was going on in Daisy's mind. She just hoped Callum did too.

He winked at Beth. 'Yes, of course I think you can have turkey, Daisy. I'm just amazed that it's taken you this long to ask.'

Daisy smiled in relief and picked up her glass of water, clinking it against Beth's. 'Phew. Just as well. This vegan business is tough.'

Callum sat down and smiled across the table at Daisy, then Beth. In that moment, it felt like a moment to treasure. She felt as though she belonged. They felt like a family.

'I'd like to make a toast.' Callum picked up his glass. 'I want to wish you both a very happy Christmas. I feel very lucky right now. Like all my Christmases have come at once.'

Beth's cheeks flushed and she could hear Daisy giggling. 'Cheers.' Beth lifted her glass.

'Here's to a Christmas to remember and happy times ahead,' said Callum.

Ruby barked, seemingly in agreement, and wagged her tail.

Beth could feel tears gathering in her eyes as she thought about how much life had changed for her in the past two months. It was okay for her to move forward with her life, to be happy and to look ahead with hope. She felt as though all her wishes had finally come true. 'It's certainly not a Christmas I'll ever forget,' said Beth happily. 'Here's to a Christmas to remember on Arran and I hope all your wishes come true. Happy Christmas everyone.'

EPILOGUE

Four months later

It was a mild spring evening and a small group had gathered in the Wee Trove. Beth took a deep breath as she clapped her hands together, looking at the smiling faces in front of her. Everybody there was connected in some way, and they were all here tonight for the same reason. Jim and Freya were here, with Murray and Rory. Daisy was standing beside her gran and Maisie, their neighbour. And Cano from Cèic, as well as Grant and Fergus from the outdoor centre had come along to offer their support, along with their partners, Thea and Amelia. Kirsty and Steve had also come along for the night, as well as Edie. The door opened, and there was a gentle ring from the bell above, and she saw Laura, the postwoman, slip in with an apologetic smile on her face. In fact, almost everyone that Beth knew on the island had come along here tonight, which was a lovely feeling. She glanced at her dad, who was sat in a chair in the corner, smiling at her. Margaret stood behind him, a protective hand resting on his shoulder.

She cleared her throat. 'Hi everyone. I just want to thank you all for coming tonight to celebrate the launch of Callum's new venture, Isla & Co. As you all know, he is a very talented man for more reasons than one.' There was a smattering of laughter as she raised an eyebrow, glancing over at Callum, who stood against the wall watching her. 'You will all be thrilled to know that he has taken up his woodwork again, and thank you Thea for being one of his official suppliers. And letting us hold this party here.'

Thea beamed at her, and Beth suppressed a chuckle as she saw Daisy give her a knowing smile. Callum was so unassuming about his talent that it had taken a huge effort to persuade him to have this celebratory launch event. He didn't see it as a big deal. However, unbeknown to him, Beth had an ulterior motive. She had a special announcement to make and wanted to gather their friends close, so she could share the good news with them all. Daisy had been instrumental in making sure tonight happened.

'Callum, would you like to say a few words?' she asked.

Callum pulled a face and came to stand beside her. 'Not really, but I will.' He laughed. 'I would just like to thank you all for coming along tonight. I appreciate all you've done for me and Daisy over the years and . . . I just wanted to say how lucky I feel to be doing what I love.'

'Hear, hear!' called Edie.

Beth watched as his cheeks flushed with embarrassment. Callum had been wondering for some time about holding some basic woodwork and joinery workshops at the community centre. With Beth's encouragement he decided to take the plunge, and had been amazed by the response. The school had approached him about holding some basic DIY sessions for the pupils, and he had told Beth in delight how much he loved teaching. The joinery was still ticking over, but diversifying had stimulated his mind and made him love his job again. Especially when he could lose himself in his combined love of creativity and wood.

'I think that's all I have to say.' He looked over at Beth.

'Well, we're not quite finished yet . . . I have one last thing to add.'

She could see Callum looking at her questioningly.

'I am so pleased to tell you that your work,' she pointed to the display of wooden bowls and cheeseboards, 'has been shortlisted in the National Creative Wood Awards.'

He looked completely astonished.

Beth shrugged apologetically. 'Jim and I decided to enter you.'

There were lots of cheers and applause. 'Congratulations Callum.' She reached over to kiss him. 'And watch this space.'

'We'll need a photo and a few words for the paper,' shouted Jim. 'It's our exclusive after all.'

Callum laughed.

'Please do join us now for a wee toast.' Beth reached for a glass of fizz and passed one to Callum. Fortunately, Thea had enlisted the help of some of her shop assistants, who had passed glasses of bubbly and juice to the rest of the guests.

'To Callum.' She raised a glass.

'Go Callum,' called Fergus.

She watched as he wiped a tear away. 'Thanks. I'm lost for words.'

'That would be a first,' muttered Grant with a laugh.

'Cheers.' Beth clinked her glass against Callum's — he looked back at her with an intensity that threatened to overwhelm. As everyone started to mingle and chat, he bent down and whispered in her ear. 'I can't believe you did this for me. I think I love you, Beth Ferguson.'

Beth's heart swooped with joy. She *knew* she loved him. In fact, she realised that she always had. Circumstances might have kept them apart all these years, but it was serendipity that had brought them back together again. They were meant to be together. Beth was so glad that she'd taken a chance and stepped into this different life and new beginning on Arran. This was where she belonged.

THE END

ACKNOWLEDGEMENTS

Writing and publishing a book is a team effort and I am so grateful to everyone who has helped to get this book out there in the world. I have lots of people to thank! As always, I would like to thank the Choc Lit and Joffe Books team for their wonderful support and encouragement. I'd like to say a particularly big thanks to Becky Slorach for her input and invaluable advice — Becky I have absolutely loved working with you! And also a huge thanks to Emma Grundy Haigh. Thanks also to Jasper Joffe, Abbie Dodson-Shanks, Tia Davis and also to Faith Marsland and proofreader Becky Wyde.

Thank you to the very talented book cover designer — Jarmila Takač — for another stunning cover!

I must also say a huge thanks to the lovely people of Arran who always make me so welcome every time I visit. Although many of the places that feature in this book are the product of my creative imagination, there are loads of wonderful coffee shops, bars and restaurants worth a visit if you do go to the island. It will always hold such a special place in my heart, and I'm delighted and grateful that these books have resonated so much with readers.

My friend, Becks Armstrong, deserves a special mention as she was an absolute legend when it came to listening to me talk about this book and offered me some brilliant insights which I will always appreciate. Thanks, Becks, for being you. Thanks also to my wonderful friends who have been really supportive in what has been a particularly tough year.

Christmas can be a really difficult time for lots of people and I hope this book might offer a wee bit escapism if the festive period is a tricky part of the year for you.

Sadly, my dad became unwell and passed away over the festive period, and I was very grateful that I had started to write this book and could absorb myself in it as I tried to navigate my way through grief. I am a great believer in using creativity as a tool to support mental health and wellbeing and I was so glad I could escape to Arran in the pages of my notebook. Writing really helped me get through those early few weeks and months.

I would like to thank the wonderful staff at the Queen Elizabeth University Hospital in Glasgow who cared so well for my dad and subsequently have looked after other loved ones this year. My family and I will never forget their kindness.

A special thanks to Dougie, Claudia and Grace for your love and support as always. And to Mum, who has always shown incredible strength, dignity and grace, but even more so this past year.

THANK YOU

I would like to thank you, the reader, for choosing to read *A Christmas Wish on Arran*. I hope you enjoyed the story of Beth and Callum as much as I loved writing it.

The island of Arran has a really special place in my heart, and I hope I have done it justice and inspired you to visit!

If you enjoyed *A Christmas Wish on Arran*, then please do leave a review on the website where you bought the book. Every review really does help a new author like me.

You can find me on Twitter, Facebook and Instagram (details on the 'About the Author' page next).

Please do get in touch for all the latest news. I look forward to chatting with you.

Huge thanks again, Ellie x

ABOUT THE AUTHOR

Ellie Henderson is the author of the Scottish Romance series, which includes her debut romance, *A Summer Wedding on Arran*, and *A Christmas Escape to Arran*, which was in the Amazon Top 100 for several weeks, and *A Christmas Wish on Arran*.

She has been a writer in residence with Luminate and Erskine Care Homes and Women's Aid East and Midlothian. This work has twice been nominated in the Write to End Violence Against Women Awards. In 2022 she was appointed as the first storyteller-in-residence at the Fringe by the Sea festival in North Berwick, East Lothian.

She is also part of the Scottish Book Trust's Live Literature Author Directory.

Ellie particularly interested in creative writing for health and well-being and run a small social enterprise in East Lothian, Sharing A Story CIC, where they use creative writing, shared reading and other creative methods to reduce social isolation and build confidence.

You can find Ellie Henderson online:
Facebook: /EllieHendersonBooks
Instagram: @elliehbooks
Twitter: @EllieHbooks

THE CHOC LIT STORY

Established in 2009, Choc Lit is an independent, award-winning publisher dedicated to creating a delicious selection of quality women's fiction.

We have won 18 awards, including Publisher of the Year and the Romantic Novel of the Year, and have been shortlisted for countless others. In 2023, we were shortlisted for Publisher of the Year by the Romantic Novelists' Association.

All our novels are selected by genuine readers. We are proud to publish talented first-time authors, as well as established writers whose books we love introducing to a new generation of readers.

In 2023, we became a Joffe Books company. Best known for publishing a wide range of commercial fiction, Joffe Books has its roots in women's fiction. Today it is one of the largest independent publishers in the UK.

We love to hear from you, so please email us about absolutely anything bookish at choc-lit@joffebooks.com

If you want to hear about all our bargain new releases, join our mailing list: www.choc-lit.com/contact

Milton Keynes UK
Ingram Content Group UK Ltd.
UKHW021321181024
2256UKWH00017B/39

9 781781 898048